SWIMMING toward the LIGHT

Other Fiction by Joan Clark

Latitudes of Melt
Eriksdottir
The Victory of Geraldine Gull
From a High Thin Wire

SWIMMING
toward the
LIGHT

JOAN CLARK

First published by Macmillan of Canada, 1990. This trade edition published by Goose Lane Editions, 2002.

Cover image: *In your eye* (detail) by Vik Kramer, © 1996.
Cover design by Paul Vienneau.
Printed in Canada by Transcontinental Printing.

10 9 8 7 6 5 4 3 2 1

National Library of Canada Cataloguing in Publication Data

Clark, Joan, 1934-
    Swimming toward the light

2nd Canadian ed.
(GLE library)
ISBN 0-86492-346-5

    I. Title. II. Series.

PS8555.L37S95 2002   C813'.54   C2002-900669-4
PR9199.3.C5227S95 2002

Published with the financial support of the Canada Council for the Arts, the Government of Canada through the Book Publishing Industry Development Program, and the New Brunswick Culture and Sports Secretariat.

Goose Lane Editions
469 King Street
Fredericton, New Brunswick
CANADA E3B 1E5

Contents

Luna Moths   1

War Stories   17

Pranks   35

Rustic Toil   51

The Loving Cup   75

Dickens's Wife   94

Colour Wheel   121

Sisters   140

The Madonna Feast   158

Margaret's Story   172

Point No Point   190

The Train Family   207

Swimming Toward the Light   218

For
Florence Mary Dodge
and
Mary Gail MacDonald

How far we all come. How far we all come
from ourselves. So far, so much between,
you can never go home again.

James Agee,
A Death in the Family

Luna Moths

There were three of them on the beach that morning, walking past the sand dunes and train tracks, gulls wheeling and mewing overhead. Their father carried Races' pitchfork, Ardith a tin bucket. Madge, the youngest, was empty-handed, a privilege fast disappearing now that she was shooting up: already she was past her father's elbow. She skittered beside him in erratic bursts, trying to keep up. Laddie was a big, broad-shouldered man with fair, sunburnt skin. In his shadow Madge did not feel long-legged and spindly, but compact and petite.

Ahead of them the clam flats spread smooth and shiny as a giant platter, rimmed by a strip of river a thin molasses colour now that it had been emptied of the sea. The outgoing tide had left behind pewter-coloured sand, ribbed like a washboard and strewn with broken shells. Once Madge had seen a seal in the river going out with the tide. Lying on its back, the seal had been rocking gently, coasting along with the water. On the flats were six large gulls, motionless as decoys. They waited until the three people had removed their shoes and socks and were walking across the wet sand before they swung to the air.

Close to the river, Laddie plunged the fork into an airhole. Madge heard the suck of water and air. She knew the clam was digging with its foot, going deeper. She half wanted it to escape, to make the chase more exciting. But her father was quick, quicker than the clam. There was a crack of shell and the pitchfork was held up, the clam speared on a tine. The clam's foot dangled in the air, helpless and limp.

"A big bugger," Laddie said. "Pull it off."

Madge pried the clam loose. She watched the slippery foot being sucked inside the shell before she threw the clam into the bucket. Laddie brought up a coven of smaller clams, their shells clamped shut, feet locked securely inside. Ardith knelt down to retrieve them.

"Thatta girl," Laddie said. "You keep up with me now."

Madge watched the bulge of muscle above her father's elbow as he levered the fork up through the sucking sand. His arms were covered with fine hairs, red-gold against his blue shirt. There were two damp circles beneath his arms, evidence of a solid, monolithic strength, a swift, sure knowledge of how the job should be done.

The gulls coasted onto the sand farther away where the river flowed beneath a train trestle. Madge ran toward them, arms flapping, sending gulls screaming into the air. She stopped and looked back at the diggers, her father bent over the fork, Ardith huddled beside the bucket. From this distance they looked small and peaceful, joined together by the darkness of their shapes against the pale expanse of sand. Madge found a large shell, knelt down and used it to scoop out an airhole. She dug jerkily, doggishly, sand flying every which way. She brought up a medium-sized clam, its foot distended into a swollen white lip. She scooped out more airholes, brought up more clams. She slipped off her pink shorts and piled the clams in the middle so they wouldn't dig themselves back into the sand. When she had built a small mound, she carried the shorts back and emptied the clams into the bucket, which by now was nearly full.

"Your mother won't like you dirtying your shorts. She just did the wash yesterday," Laddie said. "Try and be more helpful." The disapproval was in his voice, not in his face.

Madge studied her father's face, the smooth forehead, the shaved skin shiny with sweat, the large nose and ears. Her father was a high wall she couldn't scale; there was no place to get a toehold. There was no opening, no way to get inside him to know what it was like to be him looking out through those blue windows.

"A few more and we'll have enough," he said. He held the fork upright and rested his foot on it.

"Why don't you be a good girl and get me some seaweed?" he said to Madge. "There's nothing like clams steamed in seaweed." He lowered his foot and went back to work.

Their family wouldn't be eating the clams. Clams made her mother sick. They were for sailors off the ships tied up at the docks in Liverpool. Since the war had begun, Laddie sometimes had sailors to the house for poker and beer. As soon as the clams were dug, he was going back to town. They wouldn't see him again until next weekend, because after tonight he would be working night shift at the paper mill.

"All right," Madge said. This was a clear and simple way to please her father, a way she didn't have to look for. Ardith never had to look for such ways. She seemed to know exactly what their father wanted and was able to provide it. *Your father and Ardith are like two peas in a pod.* Madge's mother had said this once when Laddie was helping Ardith build a fur-trading fort for a history project, while Madge moped around the house, restless and out of sorts. Her mother made it sound as if this sameness was something she had no control over, that she despaired of, that she would change if she could, but at the same time took pleasure and pride in.

Madge brushed the wet sand from her shorts and put them on. By the time she got back to the cottage, the shorts would be dry. Her mother wouldn't care anyway. The main reason they had moved to the beach for the summer was so her mother wouldn't need to bother with things like wrinkled clothes and snarled hair.

Madge walked to the train trestle where the river pooled deep and brown. She scrambled up the embankment to the tracks that smelled of hot tar and wild roses. She crossed quickly, carefully, anticipating a foot caught beneath an iron tie, the train hurtling toward her, the engineer blowing his whistle, gesturing that she get herself unstuck. The sand on the other side of the tracks was warm and dry. Madge heard her heels squeak against it. She splashed across the shallow, frilled river mouth. Here waves broke so softly, so continuously, they hardly seemed waves at all but unravellings, rows and rows of liquid cloth being pulled apart by the gentle tug of an invisible thread. On the far side of the sandbar the water became deeper. Madge waded toward the seaweed-covered rocks, feeling put upon, unimportant, because she had been so easily dispatched upon an errand. It occurred to her that maybe her father had been trying to get rid of her in order to get the work done more quickly. At the same time, now that she was alone, she felt she had been released, set free.

She came to a tidal pool in a hollow between rocks. She saw the sideways scuttle of a crab as it disappeared beneath a curtain of brown seaweed at the bottom of the pool. She reached into the water, groping through the curtain until her fingers ached with cold. She saw a starfish splayed on the side of a rock. It was the colour of her shorts, of the roses growing beside the tracks. Madge peeled the starfish off the rock and placed it on the palm of her hand, shivering when its tentacles tickled her skin. She heard the train whistle. Dropping the starfish into the water, she yanked fistfuls of seaweed from the rocks and ran towards the tracks. She stood in the shadow of the trestle and waited for the train.

It came, the thundering engine bearing down on her, the vibrating cars swaying and groaning, shaking the ground where she stood, turning her bones to jelly. She watched the engine clatter past, deafening her. The impassive faces stared out, painted on glass, framed like movie stars on a screen. It didn't occur to Madge that some of the passengers might be anxious or afraid: a mother going to visit a sick child in a Halifax hospital, a young woman leaving home for the first time, a sailor returning to his ship two days late. Madge imagined the faces as belonging to people who were carefree and spoiled, who sat at tables covered with white cloths and were fed dessert. Their passing intruded on her aloneness, made her feel stranded, left out.

The caboose jiggled past, leaving a gust of hot, swirling air. Once again, Madge was released. She skipped over the tracks and onto the clam flats. Gulls were squawking and pecking at the holes her father had dug, now collapsing into grey mud slides. Madge ran, arms spread wide, seaweed streaming from her hands, scattering gulls. She wandered through the dunes, looking in the coarse speargrass for nests, holding one hand over her head in case the circling gulls should swoop down to peck her. She went toward a clutch of eggs. Dropping the seaweed, she got down on her hands and knees and felt in the grass. They weren't eggs at all but smooth white stones. She looked around for more eggs before she remembered the seaweed and went back for it.

By the time she found her shoes and socks, put them on, and walked back to the cottage, Laddie had already eaten his noon dinner and left for town. "Dad got tired of waiting for you," Ardith said, "*I* had to get the seaweed for him. Mum's cross at you for being late," she went on. "We have to be quiet. She's lying down."

Madge wasn't worried about her mother's crossness. These days her mother didn't have the energy to stay cross. Most of her energy had been given to the war effort. That was what she called folding bandages for the Red Cross in the bare room over the firehall, working in the sailors' canteen on Water Street, nursing survivors torpedoed by subs. For this last job she had put on a white uniform and navy blue cape and gone to the basement of the high school, which had been converted into a hospital. Dressed in her uniform, with her hair pulled back in a bun beneath her cap, her mother had looked like the nurse in the Victory Bond poster. The woman in this picture had pale skin, dark hair, a firm chin. She had her arms around two children, a boy on one side, a girl on the other.

Bombs exploded behind them, but the woman looked straight out of the picture, determined and resolute.

While their mother rested, Madge and Ardith went out to the road and into the ditch where purple vetch, black-eyed Susans, and pink lupins grew in tangled profusion. There was a numbing laziness in the heat, in the locust's dry hum, the bee's insistent buzzing. Madge didn't like being on the road in such heat. The openness, the intense sun, the insects, the length of her bare arms and legs made her feel unprotected, spied upon. It wasn't a time to be standing at all, but lying down, beneath the shade trees of Races' pasture or in the mossy spruce woods beside their cabin. Madge couldn't pass up the opportunity of catching a butterfly for Ardith, who was afraid of them. It was a demonstration of fearlessness and bravado, an easy and useful accomplishment.

Madge was hunched over a butterfly fanning its wings on a black-eyed Susan, waiting for them to close so she could quickly pinch them between her fingers, lightly, in order not to remove too much of their golden dust. It was an ordinary cabbage butterfly with yellow, brown-spotted wings. Ardith, who stood behind her with the chloroform jar, already had two other cabbage butterflies in her collection, but they had pale, silvery wings. She also had two monarchs, a red admiral, and a tiger swallowtail, all of which Madge had caught for her. These were pinned to a felt board, carefully labelled and described. Ardith had a card table set up on the porch at the cottage to hold her collections. As well as butterflies, she collected shells, which she kept in pigeonholes their father had made for her, and leaves ironed between layers of waxed paper and glued onto bristol board. At home, in his top bureau drawer, lined up in neat rows, their father had coins from different countries, match folders given him by sailors, badges he had earned when he was a King's Scout in Sydney.

The fragile wings opened, shut, opened, shut, slow, slower, the pauses longer, sleepier. There was a quivering pause stretched out like a sigh as the wings came together and stayed, becoming so thin and papery they might have been mistaken for a sliver of yellow light.

"Now!" Ardith whispered.

There was a spurt of gravel on the roadside.

Madge looked away from the butterfly just as Francis Race dropped his bike in the ditch. When she looked back, the butterfly was wobbling drunkenly over the barbed-wire fence toward the swamp.

"It's gone!" Ardith wailed. She glared at Francis Race. "It's all your fault!"

"Stupid girl," Francis said. He stood there, confident and knowing, with his bare feet and tanned chest, his pants rolled up to his knees, spears of uneven straw-coloured hair falling over his eyes. "You need a net to do it right."

"Pest," Ardith said. "Go away!"

"Can't." He grinned. "I live here."

"Boys!" Ardith huffed and crossed the road.

Francis pulled out a stalk of tender new grass and chewed on it. He stared boldly at Madge.

"Want to see inside the old boat?" he said.

He had already shown her the baby pigs in the sty, the green apples in the orchard, the black bull staked in the back pasture. Being shown the black bull was how she had got into trouble.

Madge stared at her sister's back.

Ardith turned. "You know what Mum said." She went into their driveway.

For supper that night their mother had made potato salad and devilled eggs. They sat on the screened-in verandah, plates on their knees, and looked across the road and the railway tracks, past the dunes to the sea shining smooth and blue in the sun. A fog bank hovered along the horizon; above it, white clouds piled on top of each other, huge and opalescent.

"Looks like rain," their mother said. "I hope we sleep through it."

After they had finished eating, their mother nodded toward the pitchfork standing in the corner of the verandah.

"One of you girls should return the fork to Races," she said.

"It's Madge's turn," Ardith said. "I went and got it *and* the milk."

"*I* went for the seaweed," Madge said. "Besides, Mum said *you girls.*"

Although she was trying to gain advantage from it now, *you girls* always made Madge feel angry and dissatisfied. She was disappointed that their mother couldn't take the trouble to clearly separate them into Madge and Ardith, that she lumped them together to smooth out differences.

"You were late," Ardith said. "It doesn't count."

"That's enough," their mother said sharply. "It's clear you're the one to do it, Madge."

Madge eased her thigh from the lawn chair, which had stuck to her skin, raising long, red welts.

"And make her do the dishes," Ardith said. "I did them two nights in a row."

"You wash and Madge can dry."

Ardith got up and stomped inside. The porch boards bounced beneath her weight.

"She gets away with murder around here!" she said. Their mother looked at Madge.

"You'd better take it over now, before there's any more fuss."

This was said wearily, placatingly. Madge knew that her mother was also saying *Co-operate, you know I'm not feeling well,* but she felt her mother's avoidance more strongly. Her mother's avoidance was the reason her father had given her the hairbrush last week, though it was her mother who had decided she should have it. *Fuck* was the word she'd been spanked for. *Your mother and father fuck.* That was what Francis Race had said when he was showing her the black bull. He had leaned over the pole fence and said: "The bull fucks the cows. That's how they get calves." Madge came home and told Ardith; it wasn't often she got such information first, information that was a straight forward recital of facts. Ardith told their mother.

Madge picked up the pitchfork.

She couldn't afford to hold out against Ardith. Besides, it wasn't her inclination. Her inclination was to drift like a seal with the incoming tide.

The old boat that had once belonged to Francis Race's grandfather in the days when he had been a fisherman was on the other side of the road behind the hay barn. Madge had to stand on an upturned apple box to climb inside. There was the smell of oil and stagnant water. She stood on the warped decking and looked between the broken boards at the pool of murky water below. There were grey rings of gasoline on top, yellow scum around the edges. In front of her was the cabin. It was dark and sinister-looking, with a gaping hole where the engine had been taken out. The sides of the boat came up to her chest. To Madge all this was foreign territory. She had never been in anything larger than a rowboat. What prevented her from bolting over the side was the simple fact that she had been *asked* to come aboard. That she could have huffed off like Ardith and still have had the satisfaction of being asked didn't occur to Madge. She wanted to bask in the warmth of being well-favoured, chosen, singled out.

Francis pointed to another apple box in the bow of the boat.

"You take the lookout," he said. "I'll steer."

He went into the cabin where a bicycle wheel was tied to a wooden sawhorse. He straddled the sawhorse and began turning the wheel. He made a revving noise and shouted, "Watch out for German subs!"

Madge looked through her curled-up fingers, across the dunes, scanning the shining sea.

"Where're we headed?" she asked.

"West Indies. For a load of rum."

Madge heard Ardith calling from the other side of the hay barn. She ducked down.

Ardith called again, closer this time; she had recrossed the road.

Madge crouched lower.

Francis stopped revving. He crept over the floorboards toward Madge.

"Madge?" Ardith's voice was querulous, timid. It was right there, at the corner of the barn.

Madge felt the heat rising from her cheeks, the coolness of Francis's bare arms against hers. She reached up and peeled off a large curl of black paint from the gunnel.

"Madge?"

The voice was back on the other side of the road, lingering.

Francis's mouth was against her ear.

"Lie down on the boards."

With the same stealth, the same urgency to hide and conceal from her sister, Madge stretched out, belly down, on the weathered boards.

"Not that way," Francis whispered. "On your back."

Madge rolled over.

Francis lay on top of her, his face close to hers. He had a faint barn smell.

"This is fucking," Francis said. He bobbed up and down. His face was flushed and serious.

"Madge!" Ardith was still on the road.

Francis propped himself on one elbow and fumbled inside his pants. He bobbed up and down again.

Madge felt something soft against her thigh, something pointed and tickling. She giggled.

Francis put his full weight on her.

The skin between her halter top and her shorts pinched as it was squeezed between the boards.

"You're too heavy." She gave him a shove.

Francis rolled off and onto his belly. He lay there, flat against the boards, looking red-faced and cross.

Madge jumped out of the boat onto the swampy grass. She ran to the road.

Ardith was walking into their driveway.

"Ardith! Wait up!"

Her sister kept on walking. Ardith would go inside, bring her movie magazines out to the porch, and sit on the water-stained sofa, cutting and trimming photographs for her scrapbook. She would ignore Madge for the rest of the afternoon. Madge recognized this as a trade-off for not telling their mother she had been with Francis Race. This didn't mean Madge was convinced being with Francis was wrong. Saying *fuck* outright was wrong, but she hadn't said it, Francis was the one who'd said it. What had gone on in the boat was something else. She saw Francis's red face bobbing up and down, his unsheathed, naked *thing* – she and Ardith didn't have a name for it – tickling her thigh, as a game, a game that was harmless but required secrecy and stealth in order to work. It was like watching Miss Wigglesworth undress when she forgot to pull down the blind, or Uncle Dillon take a pee in the bushes behind Grandfather Burchell's toolshed. For Madge, anything to do with naked flesh was a revelation. She felt a need to hide, to store, to cherish such revelations. Even if she could have found the words, she wouldn't have handed these tingling satisfactions over to Ardith. Madge's collections were covert, unobtrusive, easily diminished.

That night Madge and Ardith lay on the creaky metal bed under a quilt. The quilt was made of floral circlets set in squares. The petals were hexagons sewn from dimity dresses, wide satin ribbons, flannelette nightgowns faded as old wallpaper, flowers within flowers stitched together by fine threads and insulated with cotton batting. Their mother had bought this quilt from Francis's grandmother, who had made it on a wood frame set up on Races' verandah. Across the living room, in the other bedroom, Madge heard her mother cough. Madge looked at Ardith sleeping beside her. Ardith was on her back, legs spread, mouth slightly open, breathing in and out with the curtains above the bed. She looked pink, defenceless, babyish. Through the open window Madge heard the rollers thundering on the beach. The tide was coming in. It began to rain, a light freckling on the rooftop. It was like picking out random notes on an old piano. Madge waited, holding back sleep, trying to measure the size of the drops, the different sounds they made on the roof. They were coming more heavily now, large polka dots bouncing off shingles faster, thicker, faster, mounting to a pounding crescendo. Madge reached up, closed the window, then burrowed deep into the lumpy mattress, giving herself over to the rhythm of rain and surf.

In the morning she was the first one up. She tiptoed through the cool, silent rooms. A moth was clinging to the screen door that slapped shut behind her, but she didn't look at it. She was looking down at her nightgown, which she was holding above her legs so it wouldn't touch the long wet grass growing on either side of the path.

The trees around the outhouse dripped, the drops glistening on wet spruce needles. Tatters of cloud drifted over the trees, remnants of the fog that had come in with the tide. Madge hitched her nightgown higher and sat down on the outhouse seat, looking through the open doorway. It was then she saw the green moths.

They were all over the cottage, the sides, the roof, even the stone chimney. She had never seen so many moths and never this huge, luxurious kind. She was used to flimsy brown moths that beat themselves to frenzied shreds against the outdoor light. Madge pulled down her nightgown and, forgetting to hold it above the grass, walked along the path to the back door, keeping her eyes on the moths, afraid they would disappear if she looked away. The moths seemed painted on, like the faces in the train windows. Madge looked at the moth on the screen door. It had long trailing wings that flowed down from its body like a ballgown, a soft mint colour such as a beautiful woman might wear, richly draped and caught below the waist with golden clasps. These clasps were two yellow moons, one on each wing. On its head were two feathery antennae, swaying gently like fans.

Madge walked through the tall wet grass to the front of the cottage, intending to go in the porch door, but the screening was covered with moths. They went up the front of the cottage and over the top like a net. There were hundreds of them. The wonder and enchantment of it, that this green velvety net had been cast over the cottage while she had been sleeping. She went around to the back door and opened it, carefully so the moth would stay on the screen.

Ardith woke up grumpy and dishevelled, but she agreed to look. They went out to the front porch and stared at the undersides of the moths. The bodies were furry and small, so small it seemed incredible they could support such large wings. Tiny legs clung to the holes in the screen. One of the moths moved slightly, putting its legs into other holes, dragging its wings upward.

Ardith shivered and rubbed her bare arms. Ardith did not like moths any better than butterflies. There was too much potential for sudden and unexpected movement.

"They're all over the cottage," Madge said. "I'll show you."

She had to hold the screen door wide to allow Ardith safe passage. Still, the moth did not budge.

Once she was outside in the grass, looking up at the roof, Ardith forgot herself.

"Look at them!" she said. "Where did they come from?"

There was a wedge of sunlight on the roof. It shone on the wings, making them a paler, translucent green. The moths in the shade were moist and velvety.

"There's so many of them, they must be migrating," Ardith said knowledgeably, "like monarchs do."

They stood side by side in the wet grass, speaking in whispers. There was something magical about this visitation. It wasn't something to be managed or tampered with. Its magic lay in fragility and calm.

The fog vanished.

The wedge of sunlight widened, encompassed the roof.

Down by the road a locust hummed.

One by one, the moths began to lift, singly, then in groups, detaching themselves from shingles, boards, bricks, screening, rising into the air, a loose, green, fluttering cloud. The cloud rose higher, lifted over the spruce trees. At this height it began to lengthen and thin, swooping and diving like a dragon kite. The tail of the kite swung over the clearing where the sisters stood. It dipped down suddenly, one moth coming within inches of Ardith's head. She screamed and covered her nose. The scream seemed to unbalance the moth. It wobbled lower, then flew on a slant, as if its wings were unevenly weighted. It stayed close to the ground, bobbing and jerking along the wooded path toward Races' house. Madge watched it disappear in the shadows of the trees.

Ardith was on the back step.

"Look! The one on the back door is still here!" she said. "Get it. Quick!"

Madge cupped her hand over the moth. Beneath her fingers she felt the feathery antennae tickling her palm. She felt the wings quiver. Goose pimples came up on her arms.

Ardith went around to the front porch and came back with the chloroform jar.

"There!" she said triumphantly after Madge had slid the moth into the jar.

They took the moth inside. Their mother was in the kitchen putting the kettle on to heat. She looked better today, stronger, more like the woman on the poster.

Ardith showed her the bottle.

"That looks like a luna moth. They have them down south," their mother said. "I wonder what it's doing up here?"

Madge told her about them being all over the roof.

"Maybe they came north with the Gulf Stream," their mother said, "then drifted in with the fog."

"Their wings were wet," Madge said.

"They probably stopped here to dry them off. The cottage must have been the first solid spot they came to that was high enough."

Madge believed this. The moths drifting north with the Gulf Stream, just happening to land on their cottage – the randomness and chance of this impressed her.

She saw their mother as having this same randomness. There were crevices inside her, mysterious corners where she tucked away surprising bits of information like this. You would think she was miles away, not even knowing you were there when, *presto!* she would plunk some bit of information down in front of you, matter-of-factly, as if there was nothing to it at all, and walk away.

Already she had gone into the bedroom to put on her slacks.

The moth wasn't labelled until the end of the summer when they had driven back to town. After the car was unpacked and everything put away, Ardith and Laddie looked through the *Encyclopaedia Britannica* for more information. This is what Ardith printed on a square of cardboard: *Luna Moth, a species of saturniid moth. Wing spread, four inches. Light green with tail-like projections on back wings. Occurs in southern parts of North America.*

While Ardith was doing this, Madge went outside and down the driveway to the back garden which had grown luxurious and opulent during her absence. Her father didn't like gardening and had let it go. Roses had become careless and wanton, strewing their petals onto the unclipped grass. Currant bushes dripped clusters of crimson berries. Holly-hocks towered overhead as if they had sprung from magical seeds. Weeds looked unfamiliar and alien now that they had grown enormous. Madge sat in the long, lush grass, took off her shoes, and shook out the sand, not from any sense of fastidiousness or duty, but to get used to the transformation. Sitting here in the garden, surrounded by outsized plants, she felt she had shrunk. Earlier this afternoon, when they had come through the front door bringing with them their clean beach smell, their stiff towels, their suitcases and boxes, Madge felt she had grown huge. While she had been gone, the house had closed in on itself. The rooms were narrower, the ceilings lower, the air darker. Her bedroom was grey and smelt of dead flies, of being shut up. Out here in the garden the air was green with yellow openings where the sun poked through. Madge put on her shoes and stood up so she would feel tall. She walked around the garden, carefully as she would in a jungle. Round and round she walked, thinking about these transformations, about the fact that while she had been somewhere else, this fantastic and amazing growth had taken place.

War Stories

The day war broke out, September 1, 1939, Madge was sitting at the kitchen table drawing on the back of a stencil while her mother sat on a stool eating a boiled egg and listening to the BBC. Ardith was in school, Laddie at work. When the announcer's voice came crackling through the radio with the news that Hitler's army had invaded Poland, Madge's mother knocked the egg onto the floor with the spoon.

"My God," she said, "it's war!"

She slid off the stool, went into the hall, and phoned the Mersey where Laddie worked.

Initially, Madge had been too young to be much interested in the war. Had it not been for her mother's clumsiness in knocking over a breakfast egg, Madge might not have remembered the day the war began. The changes in their lives that followed the radio announcement did not make much of an impact on Madge. She was young enough to take these changes in her stride. The jars of rationed sugar labelled BETH, LADDIE, ARDITH, MADGE in her sister's neat printing; the Victory Bond parades; the curfew and air raid blinds; her mother's interminable knitting of grey socks, her frequent absences from home involved in the war effort; the men who slept in their spare room; all this Madge at first accepted as being part of everyday life, as part of their life as it was supposed to be. It was only when she was older, nine or ten, when the war was winding down and the excitement had ebbed away and her mother was confined to bed, that Madge paid closer attention to what was going on. It was her father who filled her in on what she'd missed. Laddie was full of war stories. He had a salesman's addiction to the lively anecdote. He knew how to shock and surprise, how to impress people he met on the post-office steps or in the Mersey parking lot. Thirty-five years later, Laddie was still telling Madge the same stories, almost word for word as the first time he'd told them.

You want to know about the war? You have only to look out the window at the sea. The North Atlantic, that's where our war was fought. There were two enemies out there, the weather and the U-boats. In the fall, there were hurricanes and waves high enough to swallow a ship. In the winter, there was freezing rain that iced up ships so bad some of them capsized. In the spring, it was icebergs as big as churches and that's not counting the part underneath. And fog. There was a lot of fog, which was dandy for the Germans, especially if it came with a calm sea. The U-boats liked to attack in fog so they could make a fast getaway, then sneak back for a second attempt. Those Germans sank nearly everything they came across: patrol boats, supply boats, fishing boats – it didn't matter what it was. You name it, they sank it. I suppose the more sinkings they could report to Hitler, the more medals they got. They didn't use torpedoes on smaller boats, they used bombs they carried aboard. If the Germans wanted to sink a fishing boat, they brought the sub on top so they could order the fishermen into lifeboats. They spoke through horns, megaphones, I think they're called, to make themselves heard. Once the fishermen were in lifeboats, the Germans came aboard for the ship's papers. They also helped themselves to whatever took their fancy – the compass and sextant, the flag, a trunk of spare clothes, this and that. After their boat went

*under, the fishermen had to row their dories anywhere up to
a hundred miles across open sea until they reached the nearest
spit of land. Of course, not all Germans played a dirty game.
Take that German captain off Cape Race, for instance. He
brought his sub to the surface and asked a fisherman to give
him some fish for his crew. The fisherman handed over part
of his catch and the German captain apologized for not having
any Canadian money to pay for it.*

Here, Laddie usually paused and shook his head, as if he
couldn't quite believe a German captain was capable of such
courtesy.

*Before our boys caught on, the Germans had a vessel rigged
up like a fish-dragger, with guns on her. The sub would hide
behind the vessel, see. That way, it could get in close to our
ships without anyone suspecting. Those Germans were foxy,
let me tell you. Do you know why they took a trunk of clothes
off a fishing boat? No? Well, I'll tell you. So they could dress
up like our boys, that's why. Captain Wherry off one of the
corvettes told me that. I used to bump into him sometimes
down in the naval canteen. As a civilian, I wasn't supposed
to go in the canteen, but sometimes I stopped for a chat when
I went to pick up your mother after she finished taking her
turn at the counter serving up sandwiches, cookies, snacks,
and the like. Captain Wherry told me that ticket stubs from
the Capitol Theatre on Barrington Street in Halifax had been
found in the pockets of a couple of German sailors when that
U-boat was captured out here, the one our boys towed into
the harbour after the Germans had been taken prisoner. They
also found a ticket stub to a New York play in the German
captain's pocket. That captain had been to a Broadway play
the night before he sank a Yankee ship. It was in the sub's log.
Imagine stooping that low!*

Madge had seen the submarine anchored off Waterloo
Street. She had watched people being rowed out to have a
look round it. A friend of Dickie Woods, Butch Corkum, had
gone aboard with his father. It wasn't free; Butch's father had
paid to get them on. Dickie said Butch saw pictures of women

taped to the walls above the sailors' bunks. He was disappointed the women weren't naked. He'd expected to see bare tits and bums, but the women looked as ordinary as mothers or sisters, not one of them with her clothes off.

The truth was that there were Germans walking the streets of Halifax during the war. There were gates blocking the entrance to Halifax harbour but they didn't go far enough down to keep out the subs. Halifax harbour's deep. There's a big rock ledge beneath the water. A sub could nose under the gates and hide beneath that ledge. Then it would surface at night and let off some of its crew.

Most of Madge's father's stories were, in one way or another, about the German submarines that prowled the ocean beyond the harbour – U-boats, sea wolves, tubes of death, black periscopes that glided out of the fog like phantoms. Her father had picked up these stories down on the docks where he went to talk to men off the ships, and from the sailors who stayed at their house while their ships were being repaired. During the war, ships were refitted at town docks along the south shore, destroyers, corvettes, minesweepers. It was in smaller harbours like Liverpool and Lunenberg that these ships were overhauled before joining convoys leaving from Halifax, Sydney, and St. John's. Laddie met most of the sailors who came to town because, as head of the billeting committee, it was his job to farm out every spare bed within a twenty-five-mile radius of Liverpool. Laddie was also on the air-raid committee that maintained the nighttime curfew and blackout. Besides these official duties, he kept a sharp lookout for traitors and spies.

We'll never know how many German spies were on the loose around here during the war. The fact is, the Germans could put a spy ashore almost anywhere along this coast without any of us being the wiser. With all the islands and coves we have the Germans had all kinds of room to manoeuvre. That's probably how that stranger got ashore, the one who turned up at Western Head. Rented a cottage out there. Said he was from the States. Claimed he was an artist. Used to have parties out there for officers off the ships. Used to pump them full of booze and then ask questions. Questions he had no business asking, like when convoys were leaving, what ports they were leaving from, that sort of thing. This only happened a few times before one of our officers stayed sober and started asking questions himself. He'd caught on to what that spy was up to. He must've given that artist fellow a good scare, because he disappeared soon after. Maybe he got aboard a sub when it surfaced at night to recharge its batteries and pick up radio signals. He left behind his pictures. Wally Sprouse, who lived out Western Head way, saw them. He said the artist fellow couldn't paint worth a damn, that he was as phony as a three-dollar bill.

Then there was that foreign couple that rented the big house at the end of River Head Road. Didn't stay long. People out there saw someone inside the house signalling the subs at night with a high-powered flashlight. Soon after it was reported, the military police came and took the couple away. We had a traitor here too, you know, right here in town. He was selling gas to the Germans. They found the empty barrels on Sheep Island.

Here, Laddie usually paused so Madge could ask who the traitor was. By the end of the war, Felix Brownell had left Liverpool, so people were saying his name right out. Felix had moved to the Bahamas, where he bought a sugar plantation. Ardith, who had sat beside Felix's daughter Rosemary in school, had received a letter from her describing the cane fields and the black servants who brought the Brownells their meals.

When Felix Brownell came to Liverpool before the war, he couldn't afford a post-office box. Had to take his mail through General Delivery. Had to rent a truck to start up a scrap-metal business. Later on, he bought a ship to take the scrap metal across the Atlantic to the Germans. Of course, the subs never got him, not once, which was no coincidence. Even before the war was halfway over, Felix was loaded, on his way to becoming a millionaire. He was a wily bugger. Timed his departure just right. In the fall of '44 he packed up lock, stock, and barrel and cleared out for the Bahamas. Left town before the military police could nail him.

Laddie's favourite war story wasn't about spies or traitors, however; it was about Captain Smith and the *Liverpool Packet*. Captain Smith also worked for the Mersey, so Laddie had got the story first hand, which probably explained why he liked to tell it so often.

Captain Smith was the skipper of the Liverpool Packet, *a crusty old bugger he was with a long white beard and a gimpy leg. Was on his way to Boston with a load of newsprint when a U-boat got him. The sub surfaced and the Germans came on top, three of them with machine guns. One of them, the officer in charge, ordered the men off the* Packet *and into lifeboats, Captain Smith included. Two Germans carried a bomb aboard and sank her. Afterwards, the officer called over to Captain Smith, asking him what his boat's name was. Captain Smith said the officer hadn't looked close enough at the* Packet *before she went down and wanted to put her name in his log.*

"The Liverpool Packet," *Captain Smith yelled from the lifeboat.*

The German officer asked him to repeat it, though Captain Smith said he had yelled it out good and loud the first time and there was nothing wrong with the German's English. A lot of Jerries spoke English as good as us, you know. Maybe the German officer thought the boat came from Liverpool, England. Or maybe he thought Captain Smith was pulling his leg, trying to put one over on him. I don't know. Anyway, Captain Smith shouted back, "The Liverpool Packet, *you bloody fool!"*

And those men standing there with machine guns.

That German officer never said a word, no sir. He just turned his back on Captain Smith, went down the hatch, the machine-gunners after him, and that was that. That's the truth, not one word of it a lie.

When Madge heard this story as a child, she had listened wide-eyed, astonished, not at the story but at her father. Her father's features looked as if they were carved out of rock or stone and mounted in a high place, on the side of a building or on a fortress wall. His face had seemed impervious to subtlety or change; excitements and setbacks could rain down on it and his features remained impenetrable, untouched. With the telling of this story, Madge saw a weakness, a crumbling of mortar and stone, a chink of light showing through. She saw what could impress him. She was amazed that what impressed him were the same things that impressed boys she knew, Dickie Wood and Butch Corkum. Danger, risk, foolishness; these also impressed her father.

The spare room. *The spare room,* Laddie liked to say, *was how most civilians, the women especially, fought the war. The women made sure there were warm beds and plenty of home cooking to make our boys feel welcome. During the war every spare room in town was occupied at one time or another by someone connected with the war. It was sailors mostly.*

Madge remembered the first man who had slept in their spare room. He wasn't a sailor but a man who spoke in the same high-pitched way as the radio voice from the BBC. He was Peter Hickey, an RAF instructor who stayed with their family for six weeks while he was giving a training course. The second person to sleep in their spare room was Stefan Edwardson, a Norwegian whaling captain who stayed with them three months, until his frost-bitten feet healed. After Stefan left, a string of sailors used their spare room: Herbie, Kenny, Pee Wee, Buddy, Verne, Norm. What Madge remembered most about these sailors was that they were usually laughing and joking. Arm in arm, they swaggered along the streets in their narrow-hipped trousers and comical round hats, whistling at girls and singing at the tops of their lungs:

Bell-bottom trousers, coat of navy blue,
Girls love the sailors and they love them too.

Sailor boys, Laddie called them. Some of these sailor boys were willing to play house and drink tea from the tiny china cups Madge's Aunt Margaret had given her one Christmas. Pee Wee and Kenny would play *Red Rover, Come Over* and *Run, Sheep, Run* with the neighbourhood kids. Pee Wee often teased Ardith about learning to cook so he could come back after the war and marry her. Ardith, who was three years older than Madge, disapproved of sailors. They drank too much, she said. Bess Eisner's sister had opened her school locker one morning and a drunken sailor had tumbled out. Sailors got girls in trouble. That was why the bushes at The Fort were called the *breeding grounds*. Boys went over there after school to pick up change that had fallen from sailors' pockets. It was sailors who had got Gladys in trouble. It wasn't Gladys's fault, Ardith said. Gladys didn't know any better.

Gladys Oickle had come to them from Port Mouton. This was toward the end of the war, when Madge's mother was in bed with TB and Laddie needed someone to fix meals and look after the house. Laddie wanted someone older than Gladys, but it was hard to get help during the war because so many women had joined up. Gladys had no father and her mother was dead. Gladys had been living with her mother's brother, who had seven children of his own, including a son Gladys's age.

"Now that she's sixteen, her uncle wants her out of the house," Ardith said. "That's what he told Dad."

Ardith was four years younger than Gladys, but this didn't prevent her from managing Gladys. It was Ardith who braided Gladys's fine albino-blonde hair and wound the braids around her head so they wouldn't get in the food. It was Ardith who trimmed Gladys's toenails and asked if Gladys could have a pair of their mother's old nursing Oxfords. Gladys had turned up on their doorstep wearing a pair of dirty sneakers and holding a carton of clothes tied with string.

"It's a good thing school's out and I'm here to look after her," Ardith said.

She helped Gladys feed the wash through the wringer, peel potatoes, clean out the icebox, sweep the floor, work she would have grumbled about, saying Madge should be doing her share, had their mother expected her to do it alone.

Gladys was nosy. While she and Ardith worked, she would ply Ardith with questions: what was Laddie's job at the paper mill, how much money did he make, what was wrong with their mother, did they know any sailors, what were their names, what did they look like. Ardith rattled off the sailors' names, told Gladys about Peter Hickey and Stefan Edwardson.

Ardith's missionary zeal tended to wear out quickly, especially if she was dissatisfied with the results. In Gladys's case this happened in less than a month.

"Gladys does the stupidest things," Ardith told Madge after she and Gladys had returned from picking blueberries on the hillside behind the school. "Two sailors had a tent pitched at the end of the field, beside a tree. They sat under the tree and watched while we picked. They kept whistling at Gladys and calling her to come over. I told her not to pay any attention, but she went over and got inside the tent. She stayed in there the longest time, giggling and carrying on. When she came out, her skirt was on backwards and she wouldn't help pick. She kept pulling berries off the branches and stuffing them into her mouth," Ardith said disgustedly.

Ardith's disgust centred on Gladys's failure to pick enough berries for a batch of jam. She showed no interest in what had been going on inside the tent, but Madge was interested. After Ardith had told her this story, Madge looked at Gladys in a new way. She noticed the blond ripeness of Gladys, the smooth, plump flesh that looked as if it would run with clear sweet juice if it were bitten into.

A few days after Ardith and Gladys had gone berry picking, Ardith began writing a play about war orphans that she and Bess were going to put on in the Eisners' garage. For the rest of the summer, until school started, she was seldom home, which meant Madge was left alone with Gladys.

Gladys could be foxy about her nosiness. It didn't always come out in questions. Sometimes she hid her curiosity behind pronouncements she expected you to confirm or deny. That was the form her nosiness took the afternoon she was dusting the living room while Madge lay on the chesterfield reading *The Five Little Peppers and How They Grew*. Gladys was half-heartedly flicking a cloth at tables and chairs, stopping intermittently to bite off a fingernail or pick a scab. Gladys had thick scabs on her knees, which she claimed were the result of scrubbing floors. Madge had reached the part in the story where Polly Pepper had mended the hole in the back of the stove with a scrap of shoe leather so she could bake a cake for her mother. She was trying to make the cake without butter or eggs. Madge was fascinated by Polly's goodness and cheerful determination. She seemed able to turn the worst situation into a party or game. Of course she had brothers to help her and did not have a sick mother lying upstairs.

"Your poor mother," Gladys said. "Pining away upstairs." She sighed. "It's pitiful."

Madge had only a rough idea of what *pining away* meant, but she understood *pitiful* all right. She felt that, compared with the Peppers, her own family was falling apart. She felt the urge to defend her family. She did not like Gladys using the word *poor* to describe her mother. She did not like Gladys feeling sorry for her mother.

"Mum's worn out by the war effort," Madge said. "That's what the doctor said. She's got a spot on her lung that will go away if she stays in bed."

"It's not the war effort that put her in bed," Gladys said slyly, "or the spot on her lung." She took a swipe at the mantelpiece, nearly knocking over a pair of brass candlesticks.

"What was it then?"

Madge didn't like having to ask this question, but the need to know the answer overrode any disadvantage she felt in having Gladys know something about her family that she didn't know herself.

Gladys put her hands on her hips and squinted at Madge, trying to frown. By squinting and sliding her eyes sideways, Gladys managed to convey a warning that she was about to say something that demanded attention and respect.

"Can you keep a secret?"

"Yes."

"Promise?"

"Cross my heart."

Gladys came over to the chesterfield and put her soft, pulpy lips against Madge's ear.

"Your mother's pining away for that whaling captain who stayed here, that Stefan somebody your sister was telling me about. They loved each other!"

Gladys waited for this to sink in, then she drifted to the other side of the room. She lifted the curtain and stared moonily out the window, as if she expected Stefan to come striding up the walk and rescue Madge's mother. Gladys sniffed and said in her mopey way, "It's so sad."

Madge was disappointed Gladys couldn't come up with anything better than this. She'd expected a different kind of secret, something coarser and fleshier, something closer to what Gladys had been up to inside the tent. She didn't expect anything so soppy. She understood from the way Ardith bossed Gladys that Gladys wasn't to be taken seriously, that Gladys was foolish and somewhat stupid. Madge felt silly for having been so easily taken in. She picked up her book and found her place in the story. Polly Pepper had taken the birthday cake from the oven. The cake had been blackened with smoke, but Polly was making the best of it by decorating the top with posies. Madge didn't believe Gladys. Not then, she didn't.

Although she didn't know it at the time, Madge had been the first one in the family to see Stefan Edwardson. He had waved at her from a car. It had been early in the war; she would have been four, too young for school. She was standing on the sidewalk in the shivery cold, watching her mother striding up the street, away from her. Her mother was wearing her white nurse's cap and a navy blue cape over her uniform. She was on her way to the high school, where a makeshift hospital had been set up in the basement to treat survivors from a ship that had been torpedoed outside the harbour.

Soon after her mother's figure disappeared, Madge saw a cavalcade of cars coming along the street, slowly like a funeral procession. The survivors were inside these cars, staring out the windows. Their shoulders and faces were black, their hair and beards white. One of the men raised a hand and waved at Madge as his car passed, then let it drop.

Do you remember the Norwegian, Stefan Edwardson, who stayed in our spare room after that ship went down out here? Stefan was a whaling captain but he wasn't on a whaling boat. He was on the tanker Victory Sun, *on his way to meet up with his whaling fleet in Little Norway – that's what we called Lunenburg sometimes – when a U-boat sank him. There were carloads of survivors, their bodies covered with oil from their sunken ship. They'd been floating out there all night in the dark. I was down on the docks when they were brought in. It was the dead of winter. Those men were so cold their beards were iced up, their hair was in icicles. Jesus, those buggers were cold!*

Stefan was a real nice fellow; not standoffish exactly, but quiet. Dignified, I guess you'd say. He was somewhere around thirty-five, older than the other whalers. Most of them were in their twenties. A healthier, more good-looking bunch you never saw anywhere. You don't see them coming into port much any more, not like they used to. But when they were here, those Norwegians would walk miles to keep in shape. Even on cold winter mornings, you'd see them marching down the street in a line.

The girls were crazy about them. Used to follow them all over town. One day, after a big snowstorm, when the streets had just been ploughed and there were snowbanks all over, a girl by the name of Jenny Lane threw a snowball at one of the whalers just when the line was passing in front of the post office. This Norwegian stepped out of line, picked Jenny up by the ankles, and stuck her head first into a snowbank, then stepped back in line and kept on going. It was Len Ritcey who fished her out. If it wasn't for him getting his mail just then, Jenny might've smothered to death. Now, Stefan – you would-n't've caught him pulling a stunt like that. No sir, not him.

I never saw a man who hated Germans as much as he did. He was staying with us when he heard about Hitler's troops marching into Norway. The radio was on for the BBC broad-cast from overseas, same as every morning. I was working night shift at the mill, so I had just come in. You were there too. Stefan was sitting at the kitchen table. He'd just come downstairs on his crutches for breakfast and was eating a big bowl of oatmeal Beth had made him. When the news came over the radio that Norway was occupied, do you know what he did? He took that bowl of oatmeal and turned it upside down on his head. The whole mess – porridge, brown sugar, milk – it was all over him, streaming down his face and onto his sweater. What a mess. You probably don't remember that. You were pretty young at the time.

Madge remembered. It wasn't something she would likely forget, watching a grown man dump porridge on himself and cry like a baby. Perhaps this was when the horror of war began to sink in, when she saw that it could make a grown man cry.

It wasn't too long after this – in fact, it was the day he got off his crutches – that Stefan bought the Pontiac, a light blue model with all the trimmings. Brand new, she was. He got her from Power Motors in Bridgewater. Paid cash. I drove him up so he could buy it. Had a roll of bills on him thick enough to choke a cow. I guess, being single, he could save his money. He was sure proud of that car. Two nights before he sailed, someone side-swiped it, dented the right bumper. I got it fixed for him. Stored it in Ed Bartling's garage. It stayed there until after the war, when some hooligans got into it and turned it into scrap.

After Gladys had been their housekeeper for three months, she became sluggish and lazy. She let dirty clothes pile up. She stopped changing beds or washing sheets. She wouldn't get up before Madge and Ardith left for school, so they had to make breakfast themselves. Three or four times they came home at noon to find there was no dinner. When Laddie was working the early morning shift at the mill, he carried a lunch pail, so he didn't know this was going on. The situation with Gladys didn't last more than a couple of weeks, because one morning Beth got up out of bed, came downstairs, and found Gladys bloated and crying, wandering around the house in her nightgown. That same day Laddie drove Gladys back to her uncle's in Port Mouton. Their mother's sister, Margaret, moved in with them, to take over the housework.

"Gladys is having a baby," Ardith whispered that night when she and Madge lay across from one another in their twin beds. They did most of their talking before the ten o'clock curfew. "That's what happens when you lie with sailors."

The incident with Gladys occurred in 1944. By then Madge was in grade four. She and Ardith both came home at noon, but their Aunt Margaret stayed at school. She taught at the Parade School on the other side of town. It was too far for her to walk home and back in an hour. Madge and Ardith ate sandwiches their aunt had made the night before. As soon as Ardith had finished eating she went back to school for choir practice, or drama club, or volleyball, but Madge hung around the house, putting off going to school until the last minute. Most of this time she spent upstairs in her mother's room.

Beth kept a box of chocolate bars beneath her bed. Jersey Milk. She was supposed to eat a Jersey Milk a day to fatten herself up, but she gave them to Madge and Ardith instead. Ardith always saved hers, but Madge ate hers right away. Usually her mother made her wait until after school before she'd allow her to take a chocolate bar, but occasionally she'd relent and let Madge have it at noon. One noon hour, after Madge had finished her chocolate bar, she started going through her mother's dresser drawers. This habit was a carry-over from when Madge was younger; it had dropped off since she'd started school. Madge lifted out the panties and slips, the sachets of rose petals and lavender. Her mother never minded her doing this. She had always allowed Ardith and Madge to dress up in her high heels and gloves, to try on her felt hat and rope pearls. Madge knew exactly what was inside her mother's closet and dresser drawers. She had memorized the contents of the jewellery case which was on top of the dresser. The inside of the case had tiny shelves lined with blue satin. On these shelves were a pearl necklace and earrings, a string of amber beads, her mother's nursing pin, an amethyst brooch, a gold ring with three green stones that had belonged to Madge's Irish grandmother, and a china bird pin with blue glass eyes.

The china bird pin was missing. In fact, the pin had been missing for some time without Madge noticing its absence from the jewellery case. Perhaps she hadn't been paying close attention to the jewellery. Or perhaps she'd noticed and assumed the pin was on a dress lapel inside the closet. Her mother often left jewellery pinned to clothes. This time Madge was paying attention. As soon as she noticed the pin was missing, she asked her mother where it was.

"Oh, I gave that away," Beth said.

"But it was your favourite pin!" Madge said. The pin was a white china bird with its wings spread. Not a seagull or a hawk, nothing so large. A dove possibly.

"It was only a cheap little pin I picked up in the Five-and-Ten," her mother said.

"Who did you give it to?" Madge said.

"I gave it to someone who stayed with us earlier in the war," Beth said. "A Norwegian who'd become a friend of ours. Stefan Edwardson. You remember him. He was on crutches for a while. I put the pin in an envelope with our address on it and asked him to mail it back so we'd know if he arrived home safely."

Madge looked at the place where the china bird had been. The satin was pressed down in the shape of wings. This wasn't like the surface of the sea. When you dropped something into the sea, the water swallowed it completely, even its shape disappeared.

"He didn't mail it back," Madge said, "because a sub got him."

Her mother didn't deny this. She pulled the sheet up to her chin and closed her eyes.

Madge studied the blue veins on her mother's eyelids, the black lashes on the pale cheeks, the dark, tangled hair, the lips turned down at the corners as if her mother had eaten something bad tasting or sour. Madge thought maybe this was what you looked like when you were pining away. She felt curiously distanced from her mother, as if she were staring at another woman with closed eyes whose dark hair rested on a white pillow.

The woman Madge was thinking about wasn't her mother, but someone in a story – a story that had nothing to do with Madge. In this story, a dark-haired, slender woman dressed in an emerald-green coat was stepping into a pale blue car. It was winter, but the woman was holding a picnic basket and thermos. A fair-haired man wearing a grey wool sweater was holding open the car door. Before the woman bent down to get into the car, the man leaned over and kissed her on the forehead. Then he closed the door, got in the car, and they drove away. Madge didn't know what to make of this story, especially since there was an emerald-green coat like the one the woman was wearing hanging downstairs in the hall closet.

Years later, after Madge had grown up and her mother was dead, Madge thought that Gladys, in her abstracted, hopeful way, may have hit upon something solid: that Madge's mother and Stefan had probably had a short, war-time affair, or at least a serious flirtation.

But Gladys was wrong about her mother pining away. After ten months in bed, Beth's TB was cured and she got up, cooked meals, and kept house just as she always had, and her sister

Margaret moved back to her boarding house on Union Street. The only difference in their lives was that even though ships continued to be refitted at the Liverpool docks, no more sailors stayed in their spare room because of the extra work it would make for their mother. They never again saw any of the men who had slept in their spare room during the war, though two or three of them sent Christmas cards and one of them, Verne Read, eventually became a magistrate on the West Coast.

Do you remember Herbie Piltz and Pee Wee Robson? They stayed with us for a few weeks in '43. Herbie had red hair, Pee Wee was blond. Just sailor boys, they were, both of them wet behind the ears. Herbie was nineteen; he was from Sault Ste. Marie. Pee Wee was twenty; from out west somewhere, Portage la Prairie, I think it was. Funny how it goes. Herbie was convinced he'd never get back. Pee Wee acted like he didn't have a care in the world. As it turned out, Herbie was the lucky one. Soon after they left here to meet up with a convoy, their boat was torpedoed off Newfoundland. Herbie was picked up right away. Wrote me a letter about it afterwards. Pee Wee had the bad luck. He and another fellow were found in a lifeboat by some fishermen. Both of them dead as doornails, their backs riddled with machine-gun fire. Herbie said the Germans must have been using them for target practice.

Even as a child, Madge recognized the treachery, the waste, the futility of war, though she had not, of course, used those words. From late in the war when her father began telling her his stories, Madge had known there was nothing admirable or heroic or useful about war. This knowledge was something she absorbed through the telling, along with some misgivings about her father's reliability. She felt his fervour and enthusiasm toward the war were misplaced, that her father was someone to be wary of, that his judgment was something she couldn't entirely trust.

Laddie continued to tell war stories until late in his life, when his memory began to fail. Madge thought her father told the stories to make up for the fact that he hadn't joined up because of having a family to support. *Someone has to keep the home fires burning.* Later on, Madge thought he told the stories to convince himself, as much as anyone, that the war did happen, that people like Stefan Edwardson, Herbie, and Pee Wee had slept in his spare room, eaten in his kitchen, played with his children. As long as he was able to tell his stories, he was able to convince himself that the stories were real, that they hadn't come out of a book or a movie. They hadn't come out of someone's head.

The image of the war that Madge was to carry with her into adulthood was that of a huge, rounded fin breaking the surface of the North Atlantic. The terror of watching the U-boat surface and come toward you, water pouring from its bow, while you stood on deck knowing that your life depended on something as tenuous and frightening as a German captain having a cousin living in Kitchener or Crousetown. Depended on whether there was a Captain Smith on board your ship, a man who spoke to the enemy with defiance and contempt. Depended on a German captain's sense of fair play, even, perhaps, his sense of humour. Standing in the boat, you knew you were powerless, that nothing you could say or do would make the slightest bit of difference, that it was luck and only luck that would keep you from disappearing into the sea.

Pranks

Laddie Murray liked to think of himself as a harmless prankster. He acted surprised and hurt when his wife told him that his attempts at humour were thoughtless and cruel. He was a gregarious Cape Bretoner who would give a stranger the shirt off his back and thought this generosity offset the worst of his faults. When his brother Malcolm married Marilyn George in June of 1936, Laddie kidnapped the newlyweds on the pretext of driving them from the reception in Marilyn's house to the Isle Royale Hotel in Sydney, where they were to spend the night. Laddie drove them, tin cans bouncing and clattering behind, all the way to the Telegraph Hotel in Baddeck, a distance of forty miles, too far for Marilyn to walk home. Marilyn was so put out with Laddie for this prank that she refused to speak to him for a year. Laddie was mystified by Marilyn's reaction. He thought she was being a poor sport. He remained unrepentant about the kidnapping and stubbornly refused to acknowledge Marilyn's right to be angry. In fact, whenever he retold the story, he exaggerated her huffiness, for effect. Over the years, this kidnapping story, which began as bridge-club material, gradually became absorbed into Laddie's general repertoire, popping up unexpectedly whenever conversation wandered into unfamiliar territory and needed to be hauled back.

Laddie was the only one of the Murray family who had managed to leave Cape Breton Island and stay away longer than four years. Malcolm never left the island at all except for brief holidays; he went straight from high school into his father's marine business in North Sydney, which sold sea-going equipment to fishermen and sailors. When their father, James, died of a heart attack in 1933, Bruce, Laddie's youngest brother, returned to the island to stay, bringing with him a gold medal and a science degree from McGill. He also had a job offer in Montreal, which he turned down in order to work in the family business. At this point Laddie's mother, Agnes, had been dead six years. She had drowned at age forty-four during an outing in Sydney harbour. It was after church on Sunday. She was wearing a straw boater and a long tweed skirt. The heavy skirt tangled around her legs and dragged her down. That was what Laddie had been told anyway. He was away at the time, taking pre-engineering courses at Acadia. A year after her death, he dropped out of college and went to work at the paper mill in Liverpool, where he met and married Elizabeth Burchell.

Laddie's twin sister, Harriet, was the oldest in the family by ten minutes. Harriet left the island twice a year to attend trade shows in Halifax and Toronto. Harriet owned a gift shop in Sydney, one she started herself. She carried a full line of Buchan pottery: teapots, sugar bowls, milk pitchers and plates hand-painted in Scotland. Most of her stock came from the island. There were hooked rugs and coasters made by women in Cheticamp, placemats, tablecloths, scarves and shawls woven by women in Margaree. Harriet wove herself, using patterns that settlers had brought with them in 1773 when they walked off the boat in Pictou. Harriet didn't sell coloured bangles or plastic beads, nothing as frivolous as birthstone rings with glass chip stones. Her jewellery ran to escutcheon brooches with heavy clasps, kilt pins with amethyst thistles. It was difficult to find an object inside her shop that couldn't be put to practical use.

Harriet made one trip off-island which wasn't for business purposes. She drove to Liverpool to visit Laddie. That was in September, 1938. By then Ardith and Madge had been born. Harriet took the ferry across Canso Strait and drove to Halifax. From there she followed the south shore road to Liverpool. She parked at the curb not far from Laddie's house and sat in the car for half an hour or more. Then she turned around and returned to Cape Breton, staying in Antigonish overnight. She was back in Sydney by noon the next day. It was Bruce who told Laddie; Laddie never asked Harriet why, after driving all that way, she had not come inside. Laddie treated his sister with delicacy and tact. He spoke of his brothers with a respect bordering on reverence, as if they were shepherd priests holding down a highland shieling during his absence.

The prank Laddie played on Beth's younger sister, Margaret Burchell, was to send her a valentine card with Will You Marry Me? printed across the bottom and signed with the initials H.E. The card was intended to have been sent by Harris Erb, Margaret's boyfriend of eight years who, according to Laddie, was slow getting off the mark. On the surface of it, this prank was harmless enough. What Laddie did not take into account was the fact that Margaret may have been keeping track of his misdemeanours and had accumulated enough to add him to the list of people she disliked. Margaret had known Laddie before he met Beth. They had played in the same bridge club. The night Margaret introduced Laddie to her sister, Laddie looked across the table and told Beth he was going to marry her. Margaret may have found his conceit and swagger hard to take. She may have thought that Laddie and Beth were unsuited, that they married too quickly, that they should have taken more time to get to know each other like she and Harris Erb were doing.

Harris Erb was a short, dapper man in his early forties. He wore a toupee, buffed his nails, and lived with his mother.

Harris managed the Astor Theatre in Liverpool. Madge's contact with him came whenever Ardith sent her inside the theatre to ask for movie previews of *Mrs. Miniver, Random Harvest,* or *Desperate Journey.* Ardith maintained that once these photographs – large black and white stills with a voluptuous glossy shine – were removed from the theatre window, they were thrown away, so it was all right to ask for them. Ardith preferred not to ask for them herself in case her interest in movie stars might appear trivial and misleading. She did not like to connect herself with the girl who slept beneath these photographs. After Madge came out of the theatre, she would hand the photographs to Ardith and they would walk home together. At such times there was a subdued camaraderie between the sisters that they never referred to. It had to do with an exchange of knowledge, what they knew about each other: the secret longings, the surprising pockets of boldness and daring. If nothing interrupted this truce, it might last for days, maybe weeks, Madge's satisfaction lingering whenever she looked at the stills tacked to the wall above Ardith's bed, pictures of Walter Pidgeon, Greer Garson, Errol Flynn.

It was Madge, not Ardith, who knew about the valentine prank. She was the snooper in the family, the Nosy Parker. Ardith moved about with more purpose. She had projects on the go, ambitious plans, she didn't have time to waste eavesdropping. Madge was looser, random, inclined to be lazy. She didn't recognize anything as significant until she had rolled past it. She was like a large ball made from soft material such as felt or brushed wool, the kind of surface bits and pieces stuck to as she rolled down hallways and around corners, into bedrooms and places she had no business entering. These bits and pieces clung to her haphazardly. There was no pattern to their arrangement; nothing useful could be made of this gathering; it was nothing more than an acquisitive habit.

In the mornings Madge was the last to leave for school; Ardith usually went to school half an hour early. Their Aunt Margaret left the house much earlier, before eight o'clock. Madge was upstairs in the bathroom brushing her teeth. She was careful not to close the door or turn on the water full blast so she wouldn't give herself away. She knew she was past the age of going unnoticed, of being considered too young or indifferent to care what was said in front of her.

Her father was in the room next door, sitting on her mother's bed. Madge heard him say, "Harris's back end needs a shove. Maybe Margaret will show him the valentine and he'll get the message and propose."

"I wouldn't do that if I were you," Madge's mother said.

"I've already sent it."

Madge heard her mother sigh.

"That was a mistake. If Margaret finds out you sent the valentine, she'll be furious. She'll think you were meddling. How do you know she wants to marry Harris anyway? She might like things just as they are."

Madge turned off the trickle of water and wiped her mouth on the back of her hand. Her parents' voices dropped. The conversation had changed direction. Madge knew this from her mother's laugh. Usually her mother's laugh was phlegmy and deep, like a chuckle. The sound her mother was making now was lighter, girlish. Her mother was giggling. The giggle disturbed Madge. It came from a place inside her mother she didn't know, a place where she wasn't wanted. She tiptoed to the bathroom doorway and listened.

"You know we can't," her mother said. Her voice was plaintive but wistful too, as if she wanted to be talked into something.

There was a creak of the bedsprings, a shifting of weight.

Madge appeared in the doorway of the bedroom. She had a magician's instinct for appearances. "I'm leaving now," she said.

Her mother's face turned toward the doorway.

"I thought you'd gone."

Laddie straightened himself; he had been leaning over her mother.

"Well, goodbye then," her mother said. Her cheeks were flushed. "I'll see you at noon."

"Behave yourself," Laddie said.

Wasted words. Madge was quiet in school. *Too quiet*, Miss Simms wrote on her report card. *Does not volunteer answers.*

Madge was possessive about her mother. She thought her mother needed protection, pampering. She thought she needed company, that she was lonely lying in bed all day, listening to the yellow plastic radio on the night table beside her. After school Madge would rush home and upstairs to her mother's bedroom. If her mother was asleep, Madge would stand at the foot of the bed and watch her breathe. If she was awake, Madge might ask to be told about when she had been born, though she knew the story by heart.

Madge hadn't been born in the hospital but on this very bed where her mother lay. She had been two weeks overdue, unlike Ardith who had been two weeks early. To speed up Madge's birth, Beth had jumped off the basement stairs, three steps up. *You were a nurse and you did that?* Madge would say. When the jump didn't work, Beth persuaded Betty Randall to drive her over the Western Head Road, which was bumpy with frost pits and furrows. The jolting got things going and Madge was born soon afterwards, coming so fast the doctor didn't make it on time. He was in the barber's chair getting his hair cut. Betty, who was also a nurse, helped deliver Madge. There was a shine to this story, a spunkiness, an amazing rashness that delighted Madge.

Sometimes Madge asked to be told about her mother's love affairs, *engagements*, her mother called them. Beth had been engaged to a doctor named Edward Barnes, who worked in the McKellar General Hospital in Fort William, Ontario, where Beth had trained. Unfortunately Edward's mother was the nursing supervisor at the McKellar. She kept finding fault with Beth, giving her a two-week suspension for speaking back to a patient who had rung for the bedpan eleven times in one hour. Edward did not stick up for Beth or himself when his mother chastised them for walking down the hospital steps hand in hand. Beth returned Edward's diamond ring and took a job in Montreal where, a year later, she became engaged to Carl Petrie whom she met when he was in the hospital with a broken leg, the result of a skiing accident. Carl wasn't a mama's boy, he was a playboy. He gambled. He partied too much. He didn't need a regular job because there was money in the family, an inheritance. Carl lived with his parents in a mansion in Westmount that had a suit of armour in the hall and a musician's balcony overlooking the living room. Beth had been there several times for meals. Carl's parents liked her. They told her they hoped she would straighten Carl out. They seemed to think he would grow out of his wildness. After a year's engagement, there was no sign that he would, so Beth returned the ring and moved to Bridgewater to be close to her sister and her father's second family, who had moved to Nova Scotia from Ontario.

After Margaret came to stay with them, Madge had to settle for noon hours with her mother, because her aunt beat her home after school. By the time Madge bounded up the stairs after school, Margaret would be sitting on Beth's bed in her good clothes. Margaret was a smart dresser. She wore wool dresses, stylish hats, coats with large buttons, all these in bright colours that set off her ginger-coloured hair.

The first time Margaret saw Madge dive for the Jersey Milk box beneath Beth's bed, she tapped the floor with the toe of her high-heeled shoe and said, *Aren't someone's manners missing?* Margaret disciplined people in the third person, presumably to save them the embarrassment of being directly addressed, perhaps to provide them with the opportunity to draw back and see their shortcomings in a clearer light. Madge wondered why her mother didn't tell Margaret that she was allowed to help herself to a chocolate bar. She thought it was because Margaret was a teacher. A teacher wasn't someone you corrected, a teacher corrected others' mistakes.

At four o'clock Margaret put on the vegetables for supper. Now that she had taken over the meals, they ate their big meal at night instead of noon. At four-thirty Madge was called to the kitchen to prepare her mother's tray while Ardith set the table. Laddie turned up at five. Laddie never cooked supper or put a wash through the wringer. Even with his wife in bed, he didn't. He sometimes claimed, in an abashed and bragging tone, that he couldn't boil water. In those days it wasn't expected of a man, it was seen as taking away from his manliness. Men rarely did kitchen work unless they were paid. Laddie would never stand on the back stoop and peg out laundry in the frosty air. Margaret did it on Saturday mornings, her long nails like red winter berries against the white sheets. Laddie did small house repairs, loose door-hinges, dripping taps. He rarely mowed grass or shovelled snow. When he was a boy in Sydney his family had hired help to do this kind of work.

The Murrays had lived in a large Victorian house with leaded front windows and a thick oak door. They were one of the first families on the island to own a car, a rectangular black Ford with narrow tires that frequently blew on the gravel roads over which the Murray brothers drove at top speed, honking at farmers on the top of hayracks and cows that had strayed into the ditch. Madge had seen a photo of this car, an over-exposed, brownish picture, showing Laddie leaning against the front fender, a plaid scarf around his neck, a tweed cap tilted rakishly over one eye.

That was the Murray side of the family. The substantial, mercantile side, with its bold outer face. A confident, unapologetic, clannish family that owed explanations to no one, least of all to itself.

The other side of Madge's family, her mother and aunt's side, wasn't nearly so tidy or self-possessed. To begin with, it was Irish, a fact that somehow implied intemperate mistakes and fumblings. There were holes in this family, windows left open, doors ajar. There was misfortune and disgrace.

The misfortune began when Madge's great-grandparents died of influenza, leaving Madge's Irish grandmother, six-month-old Nelly Payne, in the care of two maiden aunts in Dublin, Rachael and Margaret. The misfortune continued when Nelly fell out of an apple tree when she was sixteen and sustained a knee injury so severe she was to use a cane for the rest of her life. The injury brought her across the Atlantic to Halifax for surgery, which was only partially successful. Nelly married the surgeon's son, Norman Burchell. Norman was an electrical engineer who found work in places like Sudbury, Copper Cliff, Welland, places Nelly found barren and staid. She was someone who valued beauty and liked a good time. There were four children – Dessie, Beth, Dillon, Margaret – and several miscarriages. Norman was frequently away. Nelly drank. Twice the maiden aunts sent money and Nelly took the children to Dublin for long visits. At thirty-nine, Nelly died, not from anything as clean and swift as drowning but by complications following a miscarriage.

Beth and Margaret were sent to board in Toronto. Norman took Dessie and Dillon with him to Welland, where he was working on the canal. Dillon was retarded; he never got past grade three. He was to grow into a squat, dwarfish man with an oversized head and perfect pitch, a man who liked to whistle along with canaries. Dessie was bright enough, but he was disowned before he finished high school. He would have been about eighteen or nineteen. It was after Norman took another wife, Cassie Lewis. Beth and Margaret were still living in Toronto when the marriage and the disowning took place. They never found out what had happened, whether the marriage had something to do with it or whether Dessie had gotten into some sort of trouble with the law. Their father said Dessie had disgraced the family and ordered his daughters never again to mention his name. Beth and Margaret didn't think Dessie deserved this treatment. They couldn't imagine him as having done something horrible like murder or rape. They had known Dessie as a kind, gentle brother who used to take them to Saturday matinees and afterwards buy them shelled peanuts and the weekend funnies. They didn't think him capable of disgrace, but were shamed into silence by their ignorance of the facts.

One noon hour in April, a month before the war ended, Madge and Ardith came home at noon and found their mother hurrying around the kitchen in her grey gabardine suit, white nylon blouse, and black patent-leather pumps. By then their mother was allowed to get up for an hour or two in the mornings and again in late afternoon. Their mother had put on rouge and pinned her hair on top of her head. She looked glamorous and theatrical, moving about the kitchen in a mysterious, feverish way, pouring glasses of milk, arranging sandwiches on plates. Margaret was there too, looking smart and professional in a paddy-green suit. She was sitting at the table, a square of waxed paper on her lap, eating a sandwich made the night before. After Madge and Ardith had finished their lunch, they were sent upstairs to put on clean blouses and kneesocks, without having to wash the glasses and plates. Nothing was said about why their aunt was home at noon or why their mother was dressed up until they were back downstairs, sitting in the living room.

They wouldn't be returning to school that afternoon, their mother said. Instead, they would be visiting with their cousin, Glen Burchell, their Uncle Dessie's son. They had never seen this uncle. He lived far away, in the States. (Madge's mother had just found this out. Years later, Madge was to learn how her mother and Margaret had been kept in the dark. This was after Madge's family had moved to Cape Breton, to Murray country, and Beth was driven to making disclosures about the Irish side of the family, in self-defence.) Their mother went on to say that while they were in school this morning, there had been a phone call from Dessie's son, Glen Burchell. Glen was a U.S. Marine whose ship was tied up in Halifax for the day. He was hitching a ride to Liverpool to visit them. He would be arriving soon. Their mother didn't mention inviting

Dillon over to meet this new cousin. Dillon lived on Bristol Avenue with Madge's grandfather. Madge understood that Dillon was unpredictable and made scenes. He couldn't be trusted to behave himself.

The sisters spent the first hour waiting for Glen in the living room, Madge and Ardith taking turns at the window, their mother and Margaret sitting on the chesterfield drinking tea. Around three o'clock Ardith went downstairs to a worktable where she was making a medieval castle out of cardboard. She had painted the cardboard grey and was now cutting out window slits and a drawbridge. Madge took paper and coloured pencils downstairs and sat on the basement steps drawing pictures, to keep Ardith company. She and Ardith stayed down there until their father came home at four o'clock. He had left work early in order to meet Glen. When Madge and Ardith went upstairs, they saw Margaret standing in the hallway, arms folded across her chest, speaking to Laddie.

"I might have known it would come to this," she was saying. "We ought to have known better than to be taken in." She spoke about the morning's call with contempt, as if it had been a prank, a callous attempt to get their hopes up only to dash them down again.

"Maybe something unexpected came up at the last minute to prevent him from coming," Beth said from the living room. She was still on the chesterfield. "Guard duty or something."

"Then he ought to have phoned and told us," Margaret said. "Did he think we had nothing better to do than to sit around and wait?"

"Why don't I make some inquiries?" Laddie said. "He may have run into trouble."

Laddie was quick to offer this sort of help, to request information, to register complaints and demands through the proper channels, to act on someone's behalf. This was self-importance, mixed with kindness. At the paper mill Laddie was the person who would put a worker's case to management. (This was before the paper-makers were unionized.) He had gotten Lew Menzies rehired after he had been falsely accused of stealing Milford Robinson's watch. He had raised money to help Albert Rafuse's family after Albert had jammed his arm in a paper machine. "It shouldn't be too difficult to check with the port authorities in Halifax to find out your nephew's whereabouts."

"That won't be necessary," Margaret said. "If Glen Burchell had been serious about coming to see us, he would have turned up. I have no intention of wasting any more time on him." She turned to Madge and Ardith, who were standing at the top of the cellar stairs. "Come on, kids, you can help me get supper." Their aunt always called them kids when she was in a spirited, feisty mood.

Beth went upstairs, took off her suit, and got into bed. Madge took up her supper tray: mashed potatoes and finnan haddie poached in milk. It was six o'clock; the light in the room was a fuzzy, indeterminate grey. Beth was still wearing rouge and eyeshadow. Her hair was coming unpinned. Madge thought there was something stagey and slipshod about her mother's appearance. This was how the disappointment came out, seeing her mother as someone sloppy and unreliable.

Margaret stayed with them until May 7, 1945 – VE day. Madge was in school when the church bells started ringing and the fire sirens wailed at two o'clock in the afternoon. Miss Simms, a cautious, deer-like woman, who always wore brown and smelled of stale crackers and Noxzema, put down her speller and said in her rippling, genteel voice that class was dismissed, there would be no homework because the war was over. Books were shoved onto the floor, erasers and pencils hurled across the room. Everyone rushed for the door except Miss Simms, whose habit it was to linger in the classroom after school to tidy up, stooping between desks to pick up forgotten gym clothes and scribblers, moving slowly, staring meditatively through the window, as if she were grazing in a meadow. Outside, in the schoolyard, Madge heard car horns tooting all over town. There were shrill whistles and deep, imperious honks coming from the ships down at the docks.

Margaret wasn't home, but Madge's parents were in the kitchen with Ardith, sitting around the table listening to the overseas victory celebrations. This radio, a polished walnut box with a curved top and an opening covered with a square of beige upholstery, sat on a shelf above the table. Most mornings during the war, they had sat in front of this radio listening to the BBC broadcasts. They had gathered around the radio in the same way people gather around a fireplace or a woodstove. The ritual of listening had that kind of coziness. After the broadcast, Madge's mother made toast and sprinkled it with cinnamon and sugar. She poured sugar from one of the ration jars into the bowl for their tea.

"Just think," she said. "No more rations."

When they had finished their tea, Laddie announced he was going to plant a victory tree on the front lawn and Ardith and Madge could help. He sent them to the basement for a shovel and a bucket, and the three of them got into the turquoise Nash, Ardith sitting up front beside Laddie. They drove out of town and onto the beach road.

"You look while I drive," Laddie said.

"What kind of tree do we want?" Ardith said.

"Whatever we find that's the right size."

The tree itself didn't seem to matter, Madge thought. It was the idea of planting it.

"Nothing too big," Laddie told them.

After they had driven three or four miles down the beach road, their father pulled into a wide path that went into the trees. It was one of those muddy tracks that taper off mysteriously, leaving people wondering why it was there in the first place. Their father stopped the car, got out and walked around. Ahead was a huge oak tree with large, spreading branches. Beneath them were several saplings, slender as whips.

"One of these will do," their father said.

Ardith took the shovel out of the trunk and handed it to Laddie. The sisters stood in front of the car and watched Laddie dig. Occasionally he would give them an order – move that rock out of there, hold these branches, get the bucket out of the trunk – so they wouldn't mistake themselves for idle spectators.

When the tree had been dug and its roots put into the bucket, it was placed in the back seat with Madge, and the three of them drove home. Laddie dug a hole in the middle of the front lawn. The sisters were sent scurrying to drag out the hose, to find stakes and twine, to carry out the bag of fertilizer that was under the basement stairs. When the tree was finally planted and tied straight, Madge felt let down. The tree looked disappointing, considering all the effort that had gone into planting it. There were no leaves on its spindly branches, nothing but loose green buds, and a black gaping wound in the lawn.

That night there was a lot of drinking and singing down on the docks to celebrate the victory. There were house parties, people roaming the streets. Laddie did not join the festivities. After supper he and Buddy Titus had a couple of drinks in Billy's garage. Then Laddie brought the bottle home and he and Beth sat in the living room drinking rum from kitchen glasses. Margaret was at a beach party with Harris Erb.

At nine o'clock Madge was sent upstairs to bed. Ardith was already in their bedroom, pasting war clippings into her scrapbook. For the first time in six years there was no curfew and they did not have to pull down the green air raid blinds. They lay on their beds in the darkening night and listened to their parents' voices in the room below, the muted shouts from parties down on the waterfront.

A hundred miles up the coast in Halifax, people took to the streets by the thousands to celebrate VE day. They roamed the city, singing and dancing in the mild spring evening. No one wanted to be inside. All through the war years, people in downtown Halifax had been living in cramped quarters, doubling up to make room for the sailors and military personnel who needed a place to hang their hats. There was a lot of grumbling and discontent, because of the crowding. There were no taverns or bars, no place for people to let off steam, no place for them to kick up their heels. The canteen at the naval base closed at the usual time, nine o'clock.

People began breaking into liquor outlets, emptying shelves, carrying bottles outside. Stores were next, ordinary stores that sold groceries, clothing, jewellery. Mobs smashed windows, broke down doors, carried merchandise away. A woman was seen going inside a clothing store wearing one outfit and reappearing shortly wearing another. A man stood in front of a jewellery store and handed rings and watches to passersby. People fell or were pushed onto sidewalks littered with broken glass and had to be taken to hospital. Sensible people hurried home, locked the doors, and turned out the lights. Others stayed out all night, prowling the streets and parks. Many of these people had passed the party stage and were looking for trouble. There were fights, sexual assaults. The police were powerless to stop the violence and vandalism. They had no choice but to let people wear themselves out. By morning parts of the city looked as if they had been blitzed.

The next morning, while her parents slept in, Madge came downstairs in her nightgown and discovered her Aunt Margaret had moved out. Madge knew this from a note written on scribbler paper tacked to the kitchen wall above the shelf where the walnut radio had been. Pinned to the top right-hand corner of the page, where her aunt usually placed a coloured star, was a twenty-dollar bill. For a teacher, her aunt had terrible handwriting, but Madge was used to it and could make out the crabbed scrawl. *I'm taking the radio with me. This should be enough to buy yourselves another*, the note said. *I'm moving back to Union Street. Margaret.*

Ardith came into the kitchen, wearing a jumper and blouse. She did not like to come downstairs in the mornings until she was properly dressed.

Ardith saw her younger sister standing barefoot in the middle of the kitchen floor. She saw her point to the shelf over the table. Ardith looked at the place where the walnut radio had been. She read the note tacked to the wall.

"My God, she took the radio!" she said. "That was her wedding present to Mum and Dad."

This wasn't the sort of information Madge kept track of, but Ardith did. She knew where most of their furniture came from, whether it had been bought or given.

Ardith said, "Why would she steal our radio when she could buy one herself?"

"Maybe this was the only one she liked," Madge said.

Neither of them believed this. The sisters looked at each other and rolled their eyes. Why would their aunt do such a thing? Did she think she could just help herself to the radio and their parents wouldn't care? Or was she playing some kind of prank? Ardith, who had already lined herself up with the Scottish side of the family, made a stab at explaining it.

"It's because she's Irish," she said. "Irish people are temperamental. They do strange things like this."

Madge understood that in order to have sides you had to have differences. She saw the Murray side, which Ardith was on with their father, as straightforward and no-nonsense, confident and unmistaken, whereas the Burchell side, which she herself was on with her mother, Margaret, and Dillon, was muddled and erratic, hobbled by misfortune and bad luck. It was a side doomed to make blunders, to invite disgrace. Madge felt she should stick up for the Irish side of their family, but her aunt's theft had moved it somewhere beyond rescue. There was nothing to do but let the verdict pass.

Rustic Toil

In 1950, five years before the causeway was built, when Cape Breton could still claim to be an island, the Murray family took the ferry across Canso Strait and went to live in Sydney Mines, where Madge's father had rented them a house. The money Laddie had made from selling their house in Liverpool had gone into buying a warehouse where he was setting up a rope manufacturing business. For some time, Bruce and Malcolm, Laddie's brothers, had been encouraging him to do this, to take advantage of the post-war boom. They were putting up money to help Laddie buy equipment. The idea was that, with Laddie making the rope and them selling it in their store, they would have both ends of their business looked after. Rope was the mainstay of the marine business. Before leaving Liverpool, Laddie had turned down a job as an assistant supervisor at the paper mill. He did not like working for someone else. He and his brothers and sister had not been brought up to work for other people.

Beth Murray agreed to the move, she may even have encouraged it, but living in Sydney Mines took some getting used to. She couldn't bring in a load of laundry from the clothesline without there being coal dust on it. Soon after their move, a bra and three pairs of underpants had been stolen from the clothesline. One night about ten o'clock Madge walked into the dining room to put away a china pitcher she had unpacked and saw a man in a bowler hat standing in the flower bed, staring through the darkened window. Their house had been built over an abandoned coal tunnel. Rats lived in this tunnel. The rats came into the basement through the drain in the laundry room and dragged away washing to use in their nests. Usually it was something small: a handkerchief or a hand towel. Eventually they were to take a dresser scarf. During the next few years a rat would sometimes get loose in the basement and Madge's father would have to come home from work and kill it with the coal shovel. Madge's mother shovelled coal into the furnace, but she drew the line at killing a rat.

All this was a far cry from the town of Liverpool, where prosperous merchants built houses on solid ground and sidewalks were paved, not raked with cinders. It was a far cry from the south shore, where clean white beaches stretched for miles. What passed for a beach in this part of Cape Breton was a shingle of grey slate below Greener's Cliff, not far from the sewer outlet. People drowned cats off this cliff. Once, when Madge was walking along the beach below the cliff with Nonie Fraser, looking for a place fit to swim, she saw a dead cat float past on a board. She thought it must have fought its way out of a potato sack, climbed onto the board, and been overtaken by a wave.

The move to Cape Breton had been in mid July, the day after Ardith wrote her last provincial exam. She had finished high school. Madge was going into grade ten. Five or six weeks after the move, in August, after their furniture had been set to rights and the curtains were up, Malcolm and Bruce came to visit after church on Sunday, bringing their wives and children. Between them, they had seven children, all of them younger than Laddie's two daughters. Ardith was smart enough to escape upstairs on the pretext of having some sewing to do, but Madge, who had nothing planned, was stuck downstairs, following her cousins around, making sure they didn't ransack the kitchen cupboards or fall down the basement stairs.

One Sunday, Harriet drove over from Sydney – not for a visit, she refused to come inside. She had come to drop off a woven tablecloth, a discard she had been unable to sell in the shop. It was too rustic for her clientele, she said. The tablecloth was a raw, sienna colour, with a thick, maize-coloured fringe. Afterwards, Madge's mother said Harriet had probably made up the story about the tablecloth being a discard because she was too much of a businesswoman to admit she had taken something from the store to give away.

One Sunday in September, before Ardith went away to college, their family was summoned to Sydney to meet Great-Aunt Flora and Aunt Grace. Although they were sisters, only Flora, the elder of the two, was called Great-Aunt. Before coming to live with her sister, Aunt Grace had been married to Arthur MacKinnon for four years. Somehow, this brief, childless marriage had made Grace less formidable and more resilient, though not without her having slipped a notch or two. "Grace is without issue," Great-Aunt Flora said, as she was herself, through no fault of her own. She had never met a man she cared for enough to marry and seemed to think her sister culpable for having done so. Aunt Grace was freckle-faced and bow-legged. She wore a hairnet and an apron. Although she was well into her seventies, there was little grey in her hair, which was a dull rust colour. She was thin and badly stooped. The stoop was misleading. She moved with an agile, monkeyish grace. Great-Aunt Flora was white-haired and moved like a ship. She was heavyset and thick-shouldered. Beneath her navy rayon dress her hips were firmly girded in a bone corset, over which her bosom spilled like rising bread dough. These aunts lived in the Murray house where Laddie, Harriet, and their brothers had been born. Only now they lived on the first floor and rented out the second as an apartment.

For dinner they had roast lamb, boiled potatoes, tinned peas and carrots. There was gooseberry trifle on the sideboard

for dessert. Great-Aunt Flora had poor eyesight, Aunt Grace
had some sort of palsy. Neither one could trust herself to carve
the roast. They would not allow Laddie or Beth to carve it.
They invited Ruby Chisholm from next door to slip in the
back entryway and carve it, then slip home again, without
being introduced. Ruby was in her seventies herself, but she
could see well enough and hold a knife steady. In this house
no one entered the kitchen uninvited. You did not carry so
much as an empty water glass over the threshold. You might
catch a glimpse of the disarray in the kitchen, a disarray that
had fallen to the aunts to clean up, now that there was no
maid.

"The girls can do the dishes," Madge's mother said oblig-
ingly, after they had eaten the trifle.

"That won't be necessary," Great-Aunt Flora said. "Grace
will remove the dishes and bring in the tea." Then she turned
to Ardith and announced that, after tea, she would show her
the Murray forebears.

The parlour walls were covered with pictures of these forebears. Great-Aunt Flora named them all. Ardith was attentive,
asked questions, which Great-Aunt Flora apparently
approved of, since she answered them in some detail. Laddie
was the talker in the family, but on this occasion, humbled by
the favour bestowed on his daughter, he sat on the brocade
settee beside his wife and listened. The aunts had a glass-
fronted bookcase where they kept the Waverley novels, Rob-
ert Burns's poetry, and seven volumes of the *Highland Clans
and Regiments*. Great-Aunt Flora took down one of these
volumes and pointed out the Murray crest: a shield which
showed the image of a mermaid and a lion. Madge edged in
sideways and glanced at the page.

Tall and slender, with dark hair falling over one eye and a
loose-limbed, slouchy way of moving, Madge didn't look
bookish or scholarly, she looked indolent and uninterested,
which may have explained why Great-Aunt Flora made no
attempt to show her the picture she was pointing out to
Ardith. This was a picture of Lord George Murray, who had

landed with Bonnie Prince Charlie at Borodale and led his army at Culloden. These were the Murrays of Atholl. The Atholl residence was Blair Castle in Perthshire. Great-Aunt Flora showed Ardith a picture of the castle. Madge wandered over to the piano and looked at a framed sampler hanging on the wall above. The letters had been stitched in brightly coloured wool and flattened under glass.

O Scotia, my dear, my native soil,
For whom thy warmth from heaven is sent.
Long may thy hardy sons of rustic toil,
Be blessed with health and peace and sweet content!

"Burns liked his dram," Aunt Grace whispered. She had removed her apron and come into the parlour behind Madge. "But he could write poetry."

Afterwards, when they were driving back to Sydney Mines, Madge asked about the dram.

"It means drink," her mother said, "liquor." She turned sideways, toward Laddie. "Did you hear what Great-Aunt Flora said about Aunt Grace? She was *without issue*. I didn't think anyone talked that way any more. What a hoot they were."

"*I* thought they were interesting," Ardith said piously. "I didn't know our family had such a distinguished past."

"Well, *I* thought they were funny," Madge's mother said. "Great-Aunt Flora reminds me of those people in England who protect the crown jewels. Beefeaters, I think they're called. You know, those guards who dress in red and gold and carry a staff."

"That's enough," Laddie said sharply. The Murrays weren't a family to be trifled with. The Burchells, with their fumblings and lack of pride were fair game, but the Murrays were above mockery and banter.

The rope-making machines were second-hand. They had been bought from a man in Woodstock, New Brunswick, who had gone out of business and was selling them cheap. There were four machines altogether, one for each thickness of rope. Laddie planned to cover not only the sea-going trade, but hardware and grocery stores as well, places that sold the kind of all-purpose rope used for stringing up clotheslines or tying lumber onto the top of a car. Laddie installed the machines himself. He had built an office at the front of the warehouse, had the phone hooked up, put in a counter and two straight-backed chairs, hung the picture of a salmon leaping a waterfall on one wall. He had stationery printed up, a sign painted for the outside, bought a delivery truck from a used car dealer in Sydney, hired a man named Bernie Rideout to drive it.

Laddie went to work at the crack of dawn and came home at noon with his shirt sleeves rolled up and sawdust in his shoes, sometimes a smear of grease on his pants. After eating his dinner, he went back to work until six or later. He worked evenings and weekends. During the settling-in months, when there was money in the bank and Laddie was excited about having his own business, he was jokey and accommodating. If Beth wanted to order a peach-coloured bedspread and matching curtains from the catalogue, she was to go ahead. Ardith was given money to buy material for two skirts she was sewing for her college wardrobe. Madge was bought a second-hand bike.

By late fall, Laddie had finished the rough work and was ready to take to the road selling. He began going to work in a navy blazer, grey flannels, and a tie. He paid Madge a quarter to shine his shoes. Now that he was handling sales, he needed to look spiffy. He had hired four people to keep the plant going while he was out getting orders. Two men were running the machines. One of the women handled the packaging, the other one looked after the phone and the paperwork.

Laddie did the accounts on the weekends so he could keep close tabs on the balance sheet. It was too soon for him to show a profit. It was a question of hanging on until the business took hold, until the figures on the lower right-hand corner of the balance sheet were black. Within six months the money he had made from selling the Liverpool house had been used up, along with Malcolm and Bruce's money. Laddie's brothers told him they did not want to put any more money into the business. Perhaps they weren't yet convinced Laddie would make a good businessman. Perhaps there was a limit to how far they would go, even with their brother. Laddie ran an overdraft at the bank to handle the payroll and to help Ardith with her living expenses; her scholarship only covered tuition and books. Laddie wasn't taking out more than a subsistence salary himself. Their second summer in Sydney Mines Beth inherited some money from the Irish aunts, which she passed on to Laddie. This kept the business going for another six months, but the figures at the bottom of the balance sheet stayed red. After a year and a half selling on the road, Laddie still didn't have enough orders to pay down the overdraft. The Royal Bank manager threatened to cut off the loan.

Laddie became grouchy about his meals. They were either too hot or too cold. Beth was expected to keep a meal warm even when Laddie arrived home two hours late. He badgered Madge about her failure to turn off the lights, saying she wasted electricity because she wasn't paying the bills. One night, Madge sleepwalked through the house, turning on lights upstairs and down because she thought they had been left on.

In February, Madge was awakened in the middle of the night by thumping sounds in the hallway outside her bedroom. She smelled smoke. She got up and opened the door. Her parents were dragging a smoking mattress toward the stairs. There was a black hole in the mattress the size of a wash basin. Laddie had been smoking in bed and had fallen asleep. Beth was at the back end of the mattress. Her bare feet showed beneath her nightgown and her dark hair was dishevelled. She looked at Madge.

"It's all right," she said. "We'll put it outside in the snow. You go back to bed. Be sure to close your door and open the window."

Madge did as she was told. She didn't get close enough to her parents to know about the dram. Her parents usually waited until she was in bed before they started on the rum.

Several months later, the seat of an upholstered chair in her parents' room burned through. There were quarrels in the living room on Saturday nights. Madge heard them all the way upstairs, through two closed doors. She hadn't known her mother could fight like this. She couldn't remember her mother ever having raised her voice, let alone shouting. Madge thought her mother was being pushed too far, that Laddie was bullying her, that she needed sticking up for, that she needed to be coddled as she had in Liverpool when she lay in bed with TB. It hadn't yet occurred to Madge that her parents would keep an argument going to seek release from boredom or to distract themselves from worry.

On Monday at noon, Madge came home from school and saw the basement door open. Her mother was downstairs in the laundry room doing the wash. Madge saw her father sitting at the kitchen table, eating his dinner, his back to her. He did not turn around or acknowledge her presence, although he must have heard her opening the back door. Madge went to the top of the stairs and called her mother.

"Come down here," her mother called back.

Madge went downstairs, into the darkness. The door to the laundry room was partly ajar, but the weak light coming through the small window above the sinks barely reached the stairs. Madge opened the door wider and saw her mother in front of the washer. She wasn't feeding clothes through the wringer, she was standing still, bent over the tub. There was a grinding noise coming from the wringer.

Madge's mother had caught the front of her blouse in the wringer, between the rollers. She was hunched over the top of the wringer, her blouse pulled halfway up her back. One hand was braced against the wringer, the other against the enamel edge of the machine. She was trying to keep her breasts from going between the rollers.

How long had her mother been like this?

"The wringer's jammed," her mother said. "I can't let go to unplug the machine."

"I'll get Dad," Madge said.

"No!" her mother said sharply. "Just unplug the damn thing."

None of these goings-on reached Madge's sister. Ardith wrote home twice a month, describing her courses, her work on the university newspaper, the girls she had met in residence. Madge's mother wrote back short, encouraging notes. She usually left a space at the bottom of the page for Madge to add a few words, to save on a stamp. Madge wrote two or three breezy sentences about what she and Nonie had been up to, what movies they had seen, repeated an off-colour joke some teacher had told, nothing that required thought or disclosure. The sisters had seldom confided in each other. Early on, they had learned to keep the important things secret, to stake out territory. Madge didn't tell Ardith she missed her. She didn't know it herself. She piled the empty bed across the room with books and unwashed clothes and told herself she was glad Ardith wasn't here to boss her around. She never wrote to Ardith on her own and told her about their parents' fights or the shaky rope business. She understood Ardith had cut loose and didn't want to be pulled back. Madge became more helpful around the house, tidying up the kitchen, taking out the garbage, ironing her father's shirts, unasked. Her parents may have thought she was doing these things out of a sense of kindness and obligation, but Madge was merely trying to keep them from sliding further down.

Nonie Fraser lived two streets over from Madge, in the same direction as the school, so that Madge called for her weekday mornings. Nonie's father, Archie Fraser, was the only grocery store owner on the island to order six cases of Laddie's rope, more than Archie could sell in a year, out of kindness. Archie let people, mostly out-of-work miners, run up bills, some of which were never paid. He also delivered groceries free of charge. Two Saturdays a month, he paid Madge and Nonie a dollar each to scoop raisins and walnuts out of barrels and into plastic bags, which they weighed and stapled. Neither girl saved her money, but spent it the same day on lipstick, hair rinse, and nail polish.

The girls knew their mothers' habits: when Madge's mother played bridge, when Nonie's mother had choir practice. At these times, they went to either house, locked the doors, and leafed through novels to see what dirty passages could be found. Madge's mother belonged to the Book-of-the-Month Club. You couldn't find the type of book she received each month in the town library. Archie Fraser had a book about sex. It had a red cover and diagrams, very little writing. He kept it in his pipe stand in the living room. The stand was a small walnut box, which stood on a pedestal in front of the window, between two chairs. The book showed drawings of naked men and women standing on their heads, crouched on their knees, lying on their backs, arms and legs joined together like chain-link puzzles.

Madge and Nonie also locked the doors if Junior and Roy followed them home, expecting something in exchange for the chocolate bars, potato chips, and pop they bought the girls with their paper-route money which they earned by trudging from house to house in all kinds of weather. Once a week, usually a Friday, Junior and Roy met Madge and Nonie outside Dirty Dan's after school. The boys went to the Catholic School and lived near the mine, so they met the girls halfway, at the store, a badly weathered shack that looked more like a farm out-building than a place of business. Madge and Nonie were taken inside the store and told they could choose what they wanted. Dirty Dan, a thin man with a long, grey beard who stayed in the shadows behind the counter, kept licorice strings, bubble gum, and jaw-breakers within easy reach. The girls ignored the penny items. They were after bigger stakes, the merchandise Dirty Dan kept inside the wooden showcase or the cooler, bags of chocolate-covered raisins and nuts, bottles of fruit-flavoured pop. After the boys had paid, the four of them took the food outside to eat it, while the girls allowed the boys to walk them to one of their houses. This was as far as it went. Madge and Nonie didn't consider this courting serious. They considered it practice. They were saving themselves for the real thing. They had no qualms about running inside and locking the door, leaving the boys on the porch, where they hemmed and hawed, trying to decide whether to ring the bell or bang on the door, until they finally gave up and sauntered off, hands in their pockets.

The second year Madge lived in Sydney Mines, she and Nonie were asked to the Tri-Service Ball. They didn't call it a ball; they called it a formal. The formal was held in the school gym like the other dances, but on this occasion the boys, who were in the Reserve Army, wore their uniforms – except for their boots; they couldn't dance in boots. Madge was going to the formal with Jimmy Dean, who worked for Archie Fraser on Saturdays, at the meat counter. Jimmy often passed through the room at the back of the store when the girls were bagging, on his way to the walk-in freezer where the sides of beef and pork were hung. That was how he and Madge met. They seldom saw one another in school, except for brief glimpses in the corridor. Jimmy was a year ahead of Madge, in grade twelve. Nonie was going to the formal with Lawrence Bowser, the Royal Bank manager's son who sat across the aisle from her in grade eleven. Unlike most school dances, the Tri-Service Ball was held on Saturday night, on account of the band. There was to be a live band from Sydney, four or five musicians.

On Saturday morning, Madge and Nonie finished their bagging early and were out of the store before noon. Fortunately, Jimmy Dean was driving the delivery truck that day, so there was no need for Madge to pretend she didn't see him in his blood-stained apron, carrying animal carcasses into the freezer. Madge wanted them to appear before each other that night, transformed and splendid, as if they were seeing each

other for the first time. Jimmy Dean wasn't in the same cate-
gory as Junior and Roy. Jimmy Dean was serious.

After they had left the store, Madge and Nonie went to the
Five-and-Ten. Nonie wanted to buy nail polish, Madge a
lipstick to go with her dress. She knew the shade she wanted,
Purple Wine. She had picked it out earlier in the week. The
mauve dress was Ardith's, on a loan from college, along with
silver shoes and a silver evening purse. Once their purchases
were made, Madge and Nonie went home to get their evening
wear ready before they went on a picnic.

Madge walked halfway home before she realized she had
forgotten to go to the drugstore for her mother. She turned
around and went back downtown. Recently her mother had
developed high blood pressure and took three pills a day, one
of them before her nap. Except for the day she played bridge,
her mother took a nap every afternoon, after dinner. More
than once, Madge had opened the bedroom door and seen
her mother stripped down to her nylons and bra, sitting on
the edge of the bed, playing solitaire to relax. When her
mother got up from her nap, she would often put on a skirt
or a dress. She would do this even though she and Madge's
father seldom went out together, because Laddie worked in
the evenings.

After she arrived home with the pills, Madge ironed
Ardith's dress – Madge thought of it as a gown – and hung it
in the closet. The gown had a net overskirt and a strapless
rayon bodice. There was a net stole that went across the
shoulders at the back and was caught beneath each arm. She
wiped the silver shoes and purse with a damp cloth and laid
them on the bed with her underclothes. Then she tiptoed
downstairs to the kitchen and made two baloney-and-mustard
sandwiches. She wrapped the sandwiches in waxed paper, put
them inside her jacket pocket, and rode her bike to Nonie's.
They didn't take their bikes on the picnic. They walked. There
were places around Sydney Mines where it wasn't safe to leave
a bike without the risk of it being dismantled and resold.

The place they went for picnics was a lumpy plateau that they reached by cutting through a graveyard on the outskirts of town. The lumps were rocks concealed by last year's straw-coloured grass. A month earlier, this was where they had come to pick mayflowers. On that picnic, they had eaten their lunch while sitting on an empty powder magazine left from the war. Today, they avoided the concrete shelter and headed for a low, marshy area, which they crossed by leaping onto clumps of old grass. The swamp petered out, becoming a brook that zigzagged through the trees. There were willows leaning over the water, making shady spots where moss and ferns grew. Beyond the willows were clusters of fir trees with spaces between, places where the grass was brown and dry, sprinkled with needles and cones. Madge and Nonie were fussy about which clearing they chose, visiting one after another before settling on one that was near enough to the brook to satisfy, yet sunny in the middle. They spread Nonie's tartan rug and, flopping down, ate their sandwiches and drank their pop. Afterwards, they lay on their backs and closed their eyes, letting the sun warm their faces while they listened to the trickling water. They dozed, they might have slept, but not much. They were too excited and nerved up to sleep. They didn't start any long conversations. They were conserving energy, putting in time until that night.

Laddie arrived home later than usual for supper because the delivery truck had gone off the road and hit a large rock. It wasn't Bernie's fault, he was swerving to avoid an old man who had pulled out in front of him. The truck needed a new axle and muffler, maybe a fuel pan. Laddie didn't know where he was going to get the money for repairs. When they sat down to eat, Madge's father complained that the corn chowder burned his mouth, that there was milk on the table but no water. He dropped his knife on the floor when he was buttering a cracker. Madge picked it up and started running water for the dishes.

"Leave them," her mother said. "I'll do them later."

Upstairs, Madge washed her hair and took a bath. Swathed in a towel, she went into her bedroom and brushed her hair: eighty-three, eighty-four, eighty-five. She didn't stop until she reached two hundred. She unwrapped the towel and powdered her body with Yardley's talcum, lilac-scented, borrowed from her mother. As she was putting on her underclothes, she heard her father yell something at her mother. Madge unpinned the gown from the hanger, slipped it over her head and zippered up the side. The skirt umbrellaed outward, making her waist snug and trim. Only now did she dare look in the mirror. This was a hopeful, cautious look, not too lingering in case she should see irreversible flaws. There was a scarlet V below her neck where her blouse had been open. There was a smaller V on her nose. Madge put talcum on the sunburned spots, to tone them down. The spring sun had also reddened her cheeks, making it appear she was wearing rouge, which her father had forbidden because it would make her look like a hussy.

Madge drifted downstairs, ballerina shoes gliding from step to step. Both her parents were in the living room now, drinking tea and smoking. Her father was still hectoring her mother about the chowder, about serving meals that were too hot. Madge stood in the doorway and waited to be noticed. Now that she was dressed up, she felt like a stranger.

Her father stopped talking and looked at her.

"Well," he said. "Aren't you something."

He sounded pleased.

"A picture," her mother said, and smiled.

Jimmy Dean was long and lanky with an overgrown crew cut and mischievous brown eyes. He didn't look at all like the brooding, smouldering movie star with the same name. He laughed easily and liked to tease. Sometimes he cracked his knuckles and wiggled his ears. There was none of this tonight. Tonight, when Madge opened the door, she saw a somber young man in a khaki uniform, standing on the doorstep, holding a small white box. Madge asked him inside and accepted the box. Inside was a white chrysanthemum, tied with a silver ribbon. Madge's mother got up off the chesterfield and pinned the corsage onto the gown, while Madge's father asked Jimmy questions about the Reserve Army. Laddie couldn't meet anyone without asking a lot of questions.

A horn honked in the driveway. Madge took her shorty coat from the hall closet and she and Jimmy went outside to Lawrence's car, Gentleman Jim holding the car door open while Madge lifted her gown over the running board. Madge arranged her gown and looked at Nonie sitting up front: dependable, loyal Nonie, so pretty in her Nile-green dress. Neither of the girls talked across the boys to each other, as they did with Junior and Roy. They understood romance wasn't possible if they stuck together. They had to distance themselves from each other, to make room for it.

Jimmy Dean was a good dancer. Because this was common knowledge around the school, Madge had done some practising on her own. Nobody had known this, not even Nonie. Madge had waited until her mother had gone downtown to pick up pork chops or a chicken, an errand she preferred to do herself. While she was gone, Madge had turned up the radio and danced through the house. She had only been able to manage this twice, and now worried about being able to follow Jimmy Dean.

After the first dance, she didn't stumble much. Jimmy kept a hand on her waist and pressed it against her back when he made a turn. He sang into her ear: *I've Got You Under My Skin, Body and Soul, Love Letters in the Sand*, which took her mind off her feet. His voice was deep, guttural, as if it came from a hairy place. After four or five dances, they exchanged with Nonie and Lawrence. Then Jimmy danced with Delores Marshall and Barbara Crutcher. Nonie and Lawrence started dancing again. Rather than sideline herself with the girls standing against the wall, Madge went out the front door of the school and sat on a concrete step to cool off.

Two boys from her homeroom class, Lance and Collie, were out there smoking. Usually these boys whistled and made suggestive remarks about her, but tonight they nodded politely, Lance stealing glances at her bare shoulders. When she got up to go back inside, Collie scrambled to open the door and asked for a dance. Madge walked back to the gym, Lance on one side, Collie on the other, along the corridor with its scrubbed, grainy smell from the green janitorial cleaner, its sober-faced graduates staring down on them from wainscotted walls. Jimmy Dean was waiting for her in the doorway of the gym and pulled her away from Lance and Collie and onto the dance floor. From then on, they didn't dance with anyone else, but stood between dances on the gym floor, whispering to each other so they wouldn't be interrupted. Madge believed what was happening between her and Jimmy Dean was what she had been saving herself for. She didn't have a clear idea of what that was, but she was convinced it was more real than her ordinary life at home.

The last dance was *Good Night Irene. I'll See You in My Dreams*, Jimmy crooned into her ear as he turned them around and around, never missing a beat. Toward the end of the dance, Madge began to notice that she and Jimmy were being given the centre of the dance floor to themselves, that most of the dancers had moved out to the edges. The dance ended and the fat trumpet player, who was the band-leader, spoke into the microphone and pointed to Madge and Jimmy. "We won," Jimmy whispered. He grinned, showing a large gap where two back teeth were missing, a detail Madge noticed only peripherally. She was too caught up in what she took to be love to register imperfections. Madge and Jimmy mounted the stage and stood beside the trumpet-player while he announced they had been chosen the best dancers at the ball. Then he gave them each a record, *With a Song in my Heart*. Madge and Jimmy stayed up there all through *God Save the King*. Afterwards, they left the stage and hunted down Nonie and Lawrence. The four of them went outside to the car.

Lawrence drove them out of town, past the graveyard and the swamp where the girls had been that afternoon. He didn't take them much beyond that, perhaps a half mile more, before he pulled onto a narrow, wooded track and turned off the engine and the lights. There was a rustling of dresses and scratchy wool uniforms as bodies were shifted and rearranged. Jimmy and Lawrence rolled down the windows and lit two cigarettes. They sat in the dark listening to the frogs. Halfway through his cigarette, Jimmy threw the butt out the window and kissed Madge roughly on the lips. His lips tasted of tobacco and salt. After three or four of these hard kisses, he began nibbling Madge's lower lip, turning it down gently. It felt like chubs nipping underwater bare skin. He nibbled her neck, moved lower to where her breasts showed above her gown, eased her backwards onto the seat. Inside her belly Madge felt a pleasant sliding down. She felt her organs dissolving into liquid and trickling into a damp spot between her legs. At the same time the muscles between her legs tightened and sucked themselves in, as if they were about to hold onto something slippery and firm, something pleasant and dangerous, that they would have trouble letting go of. There was a knocking inside her ears, a fuzzy underwater sound. Far away she heard Nonie say they must be going now or her parents would have a fit. Her father would kill her if she wasn't home before midnight. Madge sat up and straightened her bodice. Jimmy groaned and lit another cigarette. He made a joke about being hard up, but Madge didn't get it. Lawrence started the car and drove them back to town. He let Madge and Jimmy off first. By the time they reached Madge's house, her belly had settled down and she had become decorous and remote.

On the doorstep, she edged away from Jimmy so he couldn't kiss her. The porch light was blazing and the living-room lights were on. She didn't want the door to fly open, to see her father appear in the pool of yellow light, demanding to know what she thought she was doing, kissing on the doorstep. "I'll call you tomorrow," Jimmy said, before he went down the steps. Madge waited until he had reached the road before she combed her hair and applied more lipstick. She opened the door and stood in the hallway, braced for an interrogating voice, either her mother's or her father's. Now she welcomed this voice. She wanted to tell her parents how she had won the record, how she had danced every dance but two, how attentive Jimmy Dean had been.

When no voice came, Madge went into the living room. Her father was on the far side of the living room, asleep in his reclining chair. His shirt was unbuttoned, as if he had started for bed and changed his mind. On the table beside him was an empty glass, an ashtray overflowing with cigarette butts.

Madge's mother was sitting on the chesterfield. There were two red spots on her cheeks, not rouge. These were splotches. She was still wearing the blue wool dress she had put on after her afternoon nap. She didn't look up when Madge came into the living room but stared at her hands, pushing down the cuticles of her left hand with the thumb of her right.

"Did you enjoy yourself?"

Madge didn't answer this. Her warning signals were up. She no longer wanted to be drawn in. She knew from the way her mother was acting that she had walked into the aftermath of a fight. She didn't want her parents' quarrel to dilute her own happiness. She knew if you told people something when they were in no mood to hear it, its importance got watered down.

Madge waved the record at her mother. "I won this," she said, carelessly, as if there had been nothing to it.

"That's nice, dear," her mother said, but the *dear* was abstracted; there was no force in it. Her mother patted the chesterfield. "Sit down."

Madge sat at one end of the chesterfield.

Her mother cleared her throat and said, "I might as well tell you now and get it over with. Your father and I are getting a divorce."

"Oh," Madge said. She might have been told that another rope machine had broken down, that Bernie Rideout had quit, that Laddie had phoned his brothers for money to buy another truck and was advised to close down the business and cut his losses. What was happening, was happening someplace else.

"The business hasn't picked up, despite your father's being a slave to it. His brothers overestimated the market on the island, and their order isn't enough to keep the business going," her mother said. "Your father will sell the business and go up north, where he can make good money and pay off our debts. You and I will go to Montreal. We'll rent an apartment close to a school and I'll find some kind of nursing work in a doctor's office, something like that."

Madge noticed her mother's voice was thicker than usual, that she slurred her words. She put this down to the fact that her mother was upset.

"Oh," Madge said again. Then she asked about Ardith.

"Ardith will stay in Halifax and continue her studies. We'll see her during the holidays, the same as we do now. All that can be worked out later." Her mother began twisting her wedding ring around her finger. "It's not Laddie's fault that the business failed," she went on. "No one could have worked harder." She began to cry.

"Can I help?" Madge asked.

By the end of next week, Madge was to think herself foolish for having asked this question, for having been duped, though at the time it was asked, her mother seemed to take the question seriously enough.

"No, thank you," she said. She took a Kleenex from the sleeve of her dress and blew her nose. Then she sat up straight, became sedate, almost prim. "It's late. You'd better go up to bed."

Madge went upstairs. If she had kissed her mother goodnight, she would have smelled the rum. If she had gone into the kitchen to put her corsage into the fridge so it would last, she would have seen the empty bottle on the counter. She would have had a head start on figuring out what was happening. She might have realized that her parents had taken temporary leave of their senses and would soon get them back.

Upstairs, Madge turned on the light and closed the bedroom door. She threw the record on Ardith's bed, unzipped the dress, and let it drop to the floor. She took off the ballerina slippers and threw them on top of the dress. She caught a glimpse of herself in the mirror and thought how ugly she looked. With her sunburned nose and bushy eyebrows, she looked like a country hick. She turned out the light and crawled into bed in her underwear.

Late the next morning, Madge opened her eyes. She saw sunlight on the walls and closed them again. She slept, awoke, slept again. Downstairs, the phone rang and was answered. Madge registered this fact, but didn't wonder if the call had been for her. Her curiosity had been temporarily disconnected. Eventually, she became hungry enough to go down to the kitchen.

Sunlight entered the window above the sink, fell on the taps, making them gleam. The sink had been scrubbed white, the countertop wiped clean. The only time the kitchen was this tidy was when her father cleaned it up, which he did on special occasions like Christmas and Thanksgiving. There was no sign of her parents. They were out – not to church, Madge's mother never went to church. They had probably gone for a drive. Why wasn't her mother packing for Montreal? The phone rang again, but Madge didn't answer. She made toast and took it up to her room to eat while she tried to study for her literature exam. She had five exams the next week. The phone rang a third time. Madge thought it might be Jimmy Dean or Nonie calling, but she couldn't bring herself to answer. She couldn't trust herself not to tell them everything, to let the messiness of a divorce and a failing business come out. She didn't feel able to put the situation in such a way that would avoid humiliation and disgrace.

If she had been able to think more clearly, she might have reminded herself that Jimmy's father was a barber with a family of eight squeezed into a small bungalow. She would have reminded herself of the time she saw Jimmy's mother in Fraser's Market with her hair up in curlers. She had two of Jimmy's little brothers with her, one holding onto the hem of her cotton housedress, the other pulling grapes from a box in the window. "Now youse stop that!" his mother said. She slapped his hand and pulled off some grapes herself. Madge would have reminded herself of a weekend the year before when Nonie's mother got in a snit because of something Archie Fraser had done and had packed her bag and gone to stay with her sister in Truro. If Madge had been able to remember these things, she might have told herself that Jimmy's and Nonie's parents were no more respectable than her own. But Madge was intent on punishing herself with a strong sense of shame. Along with this was the conviction that she had been wronged, that her parents had wrecked her first real romance. There was something perverse going on here. Perhaps Madge didn't want romance after all; perhaps she'd been scared off by sex and saw it as something to steer clear of until she was older; or perhaps she was feeling the urge to turn the punishment around.

Madge tried to memorize the poems she needed to know for the exam, but she had trouble concentrating. She kept trying to imagine what it would be like living in Montreal, to get used to the idea. She saw a small apartment on the third floor of a grey stone building, on a corner overlooking the street. There was a park close by, one or two blocks over, where old men sat on benches and there were pigeons. This was where her mother and she would walk after her mother got off work. Or they might take a bus downtown to go window-shopping or to a movie. There would be lots of stores and theatres to choose from. Madge had never been to Montreal, but she knew this much.

During the next week, Madge ignored Nonie and Jimmy Dean. Once she had started on this course of solitary confinement, she was unable to reverse it. Several times she was told by a teacher to keep her mind on her work. She didn't bother finishing the math exam. Since she was moving to Montreal, it wouldn't matter what her marks were. The schools in Montreal were bound to be different. By Wednesday, Nonie had given up trying to talk to Madge and left her alone. After Sunday, Jimmy Dean didn't phone again. He didn't try to corner her in a school corridor, which Madge thought he could have done if he'd been serious about her. On Thursday, Madge saw him walking with Barbara Crutcher. Madge didn't go to Fraser's Market; it wasn't her Saturday to work. She stayed in her bedroom and took stock. It had been a week since her parents had decided they were getting a divorce but nothing had been said about when this would happen. The suitcases were still in the basement, her mother's clothes unpacked. Her father was sleeping in the same bed as her mother and not in the spare room. Madge didn't feel relieved that her parents seemed to have patched things up. Now that she had come this far, she wanted her parents to go through with the divorce. She wanted to go to Montreal and make a fresh start. She had one more week of school and then she could go. Madge decided to say something to her mother, to bring matters to a head. She went downstairs into the kitchen. Her mother was bent over the sink, peeling potatoes.

"When are we moving?" Madge said.

Her mother jerked her head up and laughed. Was she shocked? Amused? "Moving?" she said. "Where to?"

"Montreal."

"Why would we move to Montreal?"

Madge told her mother about the divorce, her father working up north, the nursing job, and the apartment.

"That was just a silly argument," her mother said. "I forgot it days ago." She'd stopped smiling and had started to grow red. "You'd better forget it too."

"But you *said*."

Her mother cut her off. "That's enough. I told you to forget it."

"But I *want* to go," Madge said.

Madge watched her mother cut potatoes into a pot of boiling water and snap down the lid. The red had spread down her mother's neck to the collar of her blouse.

"You can set the table," she said. "Supper will be ready in half an hour."

"I'm not hungry," Madge said. She started to go back upstairs.

"By the way," her mother called after her, "don't mention any of this to Ardith."

"What's so precious about Ardith?" Madge said, though she knew.

"There's no point," her mother said. She didn't tell Madge to come back and set the table. She knew there had been some kind of damage, that something had been said that couldn't be taken back.

Madge didn't tell Ardith. Years later, she did, after their mother had died and they were clearing out old corners. It wasn't the instinct to protect Ardith that kept Madge silent all those years, though that was there. What kept her from telling Ardith was a hard core of secrecy and one-upmanship. That was at the centre of it. She knew something about their parents that Ardith, for all her cleverness, did not. It was this knowledge that kept Madge from believing that she was less worthy than Ardith, because she didn't need her parents' protection. There was also a streak of Murray pride in Madge, a nose-thumbing defiance, a stubborn belief that, contrary to being inferior to other families in Sydney Mines, her family had the edge on most. She had gotten that much out of the visit to Great-Aunt Flora and Aunt Grace. Madge didn't spend time brooding over any of this. Events intervened, took hold.

Two weeks after the Tri-Service Ball, she and Nonie picked up their friendship and kept it going by never mentioning the falling out. Jimmy Dean didn't go out of his way to talk to her when she and Nonie were bagging at the store, but he was polite enough. He started going steady with Barbara Crutcher. Even after he left Sydney Mines to join the regular army, he continued to go steady with Barbara, so he must have wanted to settle on a girl.

The next year, Madge's last year of school, Laddie closed the rope-making plant and, with his brothers' help, started up a spice-bottling plant in Sussex, New Brunswick. After Christmas, he went on ahead to get the new plant ready, leaving Madge and her mother in Sydney Mines. He took off every fourth weekend and drove back to the island for a visit, taking the ferry across the strait. By then Madge and Nonie were working Friday nights and all day Saturday at Fraser's Market, shelving goods, bagging groceries, sometimes punching the cash register. It was hard work, bending over cartons and bags, standing on their feet all day. Madge got to know the meaning of toil, what it was like to have sore feet and an aching back. Except for fifty cents a week, she began saving her wages for the day when she could get away. The fifty cents was spent on Saturday night when she went to the second show with Nonie. After the show, she went home to bed, too tired to do anything else.

One weekend, during one of Laddie's visits home, Madge came downstairs late Sunday morning and found out what she'd been up to during the night. Laddie told her how he'd put her back to bed. He said that about two in the morning he'd been awakened by the sound of the front door opening. Thinking it was a burglar, he had come quietly downstairs and armed himself with a wrought-iron bookend from the front-hall table. Then he saw Madge through the open door. She was going down the steps to the sidewalk in her nightgown and slippers, heading for the street. She was sleepwalking. Her father put down the bookend and followed her outside, creeping up behind her. He said he didn't want to wake her up suddenly and give her a scare and so had carried her upstairs as gently as he could.

The Loving Cup

Madge had this habit, not much different from reading *Screen Stars* and *True Romance*, of replaying romantic scenes from movies before she fell asleep. This was a habit she couldn't or wouldn't shake. It soothed her, was a pleasurable distraction, like a baby's pacifier or thumb; it could be counted on for gratification. These scenes were short. There wasn't much to them beyond sexual tension.

"You kissed me," Grace Kelly said to William Holden. She turned away so he wouldn't see her quivering lips, her misted eyes. She hadn't been kissed like that for years. Somehow she managed to pull herself together and say in a haughty, disdainful voice, "You may have kissed me, Mr. Dodd, but don't let it give you any ideas."
William Holden gave her a meaningful look.
"No, Mrs. Elgin," he said.

Clark Gable carried Vivien Leigh up the dark staircase to bed. You didn't see him lowering her onto the bed and getting on top. You had to imagine it. The morning after, Vivien was lying in bed alone, wiggling her toes beneath the blankets.

*Chastened by a night of tempestuous lovemaking and preg-
nant with Clark Gable's child, she looked shamefaced and
coy.*

Madge was fascinated by the effect lovemaking had on
Vivien Leigh, changing her from a manipulative, wilful
woman into a pliant, satisfied wife. Madge's voyeurism wasn't
centred on what happened in bed as much as it was on the
effect lovemaking had on the lovers, their transformation, and
on the crescendo of words and gestures leading up to the
supreme moment, the intricate and contradictory language of
lovers. She saw the path to consummation as uncertain
ground, obstructed by quicksands and switchbacks. This was
how she wanted to see it. She wasn't interested in the straight
and narrow path.

The summer Madge was eighteen, she and her mother moved
to Sussex, New Brunswick, where Laddie had started up his
spice-bottling business. He had left Cape Breton behind for
good, though he didn't know it at the time. This move took
them inland, forty-five miles away from the sea. In Sussex the
Murrays lived in an upstairs apartment next door to the movie
theatre. The apartment building was connected to the theatre
by a set of stairs. Madge would sit on the top step, beneath
the red exit sign that led into the theatre balcony, and listen
to the movies. She often put in time this way, after she had
already seen the movie and could picture what was going on.
This was when she started the habit of rerunning movies
before she went to sleep.

Madge had a job in Sussex; she had started it soon after
the move. Her father had got it for her. Earlier in the year, he
had been scouting around town for someone to help him
design a label for his spice bottles and was told about Niels
and Selda Oersted, two artists who were new to town themselves. The Oersteds ran a pottery business out of their house.

Niels and Selda didn't do commercial designs, but Selda worked up two or three drawings for Laddie. Perhaps she thought the gesture would be good for public relations, knowing people often shied away from artists, out of unfamiliarity and distrust. Not Laddie. Laddie wasn't shy or distrustful. He took on everyone as a potential customer who needed wooing. Laddie used one of Selda's designs, a large, round sun with cinnamon sprinkles on it. The design gave Laddie the idea of using the name *Sunspice* for his products. Selda refused to take any money for the design. She didn't consider it legitimate art, more like an exercise. In return for this favour, Laddie gave the Oersteds samples of his wares. Whenever he brought out a new spice, he would drop it off at the Oersteds'. That was how he found out they were looking for a young person to give them a hand, someone who wouldn't expect high wages, which they couldn't afford to pay. Now that their children had moved away, Niels and Selda needed someone to look after their display room, to deal with the public so they would be free to make pottery.

Madge couldn't start work fast enough. She was eager to get out of her parents' apartment, which was crowded with too much furniture and was stiflingly hot in the afternoons because of the flat roof. The apartment was on a corner across from the hotel and the train tracks. There was a lot of traffic on the corner and noise from trains that shunted back and forth at all hours of the day and night. The Oersteds' house was quiet and secluded, away from the main part of town. When she was inside their house, Madge felt she was in another country, a place where you kept track of light moving across the walls, where you paid attention to beauty, where it was renewed each time Niels opened the kiln. Madge thought it was her destiny to work for artists. Inside her head Madge used words like *destiny* and *fate* though she knew better than to say these words to anyone else. People would think that you were stuck-up if you used words like that in connection with yourself, that you thought yourself too good for honest work.

Until she met the Oersteds, Madge's attempts at drawing
and painting had been random, something she did on a whim.
Now that she had finished high school and was up against it,
she had decided to become an artist. It was the idea of doing
something extraordinary and unusual, something you could
do on your own, that appealed to her. This was her father's
ambition, dressed up. Madge dawdled over the image of herself sitting in front of an easel in an attic somewhere, drinking
wine and eating bread and cheese. With Madge this secret
ambition and wishfulness, this incubation of possibilities and
prospects were instinctive. They had more to do with a sense
of privacy than anything else. By the time she was eighteen,
she had moved enough that she had become used to the idea
of moving on. She wanted to get away from her parents. She
thought they wanted this, that her being around added to the
strain. Madge thought the Oersteds' marriage was on a higher
level than her parents', that their past was nobler, that their
adversity had greater significance. There was considerable
risk-taking and sacrifice in their past, which Madge mistook
for romance.

Niels had started off as a painter. He left Denmark first,
before he met Selda. In the 1920s it was still possible to buy
cheap farmland in Canada. Niels bought a quarter section in
Alberta. For three years he tried chicken-farming, but that did
little more than drain away his inheritance and discourage
him from painting. He didn't like the flat prairie landscape
and found the mountains too overwhelming to paint. He
moved east to New Brunswick, where the wooded hills and
green pastures of the Saint John River valley suited him better.
He bought a small garden farm, something that wouldn't
require too much work but would put food on the table. Niels
found clay on his land and began shaping bowls and vases.
He built himself a wheel and for two years, while he waited
for Selda to join him, taught himself to make pottery. Niels
had met Selda, who was thirteen years his junior, when he'd
stopped off in Toronto on his way east. Selda had been accompanying her father, a Danish archaeologist who was giving a

series of lectures on Norse migration at the University of Toronto. It was, Selda told Madge, love at first sight. She promised Niels she would marry him as soon as she finished school in Copenhagen. Selda was artistic and clever. She painted designs on Niels's pottery and learned to mix glazes. She and Niels had three children. For years they subsisted on porridge, eggs, vegetables. They didn't sell much pottery during these years. They refused to sell any piece with an imperfection. That was how their standards became so high. They began entering shows in Canada, Europe, and the States. They won prizes, were written up in newspapers and art magazines, became known in places like Montreal, Brussels, New York. By the time their children were in high school, they were able to do better than support their family. Two of their children had gone to university, the third married young and went to Europe. The Oersteds sold their farm and moved to Sussex. Now that they had built up a reputation, they wanted to live somewhere closer to the tourist trade.

In Sussex the Oersteds lived in a large 130-year-old house set well back from the road and surrounded by graceful, wineglass elms. Their house had high white ceilings, dormer windows, a wide curving staircase, pine floors with wooden pegs. Selda had stained the floors herself, squeezing tubes of burnt umber into the varnish. Upstairs, she had made a planked floor green, then painted on yellow flowers that looked like buttercups strewn on grass. Selda drove the Oersteds' van to auction sales, where she bought old furniture, which she stripped down to bare wood with a mixture of lye and pumice. Before summer was over, she had Madge outside in rubber boots and gloves, scrubbing the lye mixture onto an antique dresser that had been given several coats of paint. The house was filled with dressers, tables, sideboards, and chairs that had been stripped to bare wood. On the walls were paintings by artist friends of the Oersteds: Pegi Nichol, P.K. Page, Molly Bobak, Goodridge Roberts, Maxwell Bates.

Madge's job was to sell pottery and arrange displays. The two front rooms of the house, one on either side of the hallway, were display rooms. Niels had a wheel in a back room off the hallway where people could watch him work. There was another wheel in the glazing room behind the house, which was closed to the public.

Madge spent hours arranging bowls, vases, and decanters on the pine furniture. There were weavings to work with, hooked mats, embroidered cotton, and, of course, the paintings. Whenever there was a rush of customers and several pieces were sold, Madge took more pottery from the cupboards and arranged new displays.

Sometimes Madge cooked for the Oersteds. Selda was often too busy or too tired from glazing to get the evening meal. Though she hadn't been hired to do this work, Madge regarded cooking for people as cultured as the Oersteds as a privilege. She seldom cooked at home. She was used to eating what her mother cooked Laddie for supper: Welsh rarebit, creamed peas on toast, bacon and eggs. The Oersteds didn't eat food like this. They ate coarse Danish bread with sardines, pickled herring, tomato soup with dollops of whipped cream on top. This food was served on pottery plates and bowls kept on unpainted shelves. When visitors dropped in, they were served mulled wine in pottery cups. No one Madge knew drank wine. Her parents drank dark rum from peanut-butter glasses with penguins on them.

Selda had lapses of energy, usually in the late afternoon, when she would lie upstairs on the bed, holding Madge's hand and weeping, pleading with her not to let in any more visitors. Whenever this happened, Madge became fiercely protective, capable of turning anyone away from the door – the mayor, the premier – she didn't care who lifted the wrought-iron door-knocker (the mayor and premier never did). The Oersteds were talented, they were unique, they were artists. People had to learn not to barge in on them, to expect to take up their time, especially after five o'clock, when the Oersteds were entitled to eat their supper in peace. Madge never got a chance to turn anyone away, because whenever she went to answer the door, Selda, splendidly revived by the sound of the bell, would sweep down the staircase in a dirndl skirt and sandals, braids wrapped around her head. Looking girlish and confiding, she held out her hands to the visitors. Niels was a large, balding man, quiet and thoughtful. Before supper he would often go outside and sit on a sawhorse to smoke his pipe and look at the sky. Madge thought of him as a philosopher, perhaps because Selda had told her Niels was a descendant of Kierkegaard, whom Madge later looked up in the *Encyclopaedia Britannica* so she would know what he was famous for. Niels was good-natured, benevolent, self-contained, capable of ignoring visitors while raising a pot on the wheel. Sometimes he would make a small, sly joke. Mostly he left the visitors to Selda and Madge.

One of Madge's favourite pieces was a gold-speckled, earth-brown vase with a surface like pocked lava. She had bought this piece for herself out of her earnings. She hadn't taken it home because she was using it as part of an arrangement to hold dried weeds she had picked in a ditch on her way to work. There was a sold sticker on the bottom. Three brash young men, university students a year or two older than Madge, came in late one afternoon and bought the vase. Madge told herself afterwards that she wouldn't have sold it to these students if they had come in singly. The three of them together had been too much. They wore her down, hanging around for so long, hectoring her about being stubborn and mean because she wouldn't part with the vase. She had finally sold them the vase to get rid of them.

When Niels found her a half-hour later, after the students had gone, she was sitting in the display room weeping at her foolishness, her weakness; she would do anything to protect the Oersteds, nothing to protect herself. Niels asked her the students' names, what they looked like, where they lived. Madge pointed to the visitors' book, which indicated the students were from Rothesay, forty miles away. Niels glanced at the book, then went outside, sat on the sawhorse, lit his pipe, and stared at the sky. He was still there when Madge went home.

The next morning when Madge entered the display room, there was the pocked vase on the table she used for wrapping parcels. The night before, Niels had driven the van all the way to Rothesay to buy back the vase. Madge had never come across devotion like this. She thought that, through all those years when the Oersted children were babies, when Niels and Selda were eating porridge and smashing pottery, there had been this constancy between them. This devotion explained why Selda had crossed the Atlantic at eighteen to marry a poor artist much older than she. With devotion like Niels', there was no breakdown you couldn't survive, no weakness you couldn't overcome, no marriage you couldn't weather.

There were some afternoons at the Oersteds' when few people came to the door. These were usually sunny days when tourists went to Fundy Park or fishing in the Kennebecasis. It was on rainy days when tourists had nothing better to do that Madge found she had the most people on her hands. These tourists didn't buy much but hung around for hours, tramping in mud which Madge had to wipe up afterwards. They came to the Oersteds' to put in time, to browse, to watch Niels working at the wheel or Selda drawing one of her designs on a plate or bowl. The buyers were usually people who knew about the Oersteds' work beforehand and came straight to their door. People would drive hundreds of miles to make this kind of purchase. Usually they bought something large, a lamp, a decanter, or a bowl with a prize-winning glaze. On the days when few people came to the house, Madge took a sketchbook she had bought at the office-supply store, sat on a stool near the window, and sketched. Mostly she did studies of shape and size, shadow and light. She made these compositions by arranging bowls and vases on a woven runner. Sometimes she added oranges and apples from the kitchen. Once a bowl of pears.

Madge had not thought of drawing this sort of thing herself. Left on her own she would have sketched something larger, an arrangement of furniture or one end of a room. The first time she tried sketching at the Oersteds', she chose the wide, curving staircase that swept down from the second floor. Niels came into the hallway where Madge was sitting on a stool and looked over her shoulder. In his quiet, patient way, he told her it was better to draw something scaled down, preferably a group of small objects, so she could study proportion, and the light and shadow he called chiaroscuro. He arranged a vase on a pine table in the east window and showed her where the light lifted the shining surface, where shadow darkened the plane of wood. Then he left her alone to make her own arrangement.

During the next few weeks he would sometimes appear at her elbow to make suggestions and praise what she had done. She had a flair for sketching, he said, her powers of observation were strong. Sometimes Selda would come into the room when Madge was sketching and move objects around to show how many different ways it could be done. Once you learned to draw, she said, you had to learn how to design a space. You had to learn about colour. Selda took Madge into the glazing room and showed her a colour wheel. She took some paints and taught Madge how to mix colours. One Saturday, Selda presented Madge with a box of watercolours and a watercolour sketchbook, along with Madge's pay, which was inside a white envelope. Usually this envelope, with Madge's name written on it, was tucked discreetly beneath a vase or a bowl on the wrapping table where Madge would find it. It was as if Selda could not bear to spoil their friendship by handing over money directly. Perhaps she was embarrassed by how little was inside the envelope.

Madge kept her art supplies at the Oersteds', inside a cupboard at the end of the hall where tourists weren't apt to look. She didn't want to draw or paint in the hot, stuffy apartment at home, where there were pictures of kittens and sailing ships on the walls. Madge had separated her destined life with the Oersteds from her temporary life with her parents so she could continue to believe that something better lay ahead. She thought if she let what was going on around her at home take too firm a hold, she might stay in town and find herself a

better-paying job to bring in extra money. She might pay her
parents' rent, knowing money was tight. She didn't offer to
do this. She saved the money she earned, as her sister was
doing – Ardith had a summer job waitressing at the Banff
Springs Hotel – adding it to the money she had already saved
from her job in Sydney Mines.

One Friday night, Madge went downstairs and applied for
a part-time job at the snack bar in the theatre lobby, where
popcorn, soft drinks, and candy were sold. Living where she
did, she had been the first one to see the Help Wanted sign in
the window. Parnell Upham, the theatre owner, told her it
was a question of first come, first served. He was sure that
because she lived next door, she wasn't likely to be late for
work. The theatre was only open on Friday and Saturday
nights, and the work wasn't hard. After intermission Madge
was allowed to see the movie free of charge, so there was no
need to listen through the balcony door.

After she had been working at the theatre a week – by now
it was the end of July – a Mountie came into the lobby one
Friday night. He leaned against the ticket wicket, talking to
Parnell Upham and staring at Madge. The Mountie kept this
up through the intermission, then left abruptly. On Saturday
night, after the second show had gone in, he returned to the
theatre and did much the same thing. Madge ignored the
Mountie's stare, blowing a strand of hair out of her eyes as
she had once seen Greer Garson do when she was shaking a
mat out the window, pretending she didn't see Walter Pidgeon
standing below, looking up at her. Although she didn't look
at the Mountie directly, Madge was aware of the exact
moment he disappeared.

Constable Vaughan Borman didn't ask Madge out for
another week. (Later he told her he'd known she was Laddie
Murray's daughter. He said he'd avoided calling her at the
apartment because he'd been trying all week to resist temptation.) He waited until late the next Friday before returning
to the theatre. Madge was counting change when he came in.
He introduced himself and asked her to go for a drive with

him after work the next night. In his uniform Vaughan looked quite a bit like Walter Pidgeon. He was tall and dark, with a small, clipped mustache. Madge didn't think this resemblance stood up when she saw him the next night dressed in what he called his civvies: a black turtlenecked sweater, tweed jacket, and loafers. For one thing, without his boots he was shorter, about her height, and he smoked a pipe, which gave him a staid, military look that Madge didn't associate with being a Mountie. She thought of Mounties as dashing and adventurous. Vaughan was also considerably older than she (twelve years older she was to find out), and his hair was thinning in front. He drove her up the valley to Hampton, where he went into a roadside diner and came out with coffee and doughnuts, which they ate in the car. He wouldn't take her inside. He said it wasn't the kind of place he'd take a woman.

For the rest of the summer, Vaughan drove Madge somewhere two or three nights a week. Usually they went to Norton or Petitcodiac, not too far. Once Vaughan took her to Moncton for Chinese food, which you could not get in Sussex. Sometimes they drove to Sussex Corner for ice cream, then back to the railway yard, where they sat in the car with the lights turned off. On one such occasion Vaughan made a remark about Laddie's driving. He said her father couldn't drive a car without speeding. He said he would have ticketed Laddie before now, if he'd been able to catch him. Though Vaughan meant this as a joke, the comment angered Madge. "Why don't you try harder to catch him?" she taunted him. Vaughan patted her head and said, "I wouldn't want to ticket my girlfriend's father, now would I?" There was no denying Vaughan was good to her. He bought her a mother-of-pearl compact, a silver cross on a chain, and a book, *Painting from the Old Masters*, which he had gone out of his way to find. He encouraged her idea of becoming an artist, saying it was a good occupation for a woman. It was something she could do at home. Vaughan respected education, especially in a woman. He thought educated mothers raised intelligent children. He planned to marry an educated woman himself as soon as he'd saved enough money to offer her the home she deserved. With all this information inside her head, Madge was surprised by Vaughan's ardour. When they kissed and fondled, he groaned and murmured passionate endearments. He never tried to go too far. There was no danger of these sessions getting out of hand. Vaughan respected her too much to hurt her, he said.

In September Madge left for university. Since moving to Sussex she had pulled up her marks enough to earn a small scholarship at Acadia. Mostly she was required to take general courses, but she managed to sign up for a drawing class, which was her only contact with art, other than what she could pick up from library books. Her drawing instructor, Lionel Dexter, was a small-boned, fierce-looking man with slanted caterpillar eyebrows and a shrill falsetto voice. He wore a black cape to class, and when he explained something, he flapped his arms like pterodactyl wings. He was given to outbursts of temper, sometimes directed toward Madge. He would take hold of her hand and force it to draw the way he thought it should. Or he would grab the charcoal out of her hand and do it himself. Once he tore the paper from her easel and threw it in the wastebasket. Except for his favourite, a nervous, bony young man who sometimes posed for them, he carried on the same way with the other students. He called them *cows*. They had *hooves* instead of hands, he said, and were much too clumsy to draw. They were only in this course to avoid taking harder courses. He gave Madge a D. She got through her other courses with Bs and Cs. She hadn't spent much time studying.

The first week on campus Madge met Douglas Ogilvey, at a dance at the students'-union building. Doug was a third-year student, the son of a Glace Bay doctor. When Doug found out Madge had lived in Sydney Mines and her father was one of the Sydney Murrays, he invited her to join the Cape Breton Club. From then on, Madge spent too much time sitting around the students' coffee shop listening to Island jokes and becoming Doug's new girlfriend. Doug's old girlfriend, Carol Morrison, a genuine Cape Bretoner – she had been born in Inverness – hung around the club until it became evident she had been dropped. Doug was taking pre-med courses, following in his father's fôotsteps. He didn't seem serious about this and seldom cracked a book. He was an unabashed, swaggering jock, a ringleader in residence water fights and panty raids. Once Doug helped throw Marvin Leak, an English major who stammered and wrote poetry, into the duck pond in Wolfville after Marvin had been found hoarding a food parcel his mother had sent from home. When Doug and Izzy Munn flushed him out like Viking raiders (Doug looked like a Viking with his red hair and rangy build), Marvin was sitting on a suitcase inside his closet, stuffing himself with cold chicken, pickles, and date bread, which were immediately seized as booty.

More often than not, Doug was generous and open-handed with people, lending possessions and money with ease. He played the guitar and sang bawdy songs, sometimes during intermission at dances. He was popular, noticed, envied, in demand, though not for anything requiring scholarliness or contemplation.

Madge wrote Vaughan Borman. She told him she didn't want to be serious, she didn't want to be married, she wanted to be unattached. At this point she thought of Doug as an interlude. She didn't expect the relationship to last. She expected Doug to drop her as he had dropped Carol Morrison. Vaughan didn't write back. Madge bundled up his love letters written in green ink and put them in a shoebox. That summer Madge went to work at Keltic Lodge in Ingonish, Cape Breton, as a waitress. Doug had already spent two summers there working as a bus boy and porter. He said the guests at Keltic were big tippers, that the hotel manager was easy to get along with. He said they would have a good time swimming, going to staff wiener roasts and corn boils.

Madge went to a lot of beach parties that summer. She got a tan. She made enough money to pay for the fall term. Doug spent some of his wages on an engagement ring. He waited until they were back in college before giving her the ring. They were sitting in the students' coffee shop with the other members of the club. Doug slipped the ring in Madge's coffee when he was at the counter. He did it on the sly. Even the waiter didn't notice. Only Izzy Munn knew this was going to happen. Somehow Izzy managed to get everyone at their table to quiet down without telling them why. They were as surprised as Madge when she lifted a diamond ring out of her cup. The boldness and panache of her engagement made a strong impression on Madge. She was untroubled by the fact that Doug had not come straight out and asked her to marry him, that he assumed she would, or that she had come close to swallowing the ring.

Alison was conceived during a Christmas visit to the Ogilveys. A virgin when she went to Glace Bay, Madge gave in under pressure from Doug, and in defiance of his parents' dismissal of her. Dr. Ogilvey, an abrupt, taciturn man, who insisted on punctuality by ringing a small Burmese gong fifteen minutes before mealtimes, ignored Madge. Mrs. Ogilvey – Madge never did get past calling her *Mrs.* – a handsome heavyset woman with a pompadour of strawberry-blonde hair, was better at ignoring Madge without being rude. She talked about Sydney people Doug knew and avoided asking Madge leading questions. Madge had the idea Doug's parents perceived her as decorative, that they did not expect Doug to marry her, that she had been brought home for show.

Madge had a subdued Celtic beauty, dark hair, pale skin, grey eyes. Apart from her looks, she didn't make a strong impression. She relied on others to draw her out. She knew this deference was a camouflage, something she wore in others' territory, something that could be shucked off and cast away. She expected the Ogilveys to see through this. She didn't like being underestimated. She didn't like being written off, even though it was her own doing. But she felt she had come this far, she had to play it out. She went along to meet Doug's old cronies, to holiday parties, to church. She went along to bed. It wasn't sex that got Madge in trouble. It was her idea of romance. That was what put a colour wash over what was going on, over the bed where she lay with Doug, writhing and bucking in the winter twilight. Later, at parties, Madge was to joke about this rough coupling, claiming Alison's conception was at 5:45 p.m., the exact moment Dr. Ogilvey sounded the dinner gong. In fact, it had been earlier. Dinner was at six, which had given Madge and Doug fifteen minutes to scramble into their clothes and go downstairs.

They were married when Madge was eight weeks' pregnant, in a small off-campus Presbyterian church in Wolfville. Madge's parents brought a large white box with them from Sussex, a wedding gift from Niels and Selda. Inside was a white porcelain bowl on a pedestal. On the outside of the bowl Selda had painted *Margaret* and *Douglas* in blue. Selda's note explained that drinking from the loving cup was an old Scandinavian tradition. The cup was meant to be used at their wedding celebration and on anniversaries thereafter. During the reception at the Blomidon Inn, Madge and Doug drank ginger ale from the cup (the Ogilveys were teetotallers, only soft drinks were served), and toasted each other. After the wedding supper, Madge returned the cup to its box for safekeeping. For her, the cup had become a talisman, a receptacle of constancy and devotion.

Ardith, who had stood up for Madge, left soon after the reception. She was working on a Master's degree and had an essay to finish over the weekend. Madge's Aunt Margaret returned to Halifax with Ardith. By then she was teaching high school in Middle Musquodoboit and had papers to mark before Monday. The Ogilveys also left after the reception to drive back to Sydney. Madge's parents stayed in Wolfville overnight. There was no honeymoon, so the two couples spent the evening partying before going to bed. Laddie and Doug, who had hit it off when they met earlier in Sussex, spent most of the evening trading college stories. Laddie had spent two

years at Acadia before being kicked out for failing grades, so
Madge had been told. Like Doug, he had been involved in
campus high-jinks.

Madge and Doug dropped out of college. In those days, it
was difficult to get student loans. Dr. Ogilvey didn't offer
financial support, and the spice business hadn't got far enough
off the ground for Laddie to offer help. He still owed money
to the bank. Doug got a job selling pharmaceuticals. He and
Madge moved to a small apartment in Halifax, where they
spent weekends partying with student friends, who camped
on their floor, drank their beer, and emptied their fridge.
These were loud, boisterous occasions during which their
friends mimicked professors, bragged about cribbing on
exams, and made boorish asides about a busty girl named
Darla who worked in the university laundry during the day
and on her back at night. *On her back* was Izzy's way of
putting it, poking Doug in the ribs until the tips of Doug's
ears grew red. It was during one of these parties that Madge
overheard Doug telling Izzy that, during his college years,
Laddie and two others had blackballed a theology student.
They had taken the student up to the orchard behind the
women's residence and tied him to an apple tree. They had
stripped him from the waist down, shaved off his pubic hair,
and applied shoe polish to his private parts. This was the
prank Laddie had been expelled for, not for low marks.

During these parties, no one thought it necessary to keep
quiet for Alison, who was asleep in the clothes-basket on the
bed. If the stylish secretary in the apartment below sent a
message through the pipes, the bottle-opener was used to rap
out a protracted, defiant reply. Desperation not to miss out
on campus life kept these wasteful, shoddy weekends going
for a surprisingly long time. Izzy was the last to move on.
Doug finally locked him out of their apartment one night after
Izzy had put his foot through Doug's guitar on his way to the
bathroom.

Madge and Doug bought a bungalow across the harbour
in Dartmouth. Shelley was born. Madge bought baby furni-

ture, toys, a dining-room table, and a set of earthenware dishes, though she and Doug rarely entertained. Madge could never get herself organized enough to invite people in. She preferred people to drop in so they could see the chaos, the toys scattered across the floor, the fingerprints blackening the walls, the unfolded diapers on living-room chairs. People could see for themselves how unmanageable and disorderly her life had become. Their college friends seldom visited. Like Madge's sister, they had graduated, drifted away, in Ardith's case to Toronto. When he was in town, Doug took doctors out for lunch appointments. Doug never referred to his business contacts as *customers* the way Laddie did. He said *clients*. Doug wore double-breasted suits and British-made shoes. He drove a company car, an Oldsmobile, and smoked Pall Malls. Most weekdays Doug was away on the road. He covered the Maritimes; twice a year he went to Newfoundland. He came home on Fridays, too tired to make love. He and Madge made love on Saturdays and Sundays. On Saturday nights, after she had put their daughters to bed, Madge took a bath and dressed in a lounging robe or slacks and a low-cut blouse and heated up the food she had made earlier: coq au vin, beef Stroganoff, lasagna. By that time, the hockey game was over and Doug was willing to turn off the TV. Madge lit candles and put on music, Errol Garner, Nat King Cole. Doug opened a bottle of wine. Since he had started working for the pharmaceutical company, Doug had become something of a wine connoisseur, soaking off labels and pasting them in a book. After they had eaten, they went to bed and made love. That was what the preparations had been leading up to. Madge was disappointed how quickly they reached this point. She couldn't get over wanting more to happen, though she was unable to think of things to say or do to prolong the evening, to make it more interesting.

Weekday mornings, when Doug was away, Madge put Shelley in her stroller and walked Alison to play school. At that point she didn't drive. She and Doug couldn't afford a car of their own and bus service was poor. After Theo was born, Madge stopped doing this much, and Alison walked to play school alone. Madge didn't sketch or paint. She didn't even hang prints or batiks on the wall. There were travel posters on the walls: a street in Montmartre, a dancer at the Moulin Rouge, an orchard in Arles. Doug had picked up these posters on one of his trips; they had been handed out as part of a French travel promotion. Once or twice a month Madge would ask the teenager across the street to baby-sit while she took a taxi to the theatre. When she came home, she would go straight to bed while the movie was fresh in her mind and replay the romantic scenes: Gregory Peck and Audrey Hepburn hauling themselves out of the Tiber and kissing for the first time, Burt Lancaster and Deborah Kerr making love on the Hawaiian sand. She reread Vaughan Borman's love letters, then tried to imagine what it would have been like married to him. She thought Vaughan would have shown more devotion and passion than Doug. Doug was athletic and matter-of-fact in bed. He didn't spend much time at it. There were few endearments. Vaughan would have insisted on baby-sitting while Madge attended art class. He would have bought her art books and gone with her to galleries. Of course there would have been an exchange for this. There would have been demands. Vaughan might have insisted she wear a certain kind of clothes, that she treat their children differently. He might have turned out to be a fussy eater. After she had read through the letters, lingering over the one that contained Vaughan's marriage proposal, Madge put the letters back on the shelf where she kept the loving cup. She also kept the Oersteds' Christmas cards up there. These were handmade by Selda, usually one of her designs painted on folded construction paper with an encouraging note inside.

The year before Theo was born, Niels Oersted suffered a heart attack. *Suffered* was Madge's mother's word. Selda hadn't been there. She was in a craft show in Montreal. One of the Oersted daughters was at home with Niels, visiting. One evening Niels had complained to his daughter that he wasn't feeling well, gone upstairs, lain down, and died. The next year Selda moved to Saint John. Two years later she married an artist friend and moved to Sackville. She held on to the house in Sussex for several years and tried, unsuccessfully, to persuade the provincial government to turn it into an arts and crafts museum.

During the early years of her marriage, Madge would take the loving cup out of its box on their wedding anniversary and put it on the dining-room table. Before she and Doug ate one of her special dinners, they would fill the cup with wine and drink to each other. It was never Doug's idea they do this, but he might have thought of it himself if Madge had forgotten. After they had finished their dinner, Madge would rinse out the cup and put it back on the shelf. On their fifth anniversary, several months after Theo was born, Madge was too tired and distracted to remember to do this and left the cup on the table overnight, along with the dirty dishes and tubs of half-eaten food. (She had not been up to cooking that meal. Doug had sent out for Mexican food instead.) The next morning, while Madge and Doug were in bed, Shelley got hold of the cup when she was playing house with her dolls. The cup was too large for her hands. When Madge got up, she saw it lying in six or seven pieces on the hardwood floor. After breakfast, Madge sat down at the table and painstakingly glued the cup together. There were chips missing from the cracks, and the handles would not stay on, but she managed to glue the bowl onto the pedestal. This time Madge didn't return the cup to its shelf. She put it on the windowsill above the kitchen sink to use as a catch-all for safety pins, stray buttons, elastics for her daughters' hair.

Dickens's Wife

The day before Doug Ogilvey and I got married, my father took us to Halifax to shop for wedding presents. We were to do this separately. I was to choose something with my father while my mother stayed in Wolfville to work on wedding preparations; Doug was to choose something with his parents. The Ogilveys were already on their way down from Cape Breton. Doug would be driving back to Wolfville with them in the morning. With us, in the trunk of my father's car, were my remaining possessions: books, sketchpads, a painting of Selda Oersted's, a ballerina lamp, a vase, a chenille bedspread that my parents had cleared out of my room at home. We were taking these things to the apartment Doug had rented us in Halifax.

My father asked Doug if he wanted to drive. I didn't drive. Neither did my mother or sister. In those days most women didn't. Driving was primarily viewed as a male activity. The few women who drove had to put up with snide comments about the ineptitude of female drivers. *Look out, there's a female driver ahead*, my father would say, sighting her from several car lengths behind and overtaking her at the earliest opportunity. Whenever he saw my mother's sister behind the wheel, my father would put his hand over his eyes as if he were anticipating a collision.

My father and Doug had met once before, at Thanksgiving when I had taken Doug home to show off. *Show off* was the right way of putting it. I felt proud to be bringing home someone akin to my father, another Cape Bretoner, and a man to boot. You would have thought I had gone out and got myself engaged and pregnant for the purpose of presenting my father with a fully grown son. Not that I had ever heard my father say anything about wanting a son. It didn't occur to me that he might have wanted one until after Doug and my father met and I saw how quickly my father kidnapped Doug and whisked him away to view the spice-bottling plant, the old army camp, and the soft drink factory, leaving my mother and me home to stuff the turkey and make pumpkin pie.

My father was accommodating and magnanimous with strangers. It was his way of breaking the ice, of putting people at ease, of equalizing the difference between him and other people. When he handed the wheel over to Doug that day, he was acknowledging Doug's ability to get us from one place to another, he was accepting him on equal terms. Doug didn't act as if he thought equalization was necessary. He took being equal for granted. Sometimes he was overly familiar with my father. He told off-colour jokes, which offended my father's prudishness, though he didn't let it show. Doug corrected my father and dismissed his opinions as my father sometimes did with my mother and me. Not Ardith, seldom did my father correct or dismiss my sister. I attributed Doug's audacity to the fact that he was a Cape Bretoner, that he saw himself as having the right to be overbearing and know-it-all with another islander, that such arrogance and intimacy were credentials of a shared birthright though I never saw Doug act carelessly with his own father. With Dr. Ogilvey, Doug was subdued, respectful. Douglas I called him then, the only person besides his mother who did. I thought using Douglas bestowed value and honour upon him, that I regarded him with greater seriousness than other people did.

Coming back from Halifax, I sat up front with my father. Soon after we left Halifax, my father made one of his detours

to look up Cam McDougall, a Cape Bretoner from Boular-
derie who was supposed to be living somewhere in Lower
Sackville. My father was always looking for an excuse to make
a detour. It was a way of spinning out a trip, of making it
seem more like a vacation, which he seldom took. We never
did find Cam McDougall, though my father stopped at a gas
station and waylaid two passersby to ask if they knew Cam's
whereabouts. It was early evening when we reached the outskirts of Wolfville. Before we drove down the slow, winding
road into town, my father pulled into a lay-by beside an
orchard, lit a cigarette, and rolled down the window, part
way. He left the engine idling with the heater on. It was February; you couldn't sit long in a car without heat. Through
the dusk I picked out the leafless skeletons of dwarf apple
trees. I knew my father was settling in for one of his talks. I
had been given such talks on other momentous occasions in
my life: my first job, my high-school graduation, entering
college. Now I was being advised about the pitfalls of marriage. My father was telling me it wouldn't be easy, that marriage was no bed of roses.

I thought I knew this already from listening to my parents
fight, but I didn't say this. I knew my father was trying to
warn me, that he meant well. I also knew I would get the
lecture over with sooner if I said nothing to impede the flow
of words.

"One thing that helped your mother and me," he said,
speaking of the trouble in the past tense, "when the going got
rough we didn't run home with our tails between our legs.
You know what I mean?"

I knew all right. He was telling me that if Doug and I
quarrelled, I wasn't to run home with my side of the story. I
didn't think this likely. I didn't think Doug and I would fight.
I thought we were above all that.

"Most spats blow over sooner or later. It does no good to
cry on your parents' shoulders. That's one thing your mother
and I never did."

"You couldn't. Your parents were dead," I reminded him. "Except for Mum's father."

"No, but we wouldn't have anyway," my father insisted. He lifted the brim of the beige felt hat that he wore all winter, lifted it, I suppose, to relieve the tightness of the leather band against his forehead. It was then he said something unexpected and alarming. "Sometimes your mother says she doesn't love me." He threw his cigarette out the window, into the snow, and lit another one. "That's what she says."

There was something humble and confused in his voice, as if he couldn't figure out why my mother would say this. My father seldom made personal confessions. As I remember, he only made one other confession to me in his life. This confession, that my mother didn't love him, had the same effect on me as taking my possessions out of the trunk of the car and leaving them on the bare floor of an empty apartment. It made me feel irrevocably, irretrievably, cut off from childhood, that there was no way of getting back.

It was bad enough that my father couldn't afford a large wedding present like Doug's parents. (With both parents at his side, Doug picked out a five-piece set of solid mahogany, the kind of bedroom suite you sometimes see nowadays in high-priced auction rooms.) It was bad enough that my father couldn't seem to make a business succeed, that, after years of hard work, he had to run up an overdraft to pay for a small reception at Blomidon Inn. It was bad enough that the town sheriff had threatened to cut off the power to his spice-bottling plant if he didn't pay the property tax, that our family was unprotected from this kind of humiliation and disgrace. On top of all this, did I have to be told, the day before my wedding, that my mother might not love him?

I had assumed they loved each other, even if they didn't act it sometimes. It was what I wanted to believe, just as I wanted to believe I was in love with Douglas Ogilvey. Most of the time I believed this, but I had trouble sometimes, especially when Doug was grandstanding in the company of other people, telling jokes and stories, ignoring me. When this happened, I found myself working too hard at liking him, pretending to admire his bravado and careless opinions. I would opt out of the conversation, brood over my misgivings. After a while Doug would notice my withdrawal. He would put his arm around me, flatter me, make a fuss. He would kiss me in front of other people and look at me with such bold affection that I was quickly drawn alongside. Then I would tell myself that love was a kind of pain you had to put up with if you expected romance. You couldn't have love without discomfort and uncertainty. Did my mother feel this way about my father? Or did she tell him she didn't love him in order to bring him to heel? Sometimes it was hard to get through to my father. He had blind spots. He was stubborn. He liked his own way too much. Now, when I remember the time I spent sitting beside my father in the car, I think maybe my father was fishing, that he thought my mother might have said something to me about their marriage, that there might have been some female talk, that revelations and secrets might have been exchanged. Perhaps he underestimated my mother's loyalty to him or misjudged the distance I had put between my mother and myself.

My mother had her own way of warning me. Earlier that day, she'd taken the cake she'd made at home to the bakery in Wolfville to be iced. She'd also ironed my wedding dress, which she'd also made, though she hated sewing. It hung inside the closet at the foot of the bed, along with my shoes and veil. After supper I had taken a bath and gone to bed early. It must have been about ten o'clock. I was lying in bed in the dark imagining myself at the reception in my cream-coloured princess-style dress, carrying a silver plate. I saw myself moving regally from one person to another, dispensing ribboned bundles of cake. In this way I was gradually taking on some of that dreamy tolerance with which brides sometimes gild themselves in order to glide through the excitement and uncertainty unscathed.

There was a tap on the door and my mother's voice asked to come in. I got out of bed, unlocked the door, and closed it after her. We sat in the darkness facing each other, my mother halfway up the bed.

"How do you feel about tomorrow?" she said. From the smell of things I knew she and my father had been having a nightcap.

I thought this was one of her neutral questions, the requisite inquiry, until she blurted out, "It's not too late, if you want to change your mind." The words hung between us in the darkness, unclaimed. I was waiting for her to take them back.

"I mean you're only nineteen."

"I don't have a job," I reminded her. The fact was that, unless I could become an artist, I didn't want a job. I wanted to be looked after. "Besides, what about the baby? Who would look after it?"

"I couldn't," my mother said quickly. "With my blood pressure, I couldn't manage." She wanted to get that straight.

Abortion wasn't mentioned. We didn't talk about it then. I may not even have been sure what the word meant.

"Douglas and I love each other," I said loftily.

I might have gotten myself pregnant, but that didn't mean I was in trouble. After all, I had been engaged for five months, which was halfway to being married. I had the diamond to prove it.

"Good." The stamp of relief in my mother's voice was as palpable as a mark on my skin, something tattooed into the pores, something that wouldn't wash off. "Well then, good luck." My mother got up from the bed and came toward me. There was a puff of warm, moist breath as her lips touched my forehead.

I got up and followed her to the door, to lock it again.

"If I were you, I wouldn't drink any more tonight," I told her, though she was far from being drunk. I was angry that she hadn't kept her anxieties to herself. It upset me to be reminded of her powerlessness. Quite often I saved up the anger I felt toward my father and used it against my mother.

In the next four years I was pregnant most of the time. I liked being pregnant. I was seldom ill. For nine months my skin took on a rosy sheen that drained away after each birth. I carried the extra weight well, never became mountainous or awkward. My deliveries were straightforward. Just like a race horse, Ewan Forbes said after my second daughter, Shelley, was born, as if I simply dropped my daughter on the grass. I thought the doctor was complimenting me on my long legs, the ease with which I sat up on the delivery table afterwards and ate a large dinner before walking back to my room, unaided. If I had developed complications, or if any of my children had been born handicapped or deformed, I might have thought twice about becoming pregnant again. But I was lucky, each of my children emerged from the womb perfectly formed.

I enjoyed sex more when I was pregnant, or was in the process of becoming pregnant. It wasn't that lovemaking between Doug and myself improved or became more adventurous. That didn't change much. Sometimes Doug took his time and I came, sometimes he was in too big a hurry and I didn't. My enjoyment was heightened when I connected sex with procreation, when I was putting my body to that use. There was nothing religious about this. It had nothing to do with the church. It had to do with how I viewed myself. I had come to see my body as something ripe and fecund. Medium boned, with full breasts and heavy thighs, I maintained an unhurried, unflappable pace. I moved slowly, languidly. I was incapable of quick, darting movements, trim, economical gestures. I wasn't athletic. I couldn't imagine myself playing strenuous games like tennis or golf. I imagined myself as the quintessential female, one who succoured and nurtured, who gathered her children onto her lap to comfort and cradle, to nurse and feed. I took to wearing loose-fitting clothes: Doug's old shirts, baggy pants, flowered caftans I picked up in the thrift shop on Lower Water Street. Beneath these clothes my body felt generous and flourishing.

When I was lying under Doug, I would sometimes mouth words like *mount* and *ride*, words I thought a peasant might use lying on her back in a hay loft or an unploughed field. I liked damp earthy smells, raunchy pubic odours, hairy roughened skin. Sometimes I murmured the words *cock* and *stud* aloud as Doug was entering, so he would catch the rutty eroticism of the farmyard. We never talked about sex. This was the only way I knew of getting what I wanted, which was to make it as urgent and unstoppable as it seemed to be in movies and books.

Early on in our marriage, I became a nocturnal beast. There were night feedings, earaches, croup. I was used to standing in front of the kitchen window in my bathrobe and slippers, a baby over one shoulder, staring into the darkness. I kept the overhead light off so I could see the world outside, the telephone wires swooping above the back lane, a cat walking along the fence, snow sifting over the dark expanse of yard, redeeming its daytime gouges and scars. Without light behind me, no one could see me inside, but I could see them. Not that anyone was out there looking in at that hour, but I kept the light off, just in case. I liked the feeling of invisibility and secrecy, of being able to see without being seen. And the darkness blotted out the bags of garbage leaning against the wall beside the back door, the spoons and glasses piled in the sink, the greasy burners on the stove. I wasn't reminded of housework that needed doing, of work that might never be done. This was my time off. The phone never rang. Nobody came to the door. No one except the baby in my arms expected anything from me. Once I had fed or rocked the baby to sleep, the night was peaceful and undemanding. This was when I got to know my children, one at a time. These night vigils were when I did most of my reading, sitting against pillows on the chesterfield, feet braced against the coffee table so my knees could hold both the baby and the book. Now I see that this reversal of night and day, the careless way I squandered day and hoarded night, was possible because I regarded motherhood as a state of being, not a job. It wasn't an occupation for which you dressed up, or got yourself organized for. Some mothers might have seen it that way, but I never did. I saw motherhood as something you surrendered to, like the weather. It was omnipresent, pervasive, it swallowed you whole.

I liked the mild, milky smell of babies, their determined grunts, their cries, their tuneless songs. I liked their astonishment when they learned to roll over or stand without holding on. I liked the way they turned their heads in rapt attention at the sun shadows on the wall.

Most of the other couples on the street in Dartmouth, where we moved before Theo's birth, had married young and, like us, were crowding their early married years with child-bearing. In those days you were encouraged to have your children while you were young, while you still had the stamina and resilience to look after them. No one brought up a single child on purpose. Children were supposed to be better adjusted if they grew up with other siblings close to their age. And in practical terms, it was thought that if you were tied down with two children, you might as well be tied down with three or four, to get it over with. None of us used the Pill. There were too many warnings about side-effects. We stuck to the old methods. We didn't spend a lot of time trying to decide whether or not we should have babies. We went ahead and had them. It was assumed child-bearing was a part of marriage. The childless were pitied. We felt smug about this. Childless women didn't know what they were missing. We thought they were disadvantaged.

Doug and I lived in a bungalow with a yard out back. There was nothing ornamental or lush about our yard or anyone else's on the street. None of them were gussied up with wooden planters or shrubbery. There were no trees. They had been bulldozed down when the land was cleared for the subdivision. Only Nancy Rice kept a vegetable garden. The rest of us figured we didn't have the energy to look after a garden that was likely to be trampled underfoot. These yards were more like fenced playing fields and contained sandboxes, trikes, monkey bars, swings, slides, and plastic wading pools. During the day, while our husbands were at work (hubbies, Marge Putman called them), we mothers visited in one another's yards, drinking coffee or, if it was warm, iced tea, watching our children run under sprinklers bought for that purpose. Because fences were low, we were able to keep an eye on our children two or three yards away without moving from our folding chairs. There was a good-natured camaraderie among us that came from covering for each other in emergencies: rushing a child to the hospital for stitches, picking up a prescription, cashing a cheque, going for milk. Our conversation ran to toilet training, Dr. Spock, phone-in shows, recipes. We showed no inclination to move the conversation toward anything that required intellectual effort or concentration. We couldn't afford to become caught up in serious discussion. We had to keep ourselves braced for interruptions.

During these years, we didn't do much to regain our figures or glamorize our appearances beyond shaving our legs. Sometimes we trimmed hair or painted one another's fingernails, or indulged in something giddy and frivolous like stripping down to our underwear and positioning our rumps on the sprinkler. One afternoon, Lureen Santini dumped two boxes of wine grapes into a plastic pail and we stomped them in our bare feet. Lureen's husband, Tony, ordered these grapes especially for wine-making. We took turns, there was only room in the pail for one person. Marge went home and came back with a bottle of wine and glasses. While one of us tramped down the cold slithery grapes, the rest drank wine and cheered her on.

We weren't nearly as freewheeling about our husbands. We seldom talked about them beyond making oblique references to shirt-ironing, in-laws, and food preferences. Quarrels, drunkenness, verbal abuse were never mentioned. None of us was physically battered or we wouldn't have been sitting outside in the open with our bare arms and legs exposed. There didn't seem to be as much physical abuse then, or else it was better hidden. We understood that talking about our mar-

riages risked misinterpretation. We knew that if we talked
about what happened inside our houses at night and on weekends, we might let out too much. We might lose our grip,
upset the balance. Mention of new appliances, pay raises,
promotions, anything that was seen as moving us up and out
of the neighbourhood, was also avoided. It made us nervous
to think one of us might be left behind. Like women in a
harem, our equanimity and easy way with each other came
from our ability to pool our energies and our children. But
we weren't the harem of one man. We would never have
survived as concubines or numbered wives. Remaining Wife
Number One was part of the bargain we had made with our
husbands, what each of us had settled for.

During winter we moved indoors, abandoning backyards
to snowmen, tunnels, forts. We took to the phone, calling
each other in turn. Conversation was four-way as it shuttled
between the women at both ends of the line and their children.
Receivers were left dangling while one of us rushed to the
bathroom to check the medicine cabinet or the toilet, or
shouted warnings down basement stairs. To make sure nothing had been said about you, one phone call was quickly
followed by another. This used up a lot of time: there were
five of us counting Debby Rinehart, who worked in a steno
pool half days and employed a part-time housekeeper. These
conversations were less satisfying than the summer visits. Differences became more pronounced on the phone. There was
more room for misunderstanding as backgrounds came to
light. There were slips in grammar and pronunciation, sometimes a leaning toward the vulgar and coarse. Material advantages surfaced, parents who offered interest-free loans, sent
large cheques. There was more opportunity to pass judgment,
to give in to pointed remarks. We were often cranky and shrill,
inclined to whine. These were the dangerous months when
children were cooped up with measles, mumps, chickenpox.
The sky lowered, the snow fell. We could go for weeks without
seeing the sun. There were sleet storms, glare ice. Our porch
steps iced over. When Doug was away, I gave up using the

front door. The back door became a dark, shadowy hole. It took on a daunting, ominous shape. When Alison went off to school those winter mornings, I admired her for venturing forth.

One night in February, in our sixth year of marriage when Theo was wheezy and hoarse with croup, Doug came home two days early. He'd been away seventeen days instead of the usual five, attending a training session at head office in Mississauga. He had recently been made district manager of the Atlantic region. I was sleeping on the chesterfield in the living room because one of the cats had peed on our bed and the mattress was drying out. The hall light was on. One of the kids had pushed the kitchen chairs into the hallway against the front door, then covered them with blankets to make a tent. What wakened me was Doug shoving aside the chairs to get in. I remember opening my eyes and watching him stoop to take off his toe rubbers. Then he stood up and came across the room in his camel-hair coat, his hair mussed, the sting of winter in his cheeks. I was glad to see him. It wasn't his handsomeness that I welcomed but his maleness, his bulk. When Doug was away, I thought I didn't miss him, that I was getting along fine, but as soon as I saw him, I knew that all along I had been waiting for him to come back. He was carrying a box. Doug often brought me small gifts from places where he'd been. The box hovered over a pile of books and lumps of plasticine and crayons on the coffee table before coming to rest on the arm of the chesterfield, a few inches from my hand.

"For you," he said. He didn't kiss me.

"Oh, thanks." I sat up. "You're early. I wasn't expecting you." I didn't mean to sound unfriendly. I was apologizing for my grungy bathrobe and unwashed hair.

"We got through the course earlier than they figured."

"How was it?" We were always polite when we'd been apart for a while. Each time we had to start over again.

"Fine. It was good." He lifted the clothes basket from the chair, sat down, and stared at his polished brogues. "How are the kids?"

"Theo's got another earache." I had already told him about the croup. Doug phoned home two or three times a week to see how we were getting on. "The doctor says he'll have to have his adenoids out when he's older. They're so large they're blocking the tubes. They can't drain."

"Did you phone for a cleaning lady?"

Before he had gone on the training course, Doug had asked me to get someone to help me clean the house. He had made this request before, but this last time he'd been more insistent. He said he couldn't stand the mess. It embarrassed him. He couldn't bring people home. With the promotion he would need to entertain more. We could afford to pay someone to help.

I had forgotten this request, on purpose. I didn't want cleaning help. I didn't want another woman in the house. I didn't think housework was important enough to pay someone to do it. I didn't want to preside over dinner parties, to pass around hors d'oeuvres, plates of fancy dessert. I thought people who did those sorts of things were affected, that they were putting on airs. I thought of myself as a bohemian. That was the word we used instead of hippie or flower child. Also, I didn't want to spend the money. Though I didn't earn any, I worried a lot about money.

"I've been too tired to get around to it," I said. "Plus I'm pregnant."

Doug groaned and covered his face.

"It happens," I told him.

"Christ, didn't you use the diaphragm?"

"It wasn't in properly, I guess." I had a hard time telling when it was. Maybe I wasn't suited to it.

"Another kid." He still had his hands over his face. "Just when I thought we were pulling ahead."

"Well, maybe you should advise me about birth control. After all, you're the one who works for the pharmaceutical company."

He left the house after that. I heard him fall on the ice outside. I heard him curse. He drove off in the car.

When he came back half an hour later, I was lying naked on the chesterfield, except for a red bra he had bought me on a previous trip. My bathrobe was spread out beneath me. I had used a lot of rouge and eye makeup. Across my breasts was a sign I had crayoned on one of Doug's shirtbacks: *$50 a trick*. I don't know why I laid myself out like that, beyond wanting attention, and trying to be funny. I told Doug I was trying to earn money for a cleaning lady.

"Like hell you are."

"I decided you've been getting it free long enough." Which isn't what I meant. What I meant was he was the one who got out and around. I was the one stuck home with the kids.

"Come on, Madge."

There was some tenderness here, but not enough to make a difference. I didn't see the confusion. What I saw was impatience and disgust. That was what I picked up on. That was what prevented me from taking my legs from the back of the chesterfield, putting them together, sitting up, and talking sensibly. I might have flaunted the sign for hours, at least until my energy ran out. I might have made lewd gestures, got down on my elbows and knees. But Alison came into the hall and stood beneath the yellow glare of the overhead light in her nightgown and watched us. She looked frightened and wary. I saw that much before I shifted my legs from the back of the chesterfield.

Doug placed himself between Alison and me.

"Hi, Daddy," Alison said, but she didn't come any closer.

"Hi, sweetheart," Doug said. "How's my girl?"

He went into the hall and scooped her up.

"Why are you wearing your coat, Daddy?"

"I just got home."

By then I had pulled my bathrobe around me and belted it tightly. I went into the hall and stood at the end, away from the light.

"Are you all right?" I asked her.

Alison bobbed her head up and down. She had black hair
cut in bangs, which made her look solemn and righteous. She
put her palms against Doug's shoulders and pushed herself
back. "I want to get down now."

As soon as she was on her feet, she came up to me and
wrapped her arms around my thighs. I knew when I went into
the hallway that she would do this. Until we got used to his
being back, Doug would be treated as a guest.

"Can I have a drink of water, Mummy?"

I was careful to keep the bathroom light turned off so she
wouldn't see the rouge and eyeshadow. I stood in the doorway
with my arms folded tightly across my breasts, pretending she
hadn't seen me on the chesterfield.

Alison took her time drinking, watching me over the rim
of the glass. She was weighing the situation, deciding whether
or not I was responsible and trustworthy enough for her to
go back to bed.

Eric was born. Doug had a vasectomy. He said he was doing
it to make it easier for me, which I believed. This was before
he met Estelle, before I got the telephone call and the letters.

Two, then three, of my children were in school. I lost
weight, bought wool dresses, a knit suit, a matching handbag
and shoes. I wore these when I accompanied Doug to a restaurant where he entertained his clients and their wives. He
had given up on the idea of bringing them home. Gradually I
reclaimed the night for sleep. Once a week I attended an art-
appreciation class at the high school. On weekends Doug
worked on home improvements. He built a small stage in the
basement with a low railing all round, for plays, a dress-up
bin into which I tossed worn shoes and hats, clothes and belts
I no longer wore. He made a work table and installed a flu-
orescent light overhead. I spent hours at this table with my
children after school, making puppets, papier-mâché masks,
shoebox dioramas, scenes from asbestos clay. Most of this I
improvised. Some of the ideas I picked up from how-to books

I brought home from the library. I bought rolls of newsprint and tacked it to plywood sheets Doug had nailed to the walls for painting. Sometimes Lureen or one of the other mothers would look after Eric and send her older children to our basement to paint. Most of the time I carried Eric downstairs and put him in a playpen I kept down there so he wouldn't have to sit on the cement floor. I didn't have a playpen upstairs. I didn't like to confine my children. I thought it interfered with their curiosity. While I was in the basement, meals were delayed, laundry piled up, dust and clutter were ignored as I showed children how to make egg-carton tulips, coat-hanger mobiles, macaroni-and-burlap collages, painted sculptures.

I took the kids to visit my parents. It didn't work out. The kids were hard on my mother's blood pressure. The noise and confusion got on her nerves. My father was awkward around his grandchildren. He seemed to regard them as a separate species. He didn't know what to say to them.

Each summer, the first two weeks of July, we bundled the kids into the car along with a supply of diapers and toys and drove to Ingonish, where Doug's parents rented us a cottage so they could see their grandchildren. They never visited us in Dartmouth. In Ingonish we spent mornings at the beach helping the kids build sand castles, teaching them to swim, picking up sand dollars that we painted and lined up on windowsills. Those afternoons when the kids napped, Doug and I sat on the screened porch and read or made love quickly, quietly, on the rug beside the metal bed while, overhead, the breeze sucked the curtains against the screen. In the evenings Doug played the guitar and taught the kids songs. Three times a week we drove along the shore to the Ogilveys for supper.

We bought a secondhand station wagon. I learned to drive, timidly, nervously. With the kids in the car, I anticipated an accident. I didn't go far from home when I had them in the car. I stayed in Dartmouth, making short trips to the shopping centre, the library, the movie theatre, the doctor, and the dentist. One Saturday afternoon before Christmas, when Doug was home baby-sitting, I drove across the bridge to Halifax to buy Ardith a Christmas present. I went to a gift shop on Quinpool Road. After I had made my purchase, a pewter hand mirror, I came outside and found the station wagon had a flat tire. I knew about jacking up the car, taking off the hubcap, removing the bolts. But I didn't have any confidence that I could get the spare tire on securely, that the car would be safe enough to drive afterwards. I went back inside the shop and phoned Doug. I expected him to put the kids in his car and come to my rescue. "Come on, Madge," he said. "Give me a break." He was watching the Grey Cup. He told me to phone a service station. I remember standing by a roll-top desk that served as a counter, foolishly holding onto the receiver after Doug had hung up. I remember turning my back to the gift shop owner so he wouldn't see my surprise at being left high and dry. I wanted to hide the embarrassing fact that my husband had refused to help me out. The gift shop owner went outside and changed the tire. Perhaps he felt sorry for me. When I got home Doug didn't ask how I had managed. He was feeling punchy and jubilant because the Tiger Cats had won. He seemed to have forgotten about the flat tire.

Estelle Rankine was a university graduate, a chemistry major. She was two or three years younger than me. Estelle was narrow-bodied and thin. She had fine, bird-boned wrists, brown eyes, blonde hair smooth and shiny as varnished oak. She had that cool, self-sufficiency that nurses and lab technicians sometimes have, that seems to accompany a white uniform. Estelle played up the white by wearing pale lipstick and clear nail polish. She cultivated the freshness of a Breck shampoo ad and showed what most people would consider muted good taste: tiny pearl earrings, a gold watch pinned to the pocket above her breast. Estelle worked in a doctor's office to help put her husband, Warren, through dentistry. She couldn't find a lab job in Halifax. Those kinds of jobs were in Ontario and Quebec where the head offices were. Doug knew the doctor Estelle worked for. He was a friend of his father's. Since he'd become district manager, Doug had to handle a certain amount of correspondence. For a couple of years he'd used Ruby Blinkhorn, who worked out of her house. When Ruby moved to P.E.I. to live with her sister, Doug took his correspondence to Estelle. Estelle had taken secretarial courses at night school. While Warren studied at the library, she did extra typing at home, mostly term essays and reports. The only correspondence she typed was Dr. Mosher's and Doug's. Saturday mornings Doug went over to the Rankines' duplex to pick up the week's typing and dictate letters. Sometimes Estelle would drop off Doug's correspondence on her way home from work. She came weekdays when he was out of town. I would usually ask her into the kitchen for coffee, but she never stayed long. What I remember clearly was the way Estelle fixed her gaze on mine so her eyes wouldn't wander. I had the feeling she wanted to look around, open my fridge and cupboard doors, to see the bleeding roast stains, sticky food spills, the crumbs clustered like mouse droppings on the countertop, but she was disciplining herself, fastening her eyes on mine so the untidy edges of her vision fell away. By trying so hard not to see the evidence of my careless housekeeping, she gave it more weight. I thought she was guilty of pretence. I thought she was phoney.

"I don't know how you do it, Madge."

Stand it, she meant.

I was careful to wipe out any sign of plaintiveness or regret. I made jokes about the dirt and disorder, the unruliness of my children. Not self-deprecatingly, but boastfully, defiantly. On such occasions I saw myself as a good-humoured, ribald earth mother, brimming with vitality and well-being. There was nothing petty or small-minded about *me*. I was larger than life, a giantess of resilience and benign goodwill.

Estelle knit, something I never did. She did this when she and Warren were driving somewhere or watching TV. Estelle didn't like to waste time. She knit four scarves, a different colour for each of my children, wrapped them in Santa paper, and brought them around to put under our Christmas tree. On Christmas morning I knew whom the scarves were meant to impress. Estelle must have wanted to show her maternal instincts were in place. Doug made a bigger fuss over the scarves than he did the sweaters his mother had sent her grandchildren from Norway, where she and Dr. Ogilvey had gone to attend a medical convention.

Once a month, on Saturday nights, Doug and I met Estelle and Warren in a Chinese restaurant. These were informal occasions that called for something casual, offbeat. Usually I wore a floral caftan, purple or green eyeshadow, dangling hoop earrings, chunky bracelets, a large turquoise ring. I looked flamboyant, outlandish. Estelle always wore black. She had several blouses and sweaters in this colour. When she wore black, Estelle took on the slinky elegance of a leopard or cat. Black made her skin pale, almost wan. It gave her a watchful, apprehensive look. She painted her mouth a deep cherry red, which accentuated the droop in her lower lip. Sitting beside her in the restaurant, Warren looked like her younger brother. Warren's face was covered with brownish freckles. He had spiky blond hair that wouldn't lie flat. This gave him a boyish, country look. Beside him Doug looked worldly and urbane. Since our marriage, Doug had filled out, put on weight. He had lost his raw-boned lankiness, the insolent, show-off gestures. Now he moved slowly, ponderously, as if he were weighing alternatives. He pursed his lips in a way that made you think he was making respectable choices.

Doug was knowledgeable about drugs. He kept up with new products, read medical and pharmaceutical publications. He could more than hold his own with Warren. Sometimes Estelle joined the conversation. She knew more chemistry than either of them, but she was careful not to show them up. During these dinners I sat and listened. I had a rule never to talk about my children when Doug and I were out like this, which did not leave me with much to say. If the conversation had moved to novels, I would have had opinions, but nobody at the table read novels much except me.

One Saturday in March, the dinner conversation turned from pharmaceuticals and dentistry to *The Fountainhead* by Ayn Rand. Doug was the one who mentioned it.

"It's a masterpiece," he said. "The best novel I've read." Doug read one novel a year, during the summer holidays. I asked him why he would make such a preposterous statement. I didn't like the novel. There was something brittle and bloodless about it; I thought it tried to make a virtue of cruelty and egotism.

"Because it's hard hitting. It tells it like it is without a lot of bullshit," Doug said. He put his elbows on the table and shoved his behind against the back of the booth.

"Tells *what* like it is?" I could be picky when I thought someone was invading what I had staked out as my territory.

"Life," he said irritably. "What else?"

"Self-respect," Estelle said. She had read the novel too. She cupped her small, pointed chin in her hands and leaned across the table toward me. "It's about the importance of self-respect. Being true to yourself."

I recognized Estelle's look. I had seen it before, in my kitchen. The intensity, the concentration, the unwavering gaze. I knew she was shutting something out, something at the periphery of her vision, something messy and unavoidable, that was close at hand. I didn't have to walk in on them Saturday morning to find out. I knew something was going on. This wasn't something I thought about consciously, that I decided to think. Inside me an alarm had gone off, a warning, an alert.

The phone call came in the middle of next week, on Wednesday. It was before midnight, after the kids were in bed. It was a man. He said my husband was having an affair with someone I knew. It might have been Warren, holding a handkerchief over the mouthpiece. The voice had that hoarse

urgency of disguise. He might have suspected something was
going on and wanted me to blow the whistle, to bring it into
the open. Maybe he knew I was capable of fireworks, of
staging a scene that would flush out the lovers, bring them
out of hiding. I went underground instead. I rooted around
in Doug's drawers for love letters, receipts for gifts, motels.
It occurred to me Doug and Estelle might be meeting week-
nights in places not too far from Halifax, maybe Truro or
New Glasgow. I came up empty-handed. I was surprised how
few of Doug's possessions were in the house, how little evidence of his presence was there. I bought the kids new scarves
and cut up Estelle's, gluing the wool bits into a collage on the
plywood downstairs. I made a large, old-fashioned house with
a verandah and gingerbread trim. Outside there was a garden,
trees, a cat. I showed Doug the picture, but he shrugged it
off. Maybe he didn't recognize the wool. I went out early
Saturday mornings so Doug would have to take the children
to the Rankines' with him. I returned late in the day, wearing
an exaggerated air of mystery about where I'd been. Sometimes I'd gone to an art gallery or a movie. Most of the time
I spent in the library reading whatever novels were at hand:
The Black Rose, Dr. Zhivago, The Queen's Physician. I would
sometimes return from these outings in a combative, feisty
mood. After the kids were in bed I would harass Doug into
making love to me. I thought I was better at it than Estelle.

Ardith sent me a shipment of books that had been left to
her by Great-Aunt Flora. My sister kept the books on history
but she sent the poetry and novels to me, out of fairness.
There was poetry by Burns and Tennyson, complete sets of
novels by Scott and Dickens. There was also a book entitled
Unwanted Wife: A Defence of Mrs. Charles Dickens by someone named Hebe Elsna. I thought Hebe was probably a man,
though nowadays this kind of book would most likely have
been written by a woman. The chapter headings were puffed
up with Victorian righteousness and Dickensian melodrama.
"The Plot Against Catherine", "Family Chaos", "Retribution
and Forgiveness". This was the kind of thing I was in the

mood for. I left the other books in the box and sat down to read.

During fourteen years of marriage to Charles Dickens, Catherine Dickens had ten children and several miscarriages. Charles would sometimes make wry and amusing remarks about his wife's condition. With the sexual life of his characters successfully camouflaged, it must have been difficult for Dickens to pretend his own potency didn't exist. Possibly it embarrassed him.

Catherine did not have easy pregnancies. She was sickly. Her hair fell out. She had trouble with her teeth. After the death of her youngest daughter, she suffered a nervous disorder. She couldn't keep up with the large dinner parties, feeding the theatre crowd, the actors and actresses Dickens brought home.

When Charles's affair with an eighteen-year-old actress named Ellen Ternan was underway, a jeweller delivered a gold bracelet intended for Ellen to Catherine by mistake. The bracelet had been engraved with Ellen's and Charles's initials. Catherine accused her husband of infidelity, which offended Charles. He told Catherine his relationship with Ellen was based on platonic love. He said Catherine was too sensual and domestic, too ordinary to understand a relationship on a much higher plane. At his insistence, Catherine delivered the bracelet to Ellen herself, to show how wrong minded and mistaken she had been.

Dickens walled in the doorway between the matrimonial bed chamber and the dressing room where he took to sleeping on a cot. Eventually he persuaded Catherine to move out and take up residence in Gloucester Crescent, leaving the younger children in her sister's care.

Most of Dickens's children were a disappointment to him, though they were not a disappointment to Catherine, who kept in touch with them the rest of her life. Dickens was often away on reading tours, writing novels. Perhaps he felt Catherine should have done a better job with his children while he was absent, that she had let him down. As soon as they fin-

ished school, Dickens sent his sons – they were mostly sons –
to India, Australia, Canada, places from which they could
not easily come back.

When I read all this, I didn't worry about bias. It didn't
bother me that the case against Dickens was marshalled in a
heavy-handed and unscholarly way, that some of it was based
on gossip and hearsay. I took what I wanted. I was looking
for someone who had been hard done by, someone tarnished
by self-pity and blame.

Doug moved in with Estelle in mid June. By then Warren
had gone. After graduation he'd moved to Churchill, Mani-
toba, to start up a practice. I decided to wait it out. I refused
a divorce. I thought Doug would come back, because of the
kids. I thought I could forgive him, that I wanted to, that I
would get that chance. I didn't anticipate the loathing, the
weight of malice and disgust. It took a long time for me to
realize how much of this there was. Doug had visiting rights.
Every second weekend he took the kids swimming or roller
skating, to movies and country fairs. He bought them bicycles
and expensive toys. On Saturday morning when he came to
pick them up, he would wait in the car, he would never come
in. If I answered the phone before one of the kids, he hung
up and dialled again. One day the postman delivered a small,
narrow box wrapped in brown paper. Inside was a motorized
dildo, flesh-coloured. There was a battery included. The parcel had been postmarked Montreal. I thought Doug had probably ordered it from a catalogue.

Two months later a letter arrived, written on floral stationery with a border of white and yellow daisies. The handwriting had been made purposely large and childish. The letter
was postmarked Wolfville, closer to home. The letter mentioned women Doug had slept with at college, after he had
started going out with me. There was Darla White, who
worked in the laundry. Sabina Miegs, a French professor, a
divorcée with twin daughters. Doug and I had baby-sat these
twins two or three times while Sabina had gone off to a community concert or to the film society. According to the letter,

Doug had gone back to Sabina's after he had been with me. Rita Ross was another. Rita was a girl who had been on my floor in residence. I hardly knew her. I didn't even know what courses she had taken. I had the idea that Rita had written this letter, that I had slighted her in some way. I thought Doug might be seeing her again, that she was trying to shake me loose, trying to force me to let go.

Lureen and Nancy would sometimes turn up at my house with a bottle of wine, not the wine we had made from grapes we had stomped. That had been thrown out. They would send my kids outside or over to Marge's or Debby's, sit me down, and encourage me to talk. They brought me carrot muffins and coffee cake, sometimes a bouquet of flowers. Once or twice I saw them huddled outside, casting anxious glances at my house. In the mornings they phoned me about ten o'clock to see if I was out of bed. They urged me to see a psychiatrist, gave me a list of names. I never again sat with them in the yard. My skin felt transparent. I thought they could see through it, inside.

It was three years before I agreed to a divorce and cleared out. I sold the house and car, packed up my household goods and the kids, and I rode the train across Canada, to another coast. I knew I couldn't stay on this side of the country. I couldn't stay anywhere near Doug. I knew I was the one who had to go, that Doug would never live far from Cape Breton. In three years Doug hadn't said one word to me. The kids were old enough to notice this. It upset them; they didn't want to go out with him any more. I had a knack for bumping into people who thought it was their duty to tell me they weren't taking sides. Two more letters arrived, written on the same floral stationery. Did she keep a box of stationery for this purpose? No new names were mentioned, but there were more details to rub in. The question is why I opened the letters. My psychiatrist said I should have burned them unopened or torn them up, unread. I told him I was compelled by curiosity, about the contents, about myself. I wanted to know how far down I could lower myself. Sometimes I saw myself dangling on the end of a rope over the bottom of a well.

Outside Saskatoon, the kids and I were lying in our berths being hurtled through the night when there was a squeal of brakes, then a thump. The train screeched to a stop. Both girls woke up crying. Above us I heard Eric say "shit". He was six and had discovered the satisfaction in swearing. Across the aisle a female voice made a disapproving "shush!" Theo unsnapped the heavy maroon curtain, lowered his head upside down, and said, "What happened?" I pushed up the blind, but all I could see was a void of dark prairie. Our car was too far back to see what was ahead on the tracks. It might have been twenty minutes before we started up again and the kids went back to sleep.

In the morning, we dressed quickly and walked back to the dining car for breakfast. It was the last sitting. We took our time watching the fields of summer wheat slipping away from the tracks, the grain elevators leaping up on the horizon like oversized fortifications, a child's view of defence. We passed through one prairie town after another, intruding. We were like fish moving silently through an aquarium. The towns-people never acknowledged our presence, but went about their business, scarcely giving us a glance.

By the time we returned to our car, the berths had once again been packed away. The kids and I were delighted by this. We thought the porter was a magician to have performed this sleight-of-hand, to have given us back our velour seats and view window. As they had done on previous mornings, Theo and Eric went off to walk the length of the train. They liked sashaying down aisles as the train barrelled forward, bracing themselves against the swaying floor above the cou-plings. This time Shelley went with them. Alison and I took up window seats and dug books out of our carry-on bag.

"Did you get back to sleep all right?" the woman across from me asked. She had boarded the train in Winnipeg. She was a white-haired woman outfitted in a lemon-yellow polyes-ter slack suit and a white rayon blouse. She wore no makeup.

The yellow suit gave her skin a slightly jaundiced cast. I thought she was the woman who had shushed Eric the night before, that she was likely to be pious and censorious. If she had been sitting farther away, I might have ignored her, but she had taken up the aisle seat, too close for me to get away with this.

I told her I had managed some sleep.

"There was somebody lying on the tracks," the woman said. I saw Alison look up from her book. "The porter said it was a woman from a nearby reserve. The engineer couldn't stop the train on time."

I looked at the woman. She had protruding brown eyes. The area beneath them was deeply ringed and mauve-coloured, as if she seldom slept.

"Why would she do such a thing?"

There was a fretful edge to her voice. Her puzzlement was probably genuine, but I saw it as a complaint, that she thought the woman on the tracks had caused her inconvenience and discomfort, that the dead woman was interfering with her peace of mind.

"She must have been too far down," I said. "Some people get so far down they can't get back."

I thought this wasn't something that would likely happen to this woman, that she would understand. In those days it didn't take much to get my back up, to make quick judgments and dismissals.

"Oh, do you think so?" Her hand fluttered to the cameo brooch at her neck.

I opened my book.

"It must be difficult," the woman said. I thought she was referring to the woman on the tracks, until she added, "bringing up four children on your own."

She had noticed my bare ring finger. I had sold my diamond to help pay for the move. My wedding ring was packed away in a zippered case with the rest of my jewellery. I saw Alison watching us both.

"It's not so bad," I said. "I have lots of *other* women for company." I didn't want this woman's sympathy, her patronization, especially in front of my daughter. I knew I had been rude, but it didn't bother me much. I took it as a sign of toughness, that I was on my way up.

Colour Wheel

Red

When Madge was on the *Ocean Limited*, somewhere outside Mont Joli, Quebec, she picked up a man in the club car. Two cars ahead, her sons were asleep in an upper berth, her daughters in a lower, heads aligned with feet to make room for Madge when she came to bed later on. In the club car Madge selected a seat by the window, though it was too dark to see anything outside. Madge liked the seedy opulence of the heavily padded chairs, the dim lighting, the rust velvet curtains. There was something of the smoky saloon about the decor, something vulgar and tawdry.

After the waiter had brought her drink, a tall, uniformed man got up from his seat at the end of the car, where he had been watching her, and came to Madge's table. He gestured to the chair opposite Madge and said, "May I?" He spoke with a slight French accent.

"Why not?" Madge said carelessly. She was aiming for the appropriate casualness, nonchalance.

The uniform unsettled her. The gold braid on the shoulders, the officer's hat, the pressed trousers, all this spoke of order and precision, everything in its place. This wasn't the first time Madge had been attracted to a man in a uniform, but this time Madge thought the uniform was being worn by someone who was skilful and manipulative, someone who was used to picking up women. He had long, elegant fingers, manicured nails, long-lashed, languid brown eyes. In college they called eyes like his *bedroom eyes, come hither eyes.* He seemed aware of their seductiveness and was using it to pull her in. He offered a cigarette, which Madge accepted but didn't smoke, though she went through the motions. When she lifted the cigarette to her lips, her hand shook. Madge kept up the pretence of coyness and indecision by not looking at the man too closely. If she had given him a long, hard look, she might have decided she was afraid of him, that he was callous, even cruel, that it would be foolish and irresponsible to do anything more than sit there in her halter top and dangling earrings and talk to him. She might have decided to pick up her purse and go back to her children while there was still time. Instead, she stayed on and had another drink.

Eventually they went to his sleeping compartment. The bed had been made up earlier. He pulled down the blind, switched off the light, and they took off their clothes – not Madge's halter top, they were in too big a hurry to undo the knots. Madge didn't see him at breakfast. She didn't know his last name, if he was married or unmarried, if he had children. She didn't want the complications of guilt. What she wanted – and got – was carnal and raw.

When she remembers their frenzied coupling, the cramped arrangement of elbows and knees, Madge knows it wasn't sex she'd been after as much as something illicit and wayward, something that fed on contrariness and anger. It wasn't the quick flash of temper, nothing like that. It was slower, predatory, relentless. Where was this anger coming from? Not from anything that could rightly be called mistreatment or abuse, though there had been injustices and slights along the way, and it was true that she had recently been hard done by. Perhaps that was it. Or the anger might have started earlier, from watching her father's struggle to succeed, how often he had been thwarted and set back on his heels. Perhaps it went back further still, centuries, to clan feuds and bitter deprivations, when stubbornness and stiff-necked pride kept you from being wiped out. Perhaps there was a recessive, lingering knowledge of this intractability that came out later as wilfulness and perversity. Wherever it came from, Madge's anger wasn't on the surface but deeper down. It was enclosed, sealed, as if for posterity, like crimson coloured threads inside a glass paperweight.

This isn't how Madge sees it. Whenever she remembers what took place inside the sleeping compartment, she thinks of herself as being inside a bottle, a bright red bottle, carmine. The red bottle is part of a collection Madge keeps on a glass shelf in a window at the end of the hall. She likes to arrange these bottles, then stand back and look at them, noticing the way each bottle responds to the light. The bottle that started Madge on this collection is one Doug gave her early on in their marriage. The bottle, which is a murky crimson, had *Strawberry Cordial* written on it. When Doug gave it to her, there was a strawberry-flavoured liquid inside, probably a liqueur, Madge doesn't remember exactly what it was. Sometimes she thinks the bottle might have contained an aphrodisiac. This is one way of explaining why she allowed herself to have four children in six years. Sometimes she thinks the bottle might have contained some religious water, some sour-tasting potion that had to be swallowed in order to atone for the enjoyment of sex. When she wasn't busy with her children, Madge had often been preoccupied with sex. She'd known there was something puritanical going on, that she'd made a connection between childbearing and sex, that she'd enjoyed lovemaking most when she was willing herself to conceive. Madge now thinks that if Doug hadn't gotten a vasectomy, she might have kept on getting pregnant. She might have ended up like Roy Byrne's mother, who went to bed after the birth of her thirteenth child and never got up. For the rest of her life she stayed in bed and was waited on and deferred to, groomed and fed like a queen bee.

"Being female exhausted you," her psychiatrist, Aaron Blostein, told her. "All those babies so fast. No wonder you were swamped."

Aaron often made encouraging comments like this. Madge lapped them up and kept going back for more.

"I cast myself in papier mâché," Madge told him one day. "Red Riding Hood. I wasn't the girl. I was the wolf. I made myself a lascivious woman with a swollen belly, long pink tongue, and hairy ears."

Madge had started making these painted figures when her children were small. After her children lost interest in this sort of thing, Madge kept it up, making figures out of papier-mâché which she dressed up afterwards with poster paint. She paid attention to details, took pains with faces and dress. Costumes, she called them, aware of the theatricality of what she was doing. After Madge had finished Red Riding Hood, she went on to make Cinderella, Gretel, Rose Red, Snow White. She later referred to these figures as her fairy tale series. Before she moved to the West Coast, Madge entered these pieces in an art show in Mahone Bay and was amazed when they sold for $150 each. That was when she began to regard what she'd been doing as work, when she got it out of the basement and into the marketplace.

Blue

Beside *Strawberry Cordial* is an old medicine bottle Madge found washed ashore on the beach in Eastern Passage. *Take with Caution* the blue bottle warns, the message on the outside in raised letters. It's a deep cobalt blue, opaque in the light. Through a glass darkly. Her blue period. Picasso had nothing on her. After Doug left, it was Alison, Madge's eldest daughter, who brought her toast and coffee in bed. It was Alison who made sure Madge got dressed, who fed Eric breakfast while Shelley and Theo got themselves off to school. Aaron would sometimes comment on her children, what marvels they were. He said his son and daughter were arrogant and self-centred. He often confided in her during her last year of living in Dartmouth. This was after she agreed to a divorce and was preparing to pull up stakes and clear out of the East.

"I envy you moving to Victoria, living in a climate where you can grow roses in December." Aaron had already told her about his garden and greenhouse. He removed his horn-rims and rubbed the bridge of his nose where there was a tuft of dark hair. "Ruth will never leave Halifax," he said. Aaron's wife taught chemistry at St. Mary's. "She figures she's got the ideal setup here, but I'd move to Victoria in a minute." "There's room in the station wagon," Madge teased. "If you don't mind four kids and two cats for company." At that point Madge was planning to drive across Canada. "And you," Aaron said. "Don't tempt me." Madge laughed. He wasn't to take her too seriously. They had been all over the dependency thing: how staying pregnant had been a way of making sure she'd be looked after, how she'd handed over too much of herself to Doug, more than he wanted, more than anybody wanted.

"Well, I don't seem ready to leave yet," Madge said. "I don't know why." She could have added, "You, maybe it's you." This was partly true, though only slightly. Aaron was appealing in a rumpled, avuncular way. "I need more time to get myself organized," she said.

"You mustn't come here again," he said. "You don't need these visits any more and I'm too attracted to you." He sounded regretful and sincere.

Did he mean it? Or did he know her so well that he feared she'd stick around indefinitely, until she heard those words from him, until she had the satisfaction of knowing he had more than a professional interest in her.

"It's inevitable in this profession," he said.

How many women had he said this to, to get rid of them, to send them off on their own?

Yellow

Nectar of the Golden Life of Health and Vitality. This is an amber-coloured bottle that once contained a chunk of honeycomb in pale golden honey. Nowadays, even on rainy days, the bottle holds a clear, warm light. The bottle came with a book on how to raise bees which Madge bought in a craft shop in Nanaimo. During her second winter in Victoria, Madge had read up on bees. By spring she had ordered her first hive, had found a place to keep it. The previous fall, after her children were settled in school, Madge had hired herself out as an apple picker in Hector and Gussie Kost's orchard, twenty miles out of Victoria. Gussie, who was sixty-eight, could no longer pick because of the arthritis in her back and knees. Hector, a thin, agile man six years her junior, was the one who looked after the orchard. He was the one who hired Madge to pick Spartans. When she was picking, Madge would climb onto the back of Hector's tractor and hold onto his shoulders while he steered them over the uneven track, singing "Figaro, Figaro" at the top of his lungs. Madge turned out to be a good picker, twisting each apple free without breaking the next year's growth, laying the apple inside her apron pocket, carefully, without bruising or denting the skin. In addition to her pay, Hector gave Madge windfalls, which she took home and turned into jelly. He gave her permission to keep her hive in his orchard. When the apple blossoms where gone, the bees found clover and alfalfa in the adjoining field.

Her third year as a beekeeper, Madge began using bees to help the arthritis which had started up in her right elbow. She'd read up on this too. She knew there were beekeepers who claimed they never got arthritis because they kept bees. The bees' stings were supposed to be an antidote against the disease. Madge put a bee in a jar and poked her elbow into the opening. She did this every day for a week until the pain in her elbow went away. One Saturday afternoon, she carried a jar of bees into Gussie and Hector's kitchen, where they sat listening to the Texaco Opera Broadcast of *Aida*. Hector was singing *"Celeste Aida, forma divina"*, he knew every word. Madge waited until intermission before asking Gussie if she'd try the bee sting treatment. Gussie was so huge her bulk overflowed the kitchen chair, you couldn't see the chair's back or legs. She looked as if she were suspended in air.

"Nope," Gussie said.

"I bet a week's treatment on your knees would make a lot of difference."

Now that she was taking better care of herself, Madge had become something of a crusader about using natural foods and homemade remedies.

"Nope."

"Did you read that book I gave you about bees and arthritis?"

"Nope."

Gussie also refused to eat the propolis Madge scraped from the hive. Madge often ate propolis and pollen for their curative powers. Sometimes she added pollen to the dough when she was baking bread.

"She won't take your bee glue," Hector said. "But she'll take your honey."

Honey production doubled when Madge started using an Italian queen she had ordered from a California apiary. The queen was a deep golden colour with two stripes across her abdomen. She was more apt to swarm than Madge's previous Caucasian queen, but she was a better egg-layer. Before she laid her eggs, the queen was groomed and fed so she would be ready for the drones. Then she went round the hive and stung the virgin queens, to get rid of them. After the last virgin had been stung, the queen flew straight up, toward the sun, the drones mating her as she flew. She continued these mating flights for four or five days, until she had gathered a lifetime supply of sperm.

In the fall, Madge rented a stall at the farmers' market and sold her honey, along with her apple jelly and homemade bread. She also took along her bees, taping a sheet of clear plastic over the top so her customers could see the hive working. Madge told them about the sweet virtues of liquid gold, the therapeutic uses of honey. She told them how infertile females cleaned the hive and nursed the young before becoming fliers, who brought nectar and water for the hive. She told them how fliers danced outside the hive to show other workers where the flowers were. She told them how drones, after they had fertilized the queen, were either stung or allowed to starve to death. She liked to point out that a beehive was a model of efficiency and thrift.

Purple

Strictly speaking, the bottle in Madge's hand isn't purple. It's closer to a violet colour. When Madge bought the bottle three years ago in an antique shop, the dealer told her the bottle's colour would darken if she kept the bottle in the window, exposed to the light. So far this hasn't happened. The bottle is tall and thin with narrow, sloping shoulders. There are no markings on the outside to indicate what the bottle might have been used for. Madge thinks it might have contained rose water or glycerine, some bland substance that left no scent on the cork stopper. Madge's bottle collection is in a window with an eastern exposure, which means it catches the early morning light. The effect of these odd-shaped and multi-coloured bottles is something like stained glass in a church, except there's no design in Madge's arrangement, no recognizable pattern or religious motif. Three or four times a year Madge takes the bottles off the shelf to wipe them clean. Afterwards she puts them back, in different places. Usually this arrangement is random, there's no attempt at symmetry. Today Madge has decided to follow the colour wheel. Already she has the primary colours lined up and has started on the secondaries. She puts the violet coloured bottle back on the shelf and picks up the purple perfume decanter Stan bought her from a glass-blower in Arkansas last summer, after he had watched it being made.

Stan is an American who, five years earlier, followed a draft-dodging son to Canada and stayed. His wife, Annette, refused to come with him. She ran an employment agency in Little Rock and she didn't want to leave. A year after Stan left, Annette took up with one of his friends and asked for a divorce. Stan sold his advertising business in Arkansas and moved to Vancouver Island.

"Coffee on?" Madge's neighbour, Emily Moore, who lives two townhouses over, sticks her head around Madge's back door.
"Not yet but it can be."
"Good." Em closes the door behind her and throws her tote bag on the floor.

Em is an ex-elementary school teacher, whose husband died of a heart attack nine years ago. During the past three years, she has been trying to make it as a writer and illustrator of children's books. Em twirls around Madge's kitchen, her flowered skirt swishing as she turns on tiny, black slippered feet. Em usually wears ballerina slippers and full skirts, which accentuate her girlishness. She has the enthusiasm and energy of a young girl. Madge does not have this kind of energy. Her energy runs down quickly and must be carefully meted out.

"I'm going up-island to see my publisher." *My* publisher, Em says, though so far she has published only one book. Em makes the most of everything: accomplishments, disappointments, love affairs. In the eight years Madge has known her, these ups and downs have been extravagantly dramatized.

"Want to come? We could have lunch at the Black Kettle afterwards. I shouldn't be too long with my publisher. I only have to show him the preliminary sketches for my next book."

Madge had planned to spend the morning packaging two figures for a group show in Vancouver and writing up an accompanying blurb, but she changes her mind. With Stan away, she can get the packaging done tonight. She's unable to resist the temptation of returning to the Black Kettle, a restaurant owned by an old lover of hers, Farley Strike. Farley is an artist who runs the Black Kettle on the side. Madge hasn't seen him for nearly four years.

She spoons coffee into the pot, adds water, and sets the pot on the stove. "Watch this for me while I change, will you?"

Madge chooses a maroon-coloured blouse that sets off her dark hair. She hangs the silver pendant Farley gave her around her neck. She puts on a wrap-around batik skirt, sandals, and lipstick, paints her toenails maroon. She returns to the kitchen. Em is sitting at the table, drinking coffee and browsing through one of Madge's art books. Em looks up and says, "My god, Madge. We're only going for lunch."

They drive up-island to Ladysmith. While Em is inside the publisher's house, Madge finds a patch of lawn beneath a giant red alder, spreads out the car rug, lies down, head cradled on a crooked arm, and closes her eyes. It isn't Farley Strike she thinks about but Stan. Stan is in Arkansas visiting his old friend, Bitta. He's down there trying to sell his parents' acreage. Bitta is one of the women to whom Stan takes a rose during his travels. Lorraine is another. There's Shirley in Tennessee. Stan sends these women postcards, notes with recipes and clippings inside. Madge has cultivated an attitude of tolerant amusement toward this attentiveness. It's the only defence she has against greying hair, freckling hands, doubling chin. She tells herself that men who like other women make the best lovers. Sometimes she believes this.

Em is inside the publisher's house so long Madge falls asleep. When Em comes outside and wakes her up, Madge feels disgruntled, uneasy. It's past two when they pull into the *Black Kettle*. Farley will probably be gone by now. Madge knows Farley stays around for meal hours, then moves to his studio in the woods behind the restaurant. The *Black Kettle* is known for its homemade soup, wholegrain breads. They order beer and borscht. After the waitress has gone into the kitchen, they get up and look at Farley's paintings. There's no one else in the room so they're able to move easily between the red checkered tables to get close to the walls. The paintings are large acrylics showing fishermen, loggers, farmers, at work. The colours are bold, thickly applied with a palette knife. The waitress brings their food, then goes back to the kitchen.

The last time Madge and Farley were together, he had been impotent. Madge had tried to reassure him that it wasn't serious, most likely a temporary lapse brought on by fatigue; he was in the middle of preparing for a show. He had phoned her up several times after that to say he was coming to see her, but he never did. More than once he had said he wanted them to continue being friends. He meant without sex. Perhaps he had decided that kind of friendship wasn't possible with Madge, because of the way they had started off.

The waitress returns and asks if they want anything else.

"Is Farley around?"

"He's in the kitchen working on menus," the girl says.

Impulsively, Madge slips the silver pendant over her head. "Would you give him this?"

The girl takes the pendant into the kitchen, and Em says, "And I thought you came all this way just to keep me company."

The kitchen doors swing open and out comes Farley. He strides toward Madge, gives her a kiss on the forehead, his beard scratchy against her cheek, and sits down opposite, beside Em.

Madge introduces them. Farley takes out cigarettes and offers them round. Em takes one. Farley lights hers then his own. Madge watches the way they bend toward each other, the way Em lights her cigarette inside his cupped hand, how Farley inhales slowly, then holds the smoke inside as if he's timing his exhalation with Em's. Purplish smoke wafts past Madge. She notices a slight bulge above Farley's belt, a coarsening of lines across his forehead. His eyes are greener than she remembered.

He looks at Madge through the smoke.

"So what brings you this way?" he says.

"Em's been to see her publisher in Ladysmith," Madge says, then adds, "I'm tagging along for the ride."

Farley turns to Em. "What do you write?"

"Children's books. I write *and* illustrate. In fact I was just showing my publisher the preliminary sketches for my next book."

"Is that so?" Farley says. "I'd like to see them."

"I'm sure you wouldn't want to see *my* stuff," Em says. "I mean your work is *so* good."

"But I do," Farley says.

He was always kind and attentive. *Gentlemanly* Madge thinks now.

Em digs the sketchbook out of her tote bag and hands it to Farley. She puts her chin on her hands and watches his face, hopeful as a schoolgirl.

The sketches are of a fishing village, a beach, a giant seahorse, and a little girl. The story is about the little girl's attempt to persuade the villagers to help the stranded seahorse which no one but she can see.

Farley turns the pages slowly. "These are good," he says. "Very good."

"Thanks," Em says. "Coming from you, that's real praise. I haven't any formal training, you see, so I'm never sure if my work is any good. I just go by instinct."

"Best thing to do," Farley says easily.

"I've often thought I should take lessons," Em goes on. "I know I should, but somehow I'm afraid of spoiling what makes me do it in the first place. Do you think there's any danger in that, in taking lessons, I mean?"

Farley smiles. "Not if you take them from the right instructor," meaning himself.

They talk about Em's first book, which was about a mermaid who falls in love with a fisherman, about the publisher, who turns out to be a friend of Farley's, about a book of Farley's this publisher is bringing out in the fall.

"What sort of book is it?" Madge asks.

"It's oriented to the workplace," Farley says. "I'm interested in making a statement about the job as an art form. I'm writing a job description to accompany each painting." He nods at the painting on the wall above their table. It's a picture of a fisherman hauling in a net. "I've already written something to go with that one, describing how they go about catching fish nowadays, what a fisherman's day is like, what tasks he has to perform on a seiner."

"I *do* like that painting, Farley, that one in particular," Em says. She accepts another cigarette while she waves at the painting. "The colours, the boldness of the lines, it's very Degas-ish."

"You mean Cezanne-ish," Madge says.

But Em won't be slowed down. "I just *adore* your work, Farley, I really do. It's so good. I can't understand why I haven't seen it before. Believe me, when your book comes out I'll buy lots of copies and send them to friends." Em's hands dart about. "You *must* let me know when it comes out."

"Me too," Madge says. She has one of Farley's paintings hanging on her living-room wall, a painting Em has seen, a painting he exchanged for one of Madge's papier-mâché figures.

Madge tells Farley about the Vancouver show, the park-bench series she's been working on. The girl brings the bill, which Farley intercepts and puts in his pocket. He walks them to the car and tells Em about the design course he'll be teaching this fall, if she's interested in taking it. Madge has taken this course. That was how she and Farley met. Farley doesn't say anything about seeing her again. Perhaps he thinks their friendship has already received the attention it deserves.

After they have driven away, Madge says, "I didn't know you were such a flirt."

"Who, me?" Em says. The quirky lines appear at the corners of her eyes. "Never."

"Come on," Madge says. She was counting on feeling better than she does.

"Well, maybe I *was* flirting, just a bit. Farley's *such* an attractive man. But you don't need to worry about me, Madge. If you want him, I mean. That was as far as I want to go. I've had enough of men," Em says. She sounds convincing enough, speeding along the highway at seventy miles an hour, eyes resolutely on the road. Since her husband died, Em has had two affairs, none in the last three years, so maybe she means it. "The way I see it is either you care too much for a man, in which case the relationship takes too much time and energy. Or you don't care enough, in which case it's not worth the effort."

Madge doubts if she'll ever reach this kind of thinking.

"I may dye my hair," she says.

"Use Nice 'n Easy," Em advises. "You only have to touch it up every two months."

Orange

The latest acquisition in Madge's collection is an orange bottle she found in New Brunswick. When the light strikes the window, the bottle takes on the coppery glow of an autumn sun. Madge bought the bottle at a country fair in Hampton last year, when she was on her way to the airport from Sussex, where she'd been visiting her parents and her aunt. Now that she lives on the other side of the country, Madge has been spending more time getting to and from airports, sitting in waiting rooms, waiting for departures and connections.

A few miles outside Hampton, Madge saw a man in a tweed jacket, carrying a suitcase, running along the highway behind the bus that had stopped to pick up someone else. The man was close to the back wheel when the bus pulled away and sped down the highway. The man shouted and waved his arm, but the bus didn't stop. Perhaps the driver didn't see him. Madge heard the man curse as he lowered his arm. She pulled the car onto the shoulder, rolled down the window on the passenger side, and asked him where he was headed.

"The airport," he said and smiled. He had strong teeth, a Neptune beard, square shoulders. Later Madge asked herself whether she would have picked him up if he had been slump-shouldered and shabbily clothed.

"So am I," Madge told him. "What time is your flight?"

"Four-thirty," he said, then went on, explaining. "I was visiting a farmhouse up the road. I phoned a cab but it didn't show up, so I figured I'd better get out and flag down a ride."

"Well, you've got one," Madge said. "Hop in."

When he had settled himself beside her, Madge told him she planned to stop at a country fair. "It's about a mile ahead. I saw the sign back there on the road."

It turned out that her passenger, whose name was Len Vinya, was a folklorist. He'd been collecting songs from an old farmer. The farmer – he was eighty-seven – couldn't read or write but he knew more than forty songs. Len had spent two days getting them on tape.

The fair was inside a barn. It wasn't really a fair. It was more like a yard sale roofed over. Laid out on trestle tables were china jugs and chamber pots, plates with fruit painted on them, blue-and-white railway bowls, Mother's Day relish dishes, chipped enamel basins, pictures in ornate frames, a wrought iron stool painted Christmas concert gold. Madge surveyed this bold ordering of junk, looking for bottles. Among an assortment of animal salt-and-pepper shakers and Avon perfume containers Madge found a squat, orange brown bottle with *Valentine's Meat Juice* written on the side in raised letters. Len said he thought the bottle might be sixty or seventy years old. At five dollars, she couldn't go wrong. For twenty dollars he bought himself an engraving in a tarnished copper frame. The picture showed a man and a woman in a rowboat, riding a huge wave. The woman sat O-mouthed in the bow while the man bent over the oars, rowing strenuously.

On the drive to the airport, Len told Madge about his collection of early Canadian art. He had originals of Kane and Krieghoff on the walls of his house in Montreal, but he wasn't a snob. He had pictures by unknown artists, amateurs such as the artist whose work he had just bought. Like Madge, Len brought back pictures from places where he'd been, but his pictures were behind glass, not bottled inside it. The coincidence, Madge thought, two collectors meeting like this.

At the airport the coincidence seemed less likely. After they had checked their bags and were waiting for Len's flight – he was leaving earlier than Madge – Len leaned forward and

kissed her on the lips. His lips were warm, salty, accommodating. Thinking about it afterwards on the plane to Victoria,
Madge wondered if she might have willed the kiss, such was
her need for a man, even a perfect stranger.

Green

Madge's lover is a wanderer. He likes driving his van over
back country roads, discovering out-of-the-way places, camping in the off season when few people are around. He avoids
department stores and supermarkets, does his shopping in
corner groceries and farmers' markets. Stan and Madge met
in a farmers' market. Madge was shopping. She didn't have
her bees with her that day; it was March, too early to set up
her hive, but she offered to sell Stan some bread and honey
she had at home.

As soon as he was inside her townhouse, Stan noticed the
bottle collection at the end of the hall.

"Your window reminds me of a place I'd like you to see,"
he said. He picked up a miniature green Air Canada bottle
with Benedictine written on it, below a small, raised cross.
"It's a Benedictine monastery on the mainland."

"Where on the mainland?"

"South of Vancouver. How about going there with me some
day later this week?"

"I'm busy this week." Before she went that far Madge
wanted to know if her first impression would hold up. She
had learned something about self-preservation, and her curiosity was beginning to wane.

One afternoon two months later, she and Stan took the
ferry across to Vancouver and drove down the lower mainland. There was a huge, veiled sun, a mountain rising through
the haze like Fuji. Driving along the back country roads, the
rarefied air becoming clearer toward the mountain, they came
upon farms, pastures where cows grazed. The Benedictines
kept Jerseys, their hides earth brown against the Irish grass,
their heavy bodies ambling after the cow bell. Madge rolled

down the window. The bell sound was weighted, dolorous, the clapper hanging low like a cow's udder ripe for milking. One of the monks was working at the top of the drive, forking the rich, dark earth, turning it over, letting it breathe, before planting seeds. There was a mud smear on the front of his plaid shirt. He had Stan's rustic appearance, the same muscular stockiness, chest hair showing above his shirt.

"It's a farm operation," Stan said. "Their liquor-making days are over."

The monk glanced at Madge as she slid bare legs out of the van, then returned to his work. Madge was wearing a cotton skirt, sandals, a hooded blouse, her idea of church wear. She and Stan walked across the parking lot and entered a long foyer which had arched windows on one side like a cloister. Inside the door was a slotted collection box. Madge dug into her sheepswool bag for a dollar, which she pushed through the slot. A thin monk in a black soutane glided across the polished wood floor toward them and offered a tour. Stan hadn't taken the tour before. He had merely wandered around the grounds and gone inside the chapel. Now he and Madge followed their guide through a cafeteria and a classroom before mounting a staircase with concrete walls. The monk stopped on the landing to point out a painting at the head of the stairs. The painting was of Jesus raising Lazarus. The colours were watery blues and whites, cloudlike, another realm.

"One of our brothers is an artist. Completely self-taught," the monk explained. "He does these paintings between chores."

"What chores?" Stan wanted to know. He liked asking questions, knowing how things worked.

"Kitchen duty. He's one of our chefs. Dishes up some strange food." The monk gave a wry smile. "Too strange for my palate."

"Do you rotate chores?"

"Only the novitiates rotate. Once you get to be my age," the monk lifted his hands apologetically, "you stay with what you do best."

"Which is?"

"I teach mathematics."

They had come up the stairs and were on a broad balcony. Madge walked to the edge and looked down. Below them, a hillside gave way to a valley of rooftops and tall poplars. Tuscany, Madge thought, though from paintings only; she had never been to Italy.

The monk gestured toward the wall, where there were photographs of monasteries in Italy, France, Spain. Madge watched the monk's fluttering hands, the pale lips forming words. Bloodless lips, fleshless skin. But a calm smile, a soothing voice. Were the novitiates lulled by it? Did it distract them from their manhood and vigour? The art of perfect submission, devotion to ritual, the denial of self, is inexplicable to Madge. She searched the monk's face, looking for signs of discontent, unhappiness, unrest. What she saw was an untroubled countenance, smiling and serene. Where had his cancelled self gone? Madge knew where hers had gone, or at least in what bottles to look for it. Did the monk wrestle with his self every day? Or had it been purged out of him through daily prayers, duty, and obedience? The chapel bell sounded.

"Evening matins," the monk said. "We have them in the cafeteria." He led them downstairs to the front door. "The chapel is under construction but you should look at it before you go."

When they came out of the monastery, Madge saw young boys in pristine gym shorts running across the greensward. Madge and Stan strolled in the opposite direction, entering the nearby woods, which were thick with cedar and elm. Rude pathways were beaten through the ferns, whose furled tops were as pale and vulnerable as bare arched necks. They came to a mossy clearing where ivy climbed the trees. Stan removed his shirt and spread it on the moss. Lying on her back, skirt hiked up to her waist, Madge looked over Stan's shoulder at the silk-screened trees. She heard a robin's soft treble, the chiggering of a squirrel. She felt the parting of layered flesh.

She closed her eyes and imagined the purple-red labia folding around a bruised looking phallus, like some underwater creature with swaying tentacles, a sea anemone swallowing a fish. She and Stan have made love twice before. Each time Madge imagined they were beneath the sea. The slippery flesh, the milky skin, the slow, undulating rhythm made her think they were moving with the timelessness of swimming fish through lush gardens blooming with exotic flowers. This time when Madge came, she saw tiny neon rods exploding beneath her eyelids. She opened her eyes and saw golden shafts angling through the woods, sweeping down like sunlight through water, turning the forest air a shimmering green.

The matins bell sounded again. Arm in arm, Madge and Stan walked toward the chapel. Inside, they picked their way over electrical cords and steel rods until they reached the centre of the room. They looked up at the high concrete walls that curved into a dome. The dome was made of stained glass arranged the way colours were on the colour wheel: reds merging into purple, purples into blue, blues into green, greens into yellow, yellows into orange. In the slanted rays of afternoon light, the colours spun around them like jewelled planets. Through the concrete walls, they heard voices: the pure sopranos of young boys, the deeper bass of men. The stained glass, the sun, the music, Madge felt she and Stan were being lifted up and moved to the edge of the dome. They were on a rim of whirling colour. Everything they saw or did or felt was part of this giant wheel slowly turning in a circle of light.

Sisters

B eth Murray was killed in Sussex, New Brunswick, outside the old post office, beneath the town clock. It was a Friday morning in late June. The weather was sunny and cool. Traffic was slow but beginning to pick up. There were retired people out getting their mail, early tourists stopping for gas, farmers driving in for a month's groceries. Some of these farmers would have made good witnesses. When they were finished shopping at Dominion or Save Easy, they would often sit in their half-ton trucks, watching people while waiting for a family member to return from an errand or appointment. But that was usually later in the morning, closer to noon. Beth was killed earlier, between eleven-fifteen and eleven-thirty.

It was eight o'clock in the morning on the West Coast when Madge heard the news. Later that day she flew to Toronto, where Ardith lived. On Saturday the two sisters flew to Saint John, rented a car, and drove to Sussex. They had declined their father's offer to pick them up, thinking Laddie would be in no shape to drive anywhere. In retrospect, Madge thought they should have taken up Laddie's offer so they would have had time to get the facts straight, before more damage was done. There were some things that might have come out if they had got him alone first, away from their Aunt Margaret. Since the accident, Laddie and Margaret – who did not normally see much of each other though they lived under the same roof – had spent most of their time together. Margaret lived alone in the downstairs apartment at the back of the house, where she had moved after she retired from teaching in Nova Scotia. Beth and Laddie had the larger apartment upstairs. Whenever Margaret wanted to visit Beth, she'd wait until Laddie had gone to work before going up the back stairs. She made sure she was downstairs in her apartment before he came home.

When Madge walked into the living room and saw her father and aunt sitting there, she thought they looked lost, as if they had wandered off somewhere and were waiting patiently for rescue. Margaret had made an effort to appear normal. She had put green shadow over her puffy eyelids and drawn wobbly lines with an eyebrow pencil. Laddie had done nothing about his appearance. His face was unshaven. He was still wearing Friday's clothes. He kept frowning and refocusing his eyes, as if he were trying to figure out why Madge and Ardith had suddenly appeared.

The sisters sat down and got Margaret and Laddie to repeat the facts as they knew them. There were a few details that hadn't been mentioned on the phone. Beth had been crossing the street in front of the old post office, on her way back from the new post office with the mail. (This was Margaret speaking.) She was going across to Margaret, who had just returned from an errand at Moffat's Hardware and was waiting in her Volkswagen, parked under the trees, opposite the drugstore. Beth wasn't on the crosswalk, she was beside it. She was looking down at a letter she was carrying. There was a horn. The truck driver had tooted, but Beth hadn't stopped. She had gone right on walking. (Here Laddie picked up the story.) He had come along in his car about five minutes later, on his way back from showing a property in the country. A policeman had waved him along. A small group of people were gathered in front of the old post office. The policeman was trying to keep a crowd from building up, in order to make room for an ambulance. There weren't so many people that

Laddie couldn't see Beth lying on the pavement. "That's my wife over there," he said to the policeman. Then he got out of his car and went over to Beth. He knelt down and put his ear on her chest, trying to hear a heartbeat. He thought he heard something inside, but it was faint. Someone in the crowd handed him a mirror, which he held close to Beth's nose and mouth. The mirror stayed clear.

Madge and Ardith didn't write any of this down, not at first. Later, they wrote down whatever they had been told and more besides. They got busy with funeral arrangements. Because of the suddenness of the death, there were no burial instructions. Decisions were required. Despite their mother's injuries, Laddie wanted an open casket. He wanted Beth on view in the funeral home. The injuries were to the back of the head, and lower down, to the chest and legs. The face was undamaged, so a viewing was possible. Laddie wanted a church service, though Beth had not gone to church. Margaret sat silently while these decisions were made. She did not offer advice. She kept quiet about the open casket.

That evening, the truck driver who had killed Beth turned up at the door. Madge answered the buzzer, then led him upstairs. She didn't know who he was at first, though she might have guessed by his nervousness and by the streaks on his face, from crying. He looked eighteen or nineteen, maybe twenty years old. Madge led him into the living room where Ardith sat with Laddie and Margaret. They had finished what they had been able to eat of supper (a salmon-rice casserole sent in by a woman who lived in the downstairs front apartment), and were drinking tea. The young man refused to sit down but stood in the doorway and stared into the corner behind Laddie.

"I'm Ronald Parnell. I'm the one who hit your wife," he said. "I came to say I'm sorry."

This was all he got out before he started crying.

Margaret rose from her chair and went over to him. She touched Ronald's sleeve, to comfort him, to stop him crying. Margaret had rapport with young people. She still tutored students in French. Perhaps this rapport explained, as much as anything could, what happened next.

Margaret patted Ronald Parnell's arm and said, "I want you to know I saw what happened and that it wasn't your fault. My sister stepped in your way." She took her hand away. "Don't blame yourself." She went back to her chair and sat down. Ronald Parnell nodded his head up and down, but he continued to sob. He made no move to leave. What was he waiting for? What did he want? Neither Madge nor Ardith – both of them dry-eyed – tried to help him, though they had sons who, in a few years, would be close to this young man's age.

Laddie got up from his chair, went over to Ronald, and said, "It's a bad time for all of us. I want you to know there are no hard feelings."

Ronald sniffed and wiped his nose on his sleeve. Madge noticed his windbreaker was clean and his trousers pressed.

"Thanks," he said and lowered his eyes.

He made no move to go.

Ardith went up to him and said, "I think you'd better leave now."

Ronald followed her meekly to the door.

Madge went into the bedroom where she and Ardith would sleep that night, and looked out the window. She watched the young man go down the walk beneath the elms and get into a waiting car. A middle-aged woman – Madge guessed his mother – was at the wheel.

Soon after he left, Laddie and Margaret took their sleeping pills and went to bed. Madge and Ardith went outside, where they could talk. When they were on the sidewalk, well away from the house, Madge said, "Did you *hear* what Aunt Margaret *said*? 'It isn't your fault. You're not to blame. My sister stepped in your way.' I could have wrung her neck!"

"She's in shock," Ardith said. "She doesn't know what she's saying."

"Well, she'll have to retract," Madge said. "She can't go around saying the accident was Mum's fault. Mum was her own sister, for Heaven's sake."

They were walking towards Main Street. They might have walked away from the downtown area. They might have walked up the hill, past the Catholic Church and the stone drinking fountain, where there were large old houses with spreading verandahs and well-kept lawns. Once they had passed these houses, they would have come very quickly into the country, where there was the sound of frogs and the sweet smell of clover. But they were in no mood for tranquillity. They were heading in the opposite direction.

"We should go to the old post office," Ardith said. "When we were driving past there this afternoon, I noticed black tire marks. They must have been made by Ronald Parnell's truck."

The hands of the town clock were both on nine. There was plenty of light to see by.

"You're right," Madge said. "He must have braked fast to make tracks like this. Let's measure them."

They had to work around young people cruising past in souped-up cars. Twice they had to step back while the drivers sped past at breakneck speed, motors gunning. Without mufflers, the cars sounded like tanks.

"This is noisier than Yonge Street," Ardith said.

Madge and Ardith paced the length of the tire marks, counting the number of feet, twice, to make sure. Then they stood on the sidewalk and discussed the accident.

"I estimate it took approximately forty feet for him to stop after he passed the crosswalk," Ardith said. "That's how fast he was driving."

Madge looked across the street.

"I just realized something," she said. "Aunt Margaret couldn't have seen Mum hit. She was parked under the trees. The truck would have come between her and Mum."

"My God, you're right."

"Furthermore, she'd have been facing the other way, toward the railway tracks. Even if she'd turned around at the precise moment, the truck would have blocked her vision. Why did Aunt Margaret park over there anyway? There are lots of spaces on this side of the street." Madge pointed to the parking stalls in front of the old post office.

"She said she had an errand at the hardware store," Ardith reminded her. "She must have been trying to make one stop. To take Mum to the new post office, she'd have had to make two turns. Margaret would go to great lengths to avoid making a turn. She's a terrible driver."

"We need more witnesses," Ardith went on. She strode across the pavement toward the drugstore on the corner, Madge following.

A fierce energy, something bordering on grim elation, had gripped the sisters, was driving them to find out what had happened, to establish the facts, to defend their mother. And something else was providing momentum. It was the loyalty they felt toward each other. This was something the sisters never spoke of, never referred to, but took for granted. This loyalty came from a long way back, to a time when neither of them knew the word or what it meant. It came from one of them hurtling broken glass down a ravine because it had cut her sister, from fending off boys who came at them with sticks, from undertaking errands and small missions the other could not bring herself to do. It was like a pit or a stone, perhaps the core of a tree, something unchanged by layers of experience, by different wind and weather.

Madge waved a hand at the large drugstore windows. "There must have been at least one witness inside with a perfect view."

"Not perfect," Ardith said. "Remember, the truck would have blocked the view of someone inside. We need to talk to someone who was in front of the old post office at the time of the accident, to offset what Aunt Margaret said. Tomorrow, we'll ask the police. They must have a list of statements made by witnesses."

Madge and Ardith didn't get to the police station until after the funeral. The second day in town, they had to take turns sitting with their mother's body at the funeral parlour while the other one stayed with Laddie at home, listening to him talk and fielding telephone calls. Now that someone was with their father, Margaret did not come up the back stairs. After Madge had spent an afternoon with Laddie, she wrote down any observations or comments made about their mother. Ardith called it circumstantial evidence. She seemed to think this kind of documentation might help them get closer to the truth, to see the accident more clearly.

Your mother ran up to me one day last week when I came home at noon. I had just come in the door when she threw her arms around me and hugged me tight. She didn't do that kind of thing very often, you know. She told me she was so happy, she could burst.

Madge thought back to the year when her mother had been an invalid. From this Madge had gotten the idea that her mother needed to be fussed over and coddled, that she was the parent who needed pampering and displays of affection when in fact the opposite was closer to the truth. As a child Madge hadn't given much thought to what it was that made some people appear weak and others strong. She tended to take evidence at face value.

It bothered Beth that Margaret was up here so much. She was always finding an excuse to come up the back stairs. You know how much your mother needed time alone. You remember when Beth was in the hospital having that gall bladder operation. She begged me to tell Margaret not to visit her for a few days. Beth didn't want to be badgered. She wanted her privacy. She said I was the only one she wanted to see.

There was a mixture of satisfaction and wonder in Laddie's voice, that his company had been preferred over his sister-in-law's, that he had won. As far back as Madge could remember, Laddie had competed with Margaret for his wife's affection. Madge put this down to the fact that Beth and Margaret had lost their mother when they were children. For years they lived apart from their father and brothers, getting by on their own. This was when the bonding between the sisters took place, when they had to rely on each other. The bonding was strongest on Margaret's side perhaps because, as the younger of the two, she had depended on her older sister to take charge, make decisions. Madge thought if Margaret had married and had children of her own, she might have broken this bond. Perhaps not, perhaps this kind of bond could never be broken. *Beth did funny things sometimes. She was flighty. Scatterbrained, I guess you'd say. One Sunday, a few months back, she came out of the bedroom after her nap dressed in her slip and two different coloured socks, one blue, one red. "I'm ready," she said. I looked at her and said, "You're not going in the car dressed like that, are you?"*

"Dressed like what?" she said.

"In that get-up," I told her.

She looked down and saw her slip and the different coloured socks.

"I guess not," she said.

She sure looked sheepish.

Sussex was no longer under the jurisdiction of the Mounties. There was an RCMP detachment in town to serve the county. The town had its own police. Constable Sooter was in charge. Madge and Ardith went to see him, without their father. They thought it would be too painful for Laddie to come, to sit through this meeting. They hadn't told him where they were going. They had trumped up an excuse about paying the United Church minister and the organist who had played at the funeral. They had asked Margaret to sit with Laddie while they were gone.

"We've come about our mother, Beth Murray," Ardith said as soon as they were seated in Constable Sooter's office.

Constable Sooter was wearing navy trousers and a white short-sleeved shirt. He looked like someone who seldom left the office, seldom got much exercise. His skin had that kind of indoor pastiness, and his midriff was heavy with flab.

"We want to know what you've done to investigate our mother's death," Ardith said.

"There wasn't much to investigate," Constable Sooter said. "It was a straightforward accident, an open-and-shut case."

"What about the tire marks?" Ardith said. "Did you measure them?"

Constable Sooter looked surprised.

"Why would I measure them?"

"Because they run for forty-five feet," Madge said. She and Ardith had gone back to the old post office with a tape measure. "That's how far the driver had to go to stop. He was speeding."

Constable Sooter didn't deny this.

"What witnesses have you talked to?" Ardith said.

"I spoke to half a dozen of them who were in the area at that time."

"Did you take down their statements?"

"It wasn't necessary."

"Why wasn't it necessary?"

"Like I said, it was a straightforward accident."

"Did you take away the truck driver's licence?"

"No. He needs it for his job."

"What kind of police officer are you?" Ardith said.

Constable Sooter shrugged. Madge thought he had probably been asked that question before. She watched him open a desk drawer and take out a thick wad of pink slips.

"See these speeding tickets? Do you know how many people in town go over the speed limit? Doctors, lawyers, businessmen? If I arrested them all, hardly anyone would be left."

"This is a woman's life we're talking about," Ardith said aggressively. "You'd better get that straight."

Constable Sooter threw the wad of pink slips into the drawer and slammed it shut. Then he leaned toward them over the desk.

"Listen, I know you ladies are upset by what happened to your mother. That's understandable. It won't do you any good to take it out on me."

"We may take this to the Mounties," Madge told him. Madge remembered her old boyfriend, Vaughan Borman, who had been a Mountie. She recalled him as being hard-working and efficient. He wasn't here now, he'd been transferred years ago, but Madge thought the other Mounties who were based at the RCMP detachment in town might be able to help.

"It's not in their jurisdiction," Constable Sooter reminded her. "You'd be wasting your time."

"We may press charges," Ardith said.

"Suit yourselves," Constable Sooter said. He didn't show them to the door.

Outside on the sidewalk, Ardith said, "Did you ever *see* such incompetence? What an idiot! He wouldn't last ten seconds in Toronto."

Melba Weary had known their mother. She and Beth had often talked when Beth went to the drugstore to pick up her blood-pressure pills. Sometimes Beth bought sleeping pills. Those were the only medications she took. Melba Weary was a hand-some, capable woman in her mid forties, who had never lived anywhere else but Sussex, yet had somehow acquired an air of worldliness and sophistication. Although Melba wasn't a pharmacist, she had worked in the drugstore so long that people treated her as if she were. Melba often discussed the side-effects of various medications and referred to doctors by their first names. She wore a white uniform and a small wooden pin with her name on it. Melba had seen their mother on Friday morning, before the accident. She had been standing at the window near the sunglasses rack. She had seen Beth stand on the curb and open a letter. Then Melba heard the truck horn.

"Was that before or after she stepped off the curb?" Madge said.

"After. She might have gone two or three feet across when the driver honked the horn. It was like he was warning her to

back up. He was going very fast. I didn't see it happen. By
then the truck had blocked my view. They say she was caught
in the fender somehow."

"Who's *they?*"

"Clifford Mercer. He was the Baptist minister before he
retired. He lives on Floral Avenue. He was standing behind
your mother. He came in here afterwards."

"Would you be willing to give a statement of what you saw
to the police?" Ardith asked.

"Sure," Melba said. "I liked your mother." Then she added,
"He's still driving, you know."

"Ronald Parnell? *Driving?*"

"Yes, I saw him go by here yesterday. In the same truck."

"I can't believe it," Ardith said.

Melba raised her eyebrows and spread her hands. No doubt
some of her worldliness came from what she'd seen through
the drugstore windows.

Clifford Mercer was a widower. He lived alone in a small
house with a large lawn. Madge and Ardith found him squatting at the side of the house, weeding a flower bed. There was
a sprinkler running in the vegetable garden at the back. On
the grass beneath a large chestnut tree were folding lawn
chairs. When the sisters came through the gate and into the
garden, Clifford Mercer stood up, came across the grass, and
shook hands. Both sisters recognized him. He had been at the
funeral.

"You've come about your mother," he said.

"Yes."

He gestured toward the lawn chairs and they sat down.

Reverend Mercer was thin and wiry with sparse white hair.
He had the presence, the authority that is sometimes bestowed
on ministers or that they take upon themselves, out of habit
or conviction.

"We understand you saw her killed," Ardith said.

"Yes, I saw it."

"We'd like to know what you saw."

Reverend Mercer looked at them. He had very blue, penetrating eyes.

"Are you sure?"

"Yes."

"Well, then. Your mother was about three feet off the curb. Her back was to me. She had her head down like she was reading. A truck honked. Three times. The driver was coming along fast, speeding. Your mother didn't look up. She kept on going. It seemed to me she was trying to scoot the rest of the way across before the truck reached her. She got caught on the fender and was . . . well, she was thrown under the tires."

"Would you be willing to make a statement to that effect?" Ardith asked.

"Certainly."

Ardith and Madge stood up to leave.

"We may press charges," Ardith said.

Reverend Mercer didn't say, *It won't bring your mother back. What's done is done. She's in God's house now.* What he said was, "Then you should know I think it was an accident."

As they were driving back to their father's apartment, Madge said, "I wonder whose letter she was reading, yours or mine?"

That night they told their father about the two witnesses, their visit to the police. Laddie sat smoking and listening. He didn't interrupt once. When Madge and Ardith had finished presenting their case, he said, "You say that young fella is still driving?"

"Yes. The police didn't take away his licence."

Their father sat silently for several minutes. Then he said, "That's not right. That's not right at all."

"That's why we have to press charges," Ardith said.

"I see."

"We want you to think about it," Madge said. "You don't have to decide tonight, but it should be soon, so Ardith and I can act on it before we go back."

Madge thought she saw her father wince when she said the word *back*. She didn't think Laddie had come to the point of thinking about when they would leave, that he was keeping himself from thinking that far ahead. Later that night, Madge told Ardith she thought they should have another talk with Margaret, to see if they couldn't bring her around.

The next morning – it was now two days after the funeral – Laddie decided to go to the office. He ran a real estate business out of a room behind the bus terminal. He said he wanted to go over his ledger. Madge and Ardith took this as a good sign, that he would be able to keep going. As soon as they had washed the breakfast dishes and made the beds, the sisters went downstairs to see Margaret.

Margaret lived in what had once been the kitchen area of the house. The house was well over one hundred years old. It had been built in the days when there were summer kitchens. Margaret had retained what she could of its origins. She had kept the wide-planked floor and installed a Franklin stove. She had lamps made from stoneware jugs, a butter churn filled with bulrushes, an oak sideboard. Against one wall were shelves crammed with books. Margaret was a reader. Much of her reading was connected with hobbies. Since her retirement, she had taken up watercolours, painting scenes from calendars and sketching what she had seen during her walks in the country, where she went to bird watch, to pick wildflowers and mushrooms. Some of these scenes were on the walls.

Margaret served them tea in pottery mugs, which they drank sitting on their aunt's maple furniture, the sisters side by side on the chesterfield, Margaret in a chair beside the stove.

Ardith explained about their visit to the police, how they had talked to other witnesses, how they had asked Laddie to press charges. Madge told their aunt about Ronald Parnell's speeding, the fact that he was still driving the same truck.

Margaret heard them out, her face composed. When they had finished, she said, in her firm, classroom voice, "If I am called to testify, I will say that, in my opinion, the accident was Beth's fault. She walked into the truck's path."

"How could you know that?" Ardith said. "From where you were sitting, you couldn't have seen."

"I saw. I looked around and I saw." Beneath the makeup, Margaret's face had begun to collapse. She cleared her throat and moved on. "Your mother could be careless crossing the street."

Madge knew this was true. Whenever they had crossed a street together, Madge had held her mother by the arm. More than once she had yanked her mother back onto the curb, away from the oncoming traffic. Madge thought this carelessness came from the fact that her mother had never driven a car and did not take the driver's point of view.

"She walked into his path," Margaret said.

"But, she was *beside* the crosswalk," Ardith said. "Crosswalks are *for* pedestrians. The truck driver was speeding."

Margaret lifted her chin.

"I refuse to become involved in a vendetta against that young man. He has his whole life ahead of him. Your mother had lived out most of hers. She had a family, children, and grandchildren. He ought to have the same chance."

Madge and Ardith didn't remind Margaret that if she had parked the car where she should have, the accident might not have happened. They weren't prepared to go that far.

The next day, the *Kings County Record* came out with the story of the accident on the front page.

Ardith read it to Madge.

The truck, a three-ton, owned by Sprague's Paving Limited, was driven by Ronald Parnell, 23, of Sussex, who had a passenger, another employee of the same company, Clifford Webster, 21.

Ardith stopped and said, "Parnell was older than we thought."

"There was another witness," Madge said. "Constable Sooter didn't say a word about there being a passenger."

The police attached no blame to the driver, Ardith continued. *At the time of the accident, Mrs. Murray, 65, started to cross the street to return to her car after getting the mail. Traffic was light. It was stated that the driver sounded his horn and attempted to avoid striking her, but she continued on and came in contact with the front fender. She suffered multiple injuries. Death was believed to have been instantaneous.*

Ardith put down the paper.

"This article makes Mum sound like a doddering old woman," she said, "which is another reason why we have to do something. With or without Aunt Margaret's help, we have to press charges."

"Then we'll have to get started soon," Madge said. "Don't forget I have to go back to Victoria on Monday. Doug and his wife are flying out next Thursday to take the kids camping. I haven't done a thing to help them get ready."

"Couldn't Alison and Shelley get everything organized?"

"They could if they didn't have exams. They're writing them until Wednesday. Besides, I'd like to see them off. They'll be gone a month."

"Then you should go. I can stay for another week."

Quite often Ardith left her husband and two sons to fend for themselves while she went off to conferences and seminars.

"We'll have to get Dad to make up his mind," Ardith said. "We can't press charges without his say so."

Laddie couldn't make up his mind. He had read the article in the newspaper and said that it sounded like people had decided what had happened and nothing he could do would change their minds. Part of this might have been Laddie's concern for appearances. As a salesman, he cared what people thought of him. He liked to make a good impression. When Ardith pointed out that laying charges didn't have anything to do with public opinion, Laddie claimed that by trying to force him to decide, Ardith and Madge were ganging up on him. This was an old beef of their father's.

Growing up with him, the sisters had often heard him complain that he was no match for the women in his family. This had started as a light-hearted joke, the kind of thing he might pass on to his customers when he was out selling on the road. Later on, the joke turned into something more serious; it took on the harshness of an accusation. Maybe Laddie had repeated the charge so often he'd come to believe it. Maybe he'd got help from his listeners. Maybe they'd persuaded him that his wife and daughters banded together, manipulated him, did things behind his back.

On Friday, when the sisters again brought up the subject of laying charges, there was an angry outburst from their father. "I need more time," he shouted. "You can't rush something like this." He began to weep.

Madge and Ardith backed off. They got busy disposing of their mother's clothes. They emptied closets and dresser drawers. They packed up her belongings and gave them away. They kept nothing except a few items of jewellery: pearls, amber beads, an amethyst brooch, a gold ring, a nursing pin. They didn't want to admit they wanted anything of their mother's, that greed would affect them at a time like this. They made meat loaves and chicken pies and froze them, against the time when their father would be left alone. They answered letters, wrote thank-you notes.

This work drained away much of their energy and resolve. They didn't feel quite as determined to press charges against Ronald Parnell, to hound their father into going to the police. Neither of them brought up the subject again. They felt heavy, sluggish, punched full of holes. They were ashamed they no longer had the grit to follow through, that they had given in to unfairness. They felt they had let their mother down. But their mother was dead. She wouldn't care. Nevertheless, they felt that if she had been alive, she would have cared. This conviction was never to leave the sisters. Eventually, Madge was to see their regret as a ragged corner, a strip of torn material that wouldn't stay inside a box. This was what an accident was, something that could never be smoothed out, tucked under, and neatly put away. There would always be something loose, something to jar and offend.

On Monday Ardith drove Madge to Saint John, where she caught a plane. Madge felt relieved and privileged to be leaving first, to be flying up and away, back to her children. After she had been seated on the plane, this relief was overtaken by a feeling of gratitude for her sister, when she looked out the window and saw Ardith standing in front of the terminal window waiting patiently, steadfastly, for her plane to leave.

Two weeks later, Madge received a letter from Ardith, written in Sussex, just before she left town herself. Their father was doing better, she said. He was going to work every day and had managed to sell a small farm. Their aunt had put her car up for sale. The rest of the letter was about Ardith's visit to the drugstore. She had gone in there the previous day to buy shampoo and had spoken with Melba Weary.

Melba told me that a few days ago Ronald Parnell nearly hit someone else, a farmer named Norval Jenkins from Millstream. Apparently, this Mr. Jenkins was standing behind his truck, which was parked in front of Canadian Tire, lifting a chain saw into the back, when Ronald came barrelling along Main Street in the gravel truck and sideswiped him. Mr. Jenkins dropped the chain saw and leaped up onto the back of the truck. That's what saved him. I asked Melba if Mr. Jenkins would be charging Parnell, but she said she didn't think so. A lot of people, including Mr. Jenkins, have given up on the town police.

Reading her sister's letter, far away in Victoria, her house empty of children, Madge thought she saw the situation more clearly. She thought Ronald Parnell's mother had put him up to visiting Laddie. She had made him get dressed up and go apologize. Ronald wouldn't have been thinking clearly enough to have done this on his own. He might not have realized exactly what he'd done. His mother would have done his thinking for him. She would have done what she could to save his skin, to give him time. Madge thought it was something a mother would do. It was something she would do herself. It was something Ardith might do. Even knowing it was the wrong sort of protection, they would want their sons to have another chance.

The Madonna Feast

Madge and Nonie check into the cabin late Saturday –
they are getting an early start on Mother's Day. The
cabin hugs a cliff overlooking a strip of sand the colour of wet
cement. Giant logs washed ashore during winter storms, lie
on the rocks below like fallen monoliths.

Far out on the grey water, Nonie sees something dark rising
out of the waves.

"A whale!" she says, squinting, she has forgotten to put on
her glasses.

But Madge, who has become farsighted in middle age, tells
her it's a fallen tree. "The root tip sticks up like a fin."

Rain drips off trees. Madge feels the moisture seeping into
her pores. The dampness makes her joints ache, her bones
feel brittle and stiff. She looks at Nonie. Drops of water cling
to Nonie's cropped hair, yellow and coarse as wheat stubble
from years of living on the prairie. Nonie tips her head back,
parts her lips, welcoming the rain. She looks as if she could
stand in the rain for days, a porous, bulky sponge.

Madge shivers. "Let's go inside and light a fire," she says.

They carry their suitcases and baskets into the cabin, return
for firewood and kindling. A pink rhododendron blooms by
the door. Nonie picks a blossom, carries it inside, and puts it
in a bowl of water. Madge lights the fire. Nonie walks around

the large room, the kitchen, the bathroom, returns to the window overlooking the sea.

"It's lovely," she says. "Better than I imagined."

"I wanted one of the cedar cabins," Madge says. "But they don't have phones. I need a phone in case she calls."

Nonie doesn't ask about Alison. Madge has already told her about Alison's anorexia, which surfaced two years ago when Alison moved east to look for work and became a teller for the Toronto Dominion Bank.

"I told Stuart we wouldn't be near a phone," Nonie says. "It's just as well. The boys wouldn't try to telephone, but Pauline might decide to call if she has a nightmare. She might get up and dial without Stuart knowing."

While the fire crackles, they unpack their bags and put away food. Nonie has brought a basket of food with her on the plane. In it are jars of marmalade and pear preserves, espresso, miniature bottles of liqueur, Camembert, cream cheese, caviar. Madge has brought applesauce, homemade bread, croissants, bagels, honey, candles. On their way from the airport they stopped at a fish market for smoked salmon and crabmeat, at the liquor store for wine, at a supermarket for fruit, vegetables, and cream.

"How about a celebratory drink?" Madge says.

They kick off their runners and sprawl on the floor, each holding a glass of wine.

Although they have lived apart since their girlhoods in Cape Breton during the fifties, Madge and Nonie have kept in touch through letters and visits. When Madge's marriage was breaking up, Nonie flew to Halifax for a week to help out. Madge and her children have camped in Nonie's backyard in Calgary. Last year, the two friends spent an afternoon in Stanley Park when Nonie accompanied Stuart to a geological conference. For two people who have been travelling different currents since leaving Cape Breton, they feel lucky to have once again drifted into the same cove.

Madge stares at the rhododendron. In the firelight the blossom is licked with gold. Her thoughts leave the West Coast.

They wing over the prairies, travelling back to another coast, another island, to a rocky promontory jutting into the Atlantic, a scruffy hillside with barely enough soil on it to camouflage the coal mines tunnelled beneath.

"Do you remember the Mother's Day we went looking for mayflowers?" she says.

She and Nonie had begun in the graveyard on the edge of town. Leaning against two tombstones, they ate molasses sandwiches and swigged strawberry pop. Afterwards they walked around the graveyard, reading the inscriptions on the grave markers. This was when Madge and Nonie were fifteen, when their mothers were both alive.

"Susan Barton, aged 41 years / In Death's cold arms lies sleeping here, / A tender parent, Companion dear," Madge recites now.

"I remember thinking Susan was some sort of heroine," Madge says. "I had the idea Death was her abductor, that she half wanted to be carried off so the people left behind would pine for her."

"Beloved, lovely, she was but seven / A fair bird to earth, to blossom in heaven," Nonie says. Like Madge she can still remember poetry she memorized years ago. She takes a sip of wine. "It was the small white crosses that got to me. All those infant graves. Dozens and dozens."

Madge remembers the graveyard was where Otis Brogan did his drinking. Otis was a bald, shambling man, to whom nobody paid much attention. They could always tell when he'd been in the graveyard because, after he'd finished a bottle, he'd stick flowers from the grave into it and prop the bottle against a stone marker. Otis showed himself to young girls. Sometimes Madge and Nonie would taunt him into doing this, then run away. This made them feel daring, that they were flirting with the possibility of wrongdoing and chance.

"Babes in the woods, that's what we were," Madge says.

The afternoon of the mayflowers they didn't bother doing this. They saw Otis coming along the road with a brown paper bag and made for the woods.

Beyond the woods was a hill. On top of it was a disused powder magazine from the war. Inside it were dried weeds and empty liquor bottles. They sat on the grey cement walls and looked over the black coal heaps to the harbour ice. The afternoon sun poured gold onto the town, glazing the cinder streets, the rows of houses, in clear honeyed light. The cross on top of the Catholic church pierced the blue like an early star. Up there on the powder magazine, they felt a cool wind blowing off the ice. Nonie and Madge left the cement wall and started down the hillside, searching the tufted grass for rust-spotted leaves. Mayflowers grew under old grass, close to the ground. It was possible to walk right over them without knowing they were there, beneath the soles of your feet.

Madge can still recall how the possibility of not finding mayflowers and arriving home without them had filled her with panic. Mayflowers appeared in early spring, when there was leftover snow on the ground, when there was the likelihood of more snow to come. Sometimes the snow lasted until June and the time for mayflowers slipped past. You had to be lucky to find them. You had to move quickly. Together Madge and Nonie ripped apart the hillside, kicking at clumps of soil, tearing up fistfuls of grass, trying to uncover the tiny pink-white flowers whose fragrance was so exquisitely pungent that the presence of a small bouquet was everywhere inside the house.

"What I remember about that afternoon was how fierce you were," Nonie says. "You were in tears. You were frantic about the possibility of not finding mayflowers."

"Was I as serious as all that?" Madge says, though she knew she had been. She had been young enough then to feel desperate about pleasing her mother, something she grew out of later on.

"I remember we used to tiptoe around your mother," Nonie says. "We had to be careful not to close the fridge door because she was lying down." Nonie arranges herself cross-legged in front of Madge. "I never did understand that. I suppose because my mother never slowed down long enough to take a nap. She was always off playing the organ, doing church work or something. Was your mother sick or what?"

"She had high blood pressure," Madge says. "Before we moved to Cape Breton, she spent nearly a year in bed with TB. We treated her like a china doll locked inside a glass case."

"I can't remember my mother ever being sick," Nonie says.

"I used to think my mother was holding back something," Madge says. "I don't think she was. I just thought she was. Because of the glass case. We weren't allowed too close to her for fear of catching TB." Madge stares into the fire. "The fact is I was fascinated by her. I used to lie on her bed and watch her breathe. For some reason I found that interesting."

"Well, I certainly knew what made my mother tick," Nonie says. "She told me in spades. Many times. Maybe your mother left more to the imagination."

"Did I ever tell you I never wept when my mother died?" Madge says. "I always thought that was odd, considering how I felt about her."

"No, you never told me that," Nonie says. "You never said much about her death, beyond the fact that it was an accident. We never talked about it."

"She was hit by a truck when she was crossing the street. The young man who was driving the truck was back on the road the next day. He didn't even have his licence taken away. He nearly hit someone else two weeks later when he was driving the same truck. My mother's sister, Margaret, was there when the accident happened. She insisted that my mother had walked in front of the truck. She made it sound as if it was deliberate. I was so angry about all that going on that I couldn't cry."

"I don't think crying means much anyway," Nonie says. "Take me for instance. I'm so sentimental I cry over anything." Nonie tells Madge about the Saturday afternoon she dragged the ironing board in front of the TV so she could watch *Lassie Come Home* again, knowing full well she'd cry when the boy came out of the school and found the dog waiting for him. "I cried so much I didn't need to dampen the shirts." Nonie laughs. "Water, water, everywhere."

"Nor any drop to drink," Madge says, and pours more wine.

Nonie gets out lox, bagels, cream cheese, caviar. Rain drums on the roof. They hear the surf booming far below on the beach. Embers fall through the grate. There is a daybed on either side of the room and, eventually, after they've eaten the bagels and finished the wine, they tumble into bed. They close their eyes and, like fallen trees bobbing drunkenly on the waves, they drift toward the shore of sleep.

At three o'clock the phone shrills on the kitchen counter. Madge heaves herself out of sleep and stumbles over a chair on her way to answer.

"Christ," she mutters, "doesn't she know what time it is here?" *Of course she does.* Madge fumbles across the wall for the light switch, flicks it on and picks up the phone. *Steady now. You gave her the number, remember?*

"Hello."

"Mum, is that you?"

Who else would it be? "Yes, it's me."

"Mum?"

"Yes?"

"Mum. I've got to ask you something important."

Alison's voice is heavy and wet, dragged out of a swamp. Madge knows this means she's probably spent the night bingeing, that she's exhausted, her throat and stomach sore from throwing up. Madge's head throbs at one temple. She shifts the receiver to the left hand and presses her right hand against the pain.

"Fire away," she says.

"Mum." She hears Alison's intake of breath. "Mum, when Dad left, what was it that kept you alive? Was it us kids?"

There it is laid out on the ground like a dead animal, a doe. Her eldest daughter had been hunting in the woods, stalking this deer for months, maybe years, preparing to shoot it. And here it is. Thrown at Madge's feet.

Alison was the one who took over after Doug left and Madge went to bed for most of a year. The eldest of Madge's four children, Alison showed the forbearance of a saint. She was the one who was the most responsible, the most anxious and attentive, and she is now making up for it. Sometimes Madge thinks Alison is trying to find a way to sainthood, to punish and scourge herself into becoming selfless and pure-hearted. What saves Alison from going this far is righteous anger. At least this is what Madge tells herself when the anger is being directed toward her.

Madge pushes hard against her temple and concentrates on the doe. She wants to bury it but, if she does, Alison will only dig it up. Madge circles round and round, nudging the body with her foot, but it lies there lifeless on the ground.

She knows what Alison wants. She wants to be told that it was she, more than any of the others, who kept her mother alive, that when Madge's eyes finally focused on her children's faces, it was Alison's she saw most clearly. Madge has told Alison this many times. She's willing to repeat it if necessary. But if she does, Alison could say, once again, "What about me? I have no kids. Why should I stay alive?"

Madge slides to the floor and leans her head against the cold metal handle of the fridge.

"I guess," she says slowly, "I guess what kept me alive was not wanting to die."

In Death's cold arms.

"I was young. I had the rest of my life ahead of me." Madge stops. Then goes on, "Like you have."

Silence.

This is not enough.

"Since then, it's been easier," Madge corrects herself, "mostly easier. I'm fine now. Just fine." Madge feels the metal handle dig into her temple. "I have a satisfying life."

She stops, waits. Then she says, "And you can have a satisfying life too, Ally, once you get over this hump."

"Maybe I don't want a satisfying life," Alison says, and hangs up.

Pain shoots across Madge's forehead. She goes into the bathroom and rummages in her cosmetic kit for Aspirins. When she comes back, she sees Nonie lying awake watching her.

"What's her doctor say?"

"Ha! She refuses to talk to me. Weeks go by without me hearing a thing from her or from Alison. Then I'll get a call like tonight. I'm trying to stay out of it, but I feel at this stage I've got to hang in there, keep in close touch. Her doctor doesn't agree. Once I phoned and she said (Madge pitches her voice high), 'Mrs. Ogilvey, you must remember this is Alison's problem. You have to leave her alone to work it out.' " Madge switches off the light. "I wonder if she's a mother," she says and gets into bed.

In the morning Madge wakens before Nonie. She dresses and goes outside. The storm has left behind a clear blue sky, an azure sea. She chooses a path through the woods, moist and green, lush with mossy trees and bracken. She passes one of the rustic cabins. Pink clematis climbs over the chimney, spills off the roof. Purple wisteria weeps onto the grass. A slug the colour of soapstone inches along the path. Madge rubs its back with a twig as she used to as a child and the slug stretches luxuriously. She begins picking the flowering shrubs: forsythia, copper broom, rhododendron. She takes her time, enjoying the cool drops of water spraying onto her bare, warm skin. She picks until her arms are overflowing. Then she carries the flowers back to the cabin, tiptoes inside, and fills two bottles and a jar with water. She arranges the flowers and places them around the room. She puts the jar on the floor beside Nonie.

Nonie wakens, sits up.

"Get back in bed." She speaks sternly. "I'll bring you coffee."

Years ago Madge used to crawl back to bed on Mother's Day to please her children. When they were school age, her children brought her clumsily wrapped mugs, soap, bath salts, notepaper, and handmade cards, settling themselves onto the bed covers to watch her open and exclaim.

Madge gets under the covers.

Nonie serves the espresso with glasses of Bailey's Irish Cream.

Madge props herself up with pillows, leans back against the wall.

"Oh my," she says. "This is something." There are dark circles beneath her eyes.

They drink their coffee and liqueur, staring at the sea.

Nonie lights a candle, carries it into the bathroom, and takes a bath, using the new bar of sandalwood soap she has brought along. Then, while Madge bathes, watching the candlelight flicker off the white-tiled walls, Nonie makes breakfast.

She serves warm pears with whipped cream. On top of the cream are two forsythia leaves dipped in crème de menthe. This is followed by eggs Benedict, croissants.

Nonie holds a croissant in front of Madge like a microphone.

"Ms. Ogilvey," Nonie says, dragging out the *Mizz*, "would you tell me what you think of Mother's Day after all these years? I'm sure our listeners would like to hear from one of our, ah, more *seasoned* mothers."

"Seasoned, my foot. *Broken in*, is more like it."

"But the day itself?"

Madge bites the end off a croissant.

"I like it," she grins, "especially the food."

"Seriously."

"Seriously, it's just another day, or almost, now that my kids are nearly grown. Naturally I'd like my kids to acknowledge the day with a card or a note, but no fuss. A fuss embarrasses me. It reminds me of the mistakes I've made. What do *you* think of Mother's Day?"

"Well, the last few years, Mother's Day has been a charade. Except for Pauline. The boys usually forget about it. At least I think they do, especially now that they have girlfriends. I think Stuart buys the gifts and signs their names. Sometimes I think I should put a stop to such nonsense. Other times I think I'd miss it if I did. I have to admit I feel I deserve a bit of fuss." Madge dips the last of her croissant into honey and pops it into her mouth. She leans back in her chair, pats her belly, and says, "I'm absolutely stuffed."

They take their coffee outside to the deck chairs. They move the chairs into an enclosure of sunlight and sit listening to the waves far below the cliff. Madge closes her eyes.

"Pauline," she murmurs drowsily. "How's Pauline?"

After a while Nonie says, "Well she's given up thinking she's a daughter of a Czech princess, which is something."

Pauline's adopted. Nonie has already told Madge some of the difficulties she's had with Pauline. Not Stuart. Apparently Stuart and Pauline get along just fine.

"I think she was too young for the information I gave her," Nonie says. "She was only five years old when she asked me why her real mother didn't keep her."

Nonie and Pauline were lying together beside a lake in the mountains while Stuart was off fishing with the boys. Pauline had crawled into Nonie's sleeping bag. She began playing with Nonie's breasts, probing the soft flesh. She stuck a finger into Nonie's navel.

"Is that where I grew?"

"No. You grew inside someone else's belly."

"Oh. What was her name?"

"I don't know."

"If I came out of *her* belly, why didn't she keep me?"

Nonie told Pauline that her birth-mother had wanted to keep her but she couldn't. She was sixteen, still a girl herself. Nonie explained about the girl's parents, that the family managed to get out of Czechoslovakia before the Russians clamped down, that they had owned a house in Prague the size of a castle and a country place in the mountains, which they had to give up when they defected. (The social worker had told Nonie all this, it wasn't on the forms.) Nonie told Pauline the family had arrived in Canada penniless, with only the clothes on their backs. It was a large family, eight children. With all those mouths to feed the girl couldn't bring herself to tell her parents about her pregnancy. She ran away instead. Nonie told Pauline that the girl wanted to keep her but she couldn't. She didn't have a job. She was still in high school. There was no way she could support a tiny baby.

"I never should have used the word 'castle'," Nonie says. "That's what got Pauline started on the princess business. I probably told her more than she wanted to know." Nonie sighs. "Just like my mother."

"Well, she might have imagined herself a princess without your help," Madge said. "When Theo was eight years old, he was convinced he was adopted because he didn't look like the others. He made up a story about his father being a hockey player."

"When the nightmares and the tantrums started, I went to a shrink," Nonie says. "He told me I should tell Pauline her birth-mother didn't want to keep her, that she would have to face the fact that not all mothers want their children. He told me there was nothing sacrosanct about giving birth. I told him I would never tell Pauline that her birth-mother didn't want her. She was simply trying to do what was best for her daughter."

Madge doesn't ask Nonie if she remembers the woman who threw her daughters into the Bow River because she failed to produce a son, then jumped in the water herself, holding her newborn daughter. Fortunately, Pauline's birth-mother wasn't that desperate.

Instead Madge says, "I once did a piece called the *Madonna Feast*. It was part of a series I did on eating, our food rituals: you know, the birthday party, the picnic, the tea party, the wedding banquet, the Last Supper. It was when I began to take sculpture seriously." It pleases Madge that she creates painted sculptures out of something as unassuming as papier mâché, that her apprenticeship evolved when she did art projects in the basement with her children. She feels proud and oddly defiant about this, that all the time she was mothering – and mismanaging her marriage – she was transforming a mess of wet, gluey paper into her own landscape, she was finding a way to rescue herself.

"You might say it was a round table of mothers," Madge says. "There was an artist, a nurse, a secretary, a quilt maker, a teacher, a cleaning lady, a cook." She laughs. "The Virgin Mary was pouring."

For a long time neither she nor Nonie speaks. They sit listening to the sea. The tide has gone out and the water laps soothingly against the sand. Eventually they get up and stroll down to the beach. Steps have been built down the cliffside. Salmonberry bushes arch overhead, making their descent one of alternating light and shade. They clamber across the rocks at the end of the beach, searching tidal pools for exotic underwater flowers.

When they tire of poking in rock pools, they sit on a giant log beneath a red alder. The tree leans over the sand, its long drooping branches protecting them from the sun. Behind them giant trees rock softly in the breeze.

"Let's play hopscotch," Nonie says. She picks up a sharp stick and draws two rows of squares at the tideline where the sand is firm. Madge collects two crab shells, hollow orange stones. She was never good at hopscotch. As a child she lacked fluidity, was all angles and bones. But she's willing to play hopscotch now, to humour Nonie. They play with cheerful determination, dragging their knees up for each jump, then thumping heavily onto the sand on thick, peasant ankles. As they play, the tide comes in, flattened waves looping across the sand.

Madge is surprised that she would like to win this game, that she cares. Why should either of them care, both of them cut loose, drifting ashore with the tide. This need to win is the quietest of impulses, an echo, yet it teases, pokes urgently in deepest corners. *You think you don't care if you win or lose, that you've moved beyond that, but you do care, you do.* Madge recognizes the point of origin, a harsher coast where there are icebergs and mayflowers, where she often felt she was coming from behind. She still feels this. Sometimes

Madge is surprised she likes Nonie so much. Women who seem to have everything don't interest Madge. She thinks they are likely to be smug. She prefers a woman with a tougher edge, preferably a woman with plenty of mistakes in her past. A few setbacks. Disadvantages. Nonie hasn't made many mistakes. She hasn't had many setbacks. She has been lucky. Like Madge's sister, Ardith, Nonie has worked hard for advantages. They weren't handed to her, she went after them. Madge remembers Nonie used to be good at sports. She played volleyball and badminton, tennis. Even when she and Madge played cards Nonie usually won. Madge never tried to change this. If Nonie wanted to come out on top so badly (Nonie would often pull away, become aloof with concentration), then let her. If Madge had tried harder, if the odds had been on her side, she could have won oftener. Or so she thinks.

Madge watches as Nonie backs up for the final jump, crouches like a sprinter and makes a run for it. Nonie leaps over two squares, lands on one foot exactly in the middle square, bends down and picks up her shell before hopscotching lightly over the last three squares.

"I made it!"

Madge knows Nonie is so far ahead that beating her would require more energy than she is willing to give. Madge prefers to give in gracefully. That way she keeps her magnanimity intact. Madge is helped along by the rhythmic waves and moist scented air, which have entered her skin and made her lethargic and nirvanic. Lying there on the sand, she feels satiated, drugged, as if she's marooned on an enchanted isle.

"Do mermaids have children?" she asks.

"Probably," Nonie says. "After all, there are mermen."

"Then how come we don't see any merchildren?"

"They grow up fast and leave home early," Nonie says solemnly.

"Leaving their mothers free to swim the oceans," Madge says dreamily. She gets up, tosses her shell toward the middle square, and misses. When she leans over to pick up the shell, she loses her balance and flops down laughing. She rolls onto her back, leans on her elbows, and looks at her feet. There's a corn on the little toe of each foot. "See what happens to a beached mermaid?" she says. "She grows feet with corns on them." She lies back and closes her eyes. "I think I might stay in lotus-land indefinitely." "You do that," Nonie says briskly. "I'll bring us back some lunch."

Nonie goes back through the tunnel and up the cliff to the cabin. Madge feels no obligation to follow her up, to help in the kitchen. She feels like being indulged, fussed over, though not by her children. She will take whatever is being offered without apology or regret, to make up for possible inequities, disproportions. She languishes on the beach thinking *fresh crab on lettuce, Camembert, cold white wine.*

Margaret's Story

Three months before my Aunt Margaret died, she spent a week in hospital with chronic emphysema. I flew East to visit her, bringing a bouquet of daffodils, which were hard to come by in New Brunswick in February. The day after I gave Margaret the flowers, I arrived at the hospital just as she was walking down the corridor in her dressing gown, carrying the daffodils. She was taking them to Mrs. Robarts three doors along, who was dying of cancer. As Margaret later explained, Millie Robarts had endured a hard life. Her husband, a notorious womanizer and a poor provider, had been electrocuted in a freak accident, leaving his invalid wife penniless, with a crippled son to care for. I was sure the Cambodian refugees known as the Tieu family had the electric kettle I had given Margaret two Christmases ago, as well as the toaster oven my sister Ardith had sent. There was no sign of either appliance in Margaret's apartment, where I stayed during my visits. The portable TV Ardith had given Margaret had also disappeared. No doubt there were other gifts spread around town. Margaret had a strong sense of deprivation. She was vigilant against the possibility that her life would become easy or soft. It was impossible to give her anything she would keep.

Margaret died in hospital a week before Easter, of cardiac arrest brought on by emphysema. Except for a nurse, she was alone. The nurse phoned us the news. I arrived in Sussex a day before my sister. She had to stay in Toronto to invigilate exams. Ardith taught history at York University.

Margaret lived at one end of a badly stained brick building called Hotel Sussex. This was where she moved after my mother was killed and my father, Laddie, remarried and moved back to Liverpool. The hotel was beside the railway yard and across from the theatre where I worked evenings the summer I was eighteen. Like the railway station, the hotel had seen better days. Since rail passenger services had been cut back, the motels on the Trans-Canada Highway picked up the transient business. The hotel had to find other ways to keep going. The owner had taken over the adjoining building and turned it into apartments. The hotel itself had become a rooming house. It was now home to a handful of men who did seasonal work around town: wood splitting, snow shovelling, window cleaning. Between jobs they sat on cracked leather chairs in front of the lobby window, where the owner's wife kept a row of geraniums planted in old juice cans. The front of Margaret's apartment had large store windows covered with Venetian blinds. Before the hotel had taken over this building, it had been the town's liquor outlet. There was a small window in Margaret's bedroom, another in the kitchen. Neither of these admitted much light, which made the apartment dark and gloomy. There was a pervasive smell of rotting wood and damp plaster. It upset my sister that Margaret lived in such a dismal place. She felt our aunt had come down in the world, that she deserved better. Margaret had been amused by Ardith's distress. She thought it was misplaced. Our aunt claimed she had everything she wanted. By that she meant the basic necessities.

Margaret had made some effort to fix up the apartment, to put her stamp on it, for a time. In the living room there was her butter churn with the bulrushes inside like tall Egyptian reeds. There were vases of dried flowers, watercolour scenes on the wall, her red maple furniture, her old oak sideboard. There was a lot of pottery scattered about, bowls, jugs, and a small terra-cotta urn. The apartment was cluttered. There were books and papers piled on chairs and tables, scraps of paper tucked under lamps.

During her school-teaching days my aunt had been a strict enforcer of tidiness and order. But these last few years, after she had retired from teaching, she did not seem to notice clutter or disorder. She did not seem to notice dirt. There were dustballs under the furniture, mud tracked onto the braided rug. Like many elderly people, Margaret had let housework slide. I walked through the small rooms, taking stock. I decided to begin sorting books. This was an easy, undemanding task, something I would manage until my sister showed up. Soon after I began working, I found a list. It was sticking out of a book entitled *Edgar Cayce on Diet and Health*. The list was entitled *People I Have To Forgive*. Beneath the title were these names:

> *David Seward*
> *Harris Erb*
> *Annie Thompkins*
> *Bob Rafuse*
> *Muriel Wainright*
> *Laddie*

Except for my father and Harris Erb, I didn't recognize these people. Harris Erb had been a boyfriend of my aunt's when she lived in Liverpool. Presumably the others had been friends or acquaintances. One or two might have been school principals. My aunt had a low opinion of school principals. She regarded them either as spineless weaklings or overbearing tyrants.

There were other lists in Margaret's apartment: under the telephone, beneath a hooked table mat, inside other books. Some of these lists were chores Margaret had set herself: laundry, errands, doctors' appointments. Others were bibliographies for further reading. Most of them had to do with hobbies she pursued: bird-watching, painting, archaeology. Between the pages of *Inside Tutankh-Amen's Tomb* she had simply written "Read further in this area". Some of Margaret's books were heavily underlined in ink. Much of the underlining dealt with the occult and self-help: *Healing with Mind Power, The Opening of the Wisdom Eye, Seth Speaks*. These books went into a pile for Margaret's Quaker friends who lived on farms or had country places outside Sussex. I wasn't about to let this type of book loose in town, not with my aunt's name scrawled inside. My aunt lived a private, secretive life. Except for the Quakers, she didn't belong to religious groups or community organizations. She did good works and kept to herself. I thought people might think she had gone queer in the head if they were to find out what she had been reading; they might think she had been some kind of a heretic or a cult follower. The books on gardening, photography, birds, mushrooms, and flowers were safe enough to go into a pile for the town library. The books on history and archaeology went into a pile for Ardith. I set the art books aside for myself.

My aunt never married. After attending Normal College in Truro, she taught elementary school in Liverpool for fifteen years, following which she put herself through Mount Allison University. When she finished her degree, she taught high-school French in Halifax and Middle Musquodoboit. During her early school-teaching years, Margaret's hair had been thick and copper-coloured, worn in a roll at the back. I remember seeing a photograph of her once dressed in a fur-collared coat, wearing pointed shoes with straps and a cloche hat. She was standing on the running board of Harris Erb's Dodge. According to my mother, Margaret's relationship with Harris had been a serious attachment. People assumed they would marry. Harris did not have to work. His family owned land, rental properties, the Astor Theatre, which Harris managed. During the winters, Harris took himself off on exotic trips to places like Machu Picchu, Rhodes, Luxor.

Margaret travelled too, though not with Harris. She spent a year in Paris, at the Sorbonne. She went to Dublin to visit the Irish aunts. Over the years, these aunts had taken on an almost legendary significance, because they lived far away and their existence depended on random pieces of information that had been handed down to me. Their names were Rachael and Margaret Payne. Aunt Margaret and I had both been named after Margaret Payne.

The aunts were well off and liked to bet on horse races. They lived in a big house in Dublin, on what my mother referred to as an estate. Twice my grandmother Nelly, who had been brought up by these maiden aunts, took my mother and Margaret, their brothers Dessie and Dillon, to Dublin for visits. I remember my mother telling me about a shark that followed their ship back to Canada after the second visit. Midway across the Atlantic, a woman aboard the ship died and her body was wrapped in a shroud and placed on deck. Soon after, a large fin appeared behind the ship, in the wake. It stayed there, following the ship for days until it came close to land.

A year after this trip, Nelly had a fatal miscarriage and the family broke up. My mother and Margaret were sent to board with a Mrs. Wheeler in Scarborough, close to good schools. My grandfather, Norman, took Dessie and Dillon with him to Welland, where he had a job working on the canal. It was assumed the boys were better at roughing it, living in make-shift quarters and camps. Mrs. Wheeler expected my mother and Margaret to do the housecleaning, to stand on chairs and tables and wash ceilings and walls, to rub the furniture with lemon oil and scrub the floors. My mother and Margaret never saw anything of the clothing allowance their father gave Mrs. Wheeler to buy them winter coats and boots. Their old boots leaked and had to be plugged with newspapers. After they had been living in Scarborough a year, Margaret scalded her ankle as she was pouring hot water from the kettle into the scrub bucket. For weeks the wound festered and wouldn't heal. She wasn't permitted to visit a doctor. My mother waited until Mrs. Wheeler had gone to Dundas to visit a brother before packing two suitcases and getting Margaret and herself onto a streetcar, then onto a bus, then a converted coal truck, which took them to Leaside, where my mother had the address of a woman named Bertie Roach. Bertie had been a school friend of Nelly's in Dublin and had kept in touch with my mother after my grandmother's death. The sisters were to stay with this kind woman for three years; even after my grandfather married Cassie Lewis they stayed. Bertie was childless and enjoyed spoiling them. She sewed them dresses and winter coats. My mother was twelve, Margaret eight, when they ran away to Bertie. Because of their ages I have never been able to shake the picture of my mother and Margaret as orphans adrift at sea. They are in a small boat being trailed by a large fin. This is a highly coloured, mawkish notion, one my mother did not share. She was offhand and matter-of-fact about hers and Margaret's misfortune. She thought hard times straightened your backbone, toughened you up.

I have a picture of my aunt picking buds off the tree we planted on the lawn in front of our house in Liverpool. It was the end of the war. My father had planted the tree to mark the Allied victory. The tree was an oak sapling, not the usual kind of tree you saw in town. People planted maples, chestnuts, and flowering shrubs on their lawns. They left oak trees in the woods. That could have been the reason Margaret picked the buds off the tree, because she disapproved of my father's choice. As it turned out, Margaret may have helped the tree along. It grew so large that eventually it had to be cut down because it interfered with the electrical wires. I didn't see my aunt picking the leaves off the tree. No one saw her. We were in bed. Margaret had been staying with us for part of that year and had chosen VE day to leave. I say VE day but it was early next morning, after she returned from a beach party with Harris Erb. Margaret also took the walnut radio that had been one of my parents' wedding presents from our kitchen shelf. Then she picked the buds off the tree, as an afterthought. This is what I believed. I thought Margaret had done these things out of spite, to get even with my father for sending her a valentine with Harris Erb's initials on it. Margaret had not liked my father, maybe from the start. My mother told me that when she told Margaret she intended to marry Laddie, Margaret had broken down and cried. She said she thought she and my mother would be setting up housekeeping together. She had a small house picked out for them down by The Fort. It had a stained-glass panel over the door and a white picket fence.

Margaret wrote. After she retired from teaching she bought a typewriter, which she kept on a desk in the bedroom. At first she wrote nature articles about bird-watching, mushroom hunting, wildflower drying. She sent these articles to *Readers' Digest* and *Nature Canada*. They were returned without comment. She began writing thinly disguised fiction, sometimes not even bothering to change the names of people living in the town: anecdotal stories about a browbeaten wife being helped by a neighbour's kind gesture, a young man who was relieved to be caught stealing and mended his ways, an invalid widow who gained strength after a day's outing at the beach. I had known about the nature articles but not about the stories. I didn't find those until after I had finished sorting books and was going through the desk drawers. The drawers were crammed with long, descriptive passages about people, conversations with neighbours, explanations about why they talked and acted the way they did. There were several pages that described situations Margaret wanted to write about.

Willing worker at Stedman's imposed upon. Plump, pleasant cashier. Worked up to the point of crying. She is told to take care of the stationery supplies, stock up the school supplies, etc. "I'm too busy to talk now. It's about time some of the younger girls did their share of the work. I have my hands full enough with the cash register." She is always ready to tramp around and find a special shade of stockings for a customer.

Don't know her name. Comes from the country. Loves flowers. (Would make a good foil for Annie Thompkins who is the opposite.)

The aggressive person, who often has considerably less ability than the shy person, nevertheless gets ahead faster. The biggest mouth gets the biggest worm. The self-effacing person who waits for people to draw him out is often the most interesting and rewarding. (Example: Hiep Tieu.)

Do animals have a sixth sense? Of all the home-owners on a street, most of whom would not go to the bother of having a pet, a stray cat comes along and brings her starving kittens to the one person who would. (George Eliot used this device when building up the character of some man.)

I thought this story idea probably went back to the time when Margaret was living in one of the lower apartments in the same house where my parents lived. There had been a large garden out back where Margaret's cat, a stray, had prowled. Before moving to Hotel Sussex, Margaret had given away this cat. There was too much traffic outside the hotel, and the doctor had said the cat was bad for her emphysema.

Margaret interspersed her writing notes with pep talks, words of encouragement, exhortations. Apparently she was unable or unwilling to stop the compulsion of being a student.

Having to save painfully in order to acquire things like a trip, higher education, a winter coat, teaches you the self-discipline to live within your income. But this habit of saving money can also turn you into a penny-pincher, which is ugly and of no use to anybody. Watch this. Spend money on books, painting supplies, photography, growth of any kind.

My aunt obstructed passageways she didn't want entered. She simply ignored a question she considered improper or didn't want to answer, such as my sister's inquiry about how Margaret was managing on a teacher's pension. Ardith thought Margaret was barely getting by and was in need of financial help. This wasn't the kind of question I would have asked. I would have asked about Harris Erb. I would have asked why he and Margaret hadn't married, if sex had got in the way, or drink. Harris had a reputation for going on binges. I would have wanted to know if Margaret had wanted to marry Harris or if, because she couldn't have my mother, she preferred to live by herself. Margaret made a profession of loneliness. She worked at it. She knew it demanded study, preparation. Until she died, she got up early, dressed in a sweater and skirt, sometimes a dress. She put on makeup, kept her nails and her hair touched up. She found excuses to go outside, pursued hobbies, made herself useful to others. I wanted to know how she had managed this. I knew it had to do with concentration, self-centredness. I thought secrecy had a lot to do with it. My aunt had put some thought into maintaining this secrecy. Tucked beneath the telephone was a list she used to deflect inquiries about herself. This list was intended to help steer conversation toward what she considered useful and enlightening talk.

Topics of Conversation
1. *Job Opportunities – How can you expect students to work hard in school if there are no jobs?*
2. *The Political Mess in Ottawa – Civil servant mandarins are mainly interested in protecting their jobs.*
3. *Contemporary Painting – Too many paintings resemble photographs.*

I found a story about a retired teacher who kept a cat she was forced to give away. It was a long story, long enough to be a novella. It took me an hour or more to read it. The writing was clichéd, wooden, amateurish. Of course I knew I was prying, taking unfair advantage, entering places that until now had been closed to me, to anybody. I knew I had no right to read these awkward early drafts, drafts never intended to be read, that I could do this only because my aunt was dead. It was one thing to make deductions about her when she was alive to protect herself. It was quite another to have free rein when she was no longer here. None of this prevented me from reading on. I had been a snooper all my life and would go on peeling away layers to see what was beneath.

Hunger eventually compelled me to stop. I put the notes and stories I had uncovered so far into a plastic bag for burning and went into the kitchen to see what I could find for supper. The fridge was jammed with several varieties of juice, pickles, relish, jelly, mayonnaise. There were half a dozen unopened cans of tuna and salmon, a large tin of ham. There was chocolate cake and a tin of cookies. My aunt often took cake and cookies round to people who didn't bake themselves. The shelves on the fridge door were full of baking supplies: packages of raisins, dates, coconut, almonds. I was bewildered by all this food. There was nothing here I could heat up quickly. I didn't want the bother of cooking a meal. I closed the fridge, put on my raincoat, and walked up the street to a deli I had noticed earlier when I had driven into town.

Inside the restaurant a young Malaysian was waiting on tables. There were half a dozen men in the restaurant, one of them a man I had seen sitting in the lobby window of the hotel. I ordered pea soup and salad. When the Malaysian brought these to my table, I asked if he knew Hiep Tieu. He shook his head.

About eight years ago, my aunt had begun helping a young Cambodian refugee named Hiep Tieu with his English. One of the town's churches had sponsored a family of boat people. Hiep was the oldest of five children. He had already finished school in Cambodia, but attended school in Sussex to improve his English. He wanted to become a doctor. I had been told all this in Margaret's letters. The last I had heard about the

family, Tieu and his younger brother had moved to Toronto
looking for work.

When I returned to the apartment, my sister phoned to ask
me if I would pick her up at the Saint John airport in the
morning. Then she asked what I had accomplished so far.
After the phone call I stopped reading Margaret's writing and
got to work cleaning, so I could show my sister I hadn't been
wasting my time. I started with the bathroom, because it was
the smallest room. That way I could say I had one room
finished.

I began to find money, a roll of fifty-dollar bills held
together by an elastic band, shoved behind an Aspirin bottle
in the medicine cabinet, another bundle beneath the towels in
the linen closet. The next day I was to find more of these
bundles: beneath my aunt's jewellery box, under the paper
liner in a dresser drawer, inside an old purse. Altogether I was
to find eight hundred dollars. Some of this may have been
absent-mindedness. It wasn't senility. Margaret never forgot
my birthday or my children's.

I found large caches of food. Six boxes of Baker's chocolate,
nine bottles of Kikkoman soya sauce, fourteen cans of Dole
pineapple were stashed on the bottom shelves of the linen
closet. On the floor of the closet were gallon jars of lentils,
lima beans, noodles, macaroni, three kinds of rice, oatmeal.
There were quart jars of wheat germ, dried parsley and mint.
My aunt couldn't possibly have expected to use all this food.
I thought the supplies of food and bundles of money must
have been stockpiled, not against nuclear attack – the holo-
caust wasn't one of Margaret's preoccupations – but against
the unexpected and the unanticipated, against a sudden detour
that might have left her stranded in unknown territory, a place
where there were no roads or maps.

The Saint John airport was fogged in. Ardith's plane was
rerouted to Fredericton. I drove north, following the river.
Under normal conditions this river often went unnoticed in

places where it was hidden behind bushes and trees as it wound past farms and fields. It had been a spring of heavy rains. The river had overflowed its banks, spreading itself so wide that the landscape had become an enormous lake with the road running through its middle. Elm trees stood shin deep in water; only the top halves of fence posts were visible. Clumps of grass were caught on barbed wire like knots of wool. Barns were stranded. In one place an entire farm had become an island. There were gulls and ducks on the water.

Coming back from the airport, Ardith and I saw a young moose on the far side of what had once been a field. It was down on its knees, drinking. I stopped the car, rolled down the window so we could watch. After a while, the moose got up and loped into the woods. I drove on.

Ardith looked across the drowning landscape and sighed.

"There's so much to do in the next few days," she said. "All her stuff to sort through and dispose of: the committal service, the will, paying the bills, disconnecting the phone, that sort of thing. We should divide up the work. It'll go faster that way."

All along I had known Ardith would take over the arrangements. I had been counting on it. That was why I had the time to read Margaret's writing.

"I'll go see the lawyer first thing," Ardith went on. "You should probably check with the funeral parlour and find out if the ashes have arrived so we can decide on a time for the committal service. I suggest we have it the day after tomorrow, before the weekend. We'll have to pick out a tombstone."

"Maybe she didn't want a tombstone," I said.

I could imagine Margaret's ashes scattered somewhere in the country, in the woods or across the meadows. I could imagine the ashes floating on the sea, or on these flooded fields.

"You know Margaret would want to be buried beside Mum," Ardith said.

She took a leather notebook out of her shoulder bag and began listing what needed to be done.

"Look," I said.

I pointed to a man who was rowing away from a barn. There was a pig in the boat with him, in the stern.

I could have phoned about the ashes, but I knew the funeral parlour occupied the Oersteds' old house where I had once worked. Five years after I left Sussex, when I was married and living in Dartmouth, Niels Oersted died suddenly of a heart attack. After the burial, Selda closed up the house, moved away, remarried. She held onto the house for years, wanting to see it used for an arts and crafts museum. Eventually she sold it and the house was divided into apartments. It became rundown, in need of repair. I wanted to revisit the house. I told Ardith to take the car to the lawyer's, I would do my errand on foot.

Recently the house had been fixed up. There was a synthetic carpet on the front steps, a carpet so green I was sure it must glow in the dark. There were aluminum windows, a wide aluminum door. I let myself in and stood facing the broad, curving staircase. I was surrounded on all sides by a rose-coloured carpet and expensive wallpaper. There was a crystal chandelier hanging in the hallway. In one of the rooms I saw a pulpit where Niels's wheel had been. There were metal flower stands, candelabras, microphones, rows of chairs. I climbed the staircase and went toward the back of the house, looking for someone to ask about the ashes. I ran smack into a showroom where caskets were displayed. Most of the caskets were laminated wood in brown or ivory. Some were upholstered in Italian brocade, the sort of material used in women's purses. One of the caskets was lined in deep blue satin, the colour of an *Evening in Paris* perfume bottle.

A man in a grey business suit came up to me and led me into an office that had once been Selda's bedroom. On my way down the hall I caught a glimpse, through a half-opened door, of the bathroom window. A pink mermaid with yellow hair had been painted on the glass. Her eyes were closed and she was lying back, as if she were sleeping on the sea. I couldn't remember if one of the Oersteds' daughters had painted this mermaid or Selda herself. She had once painted buttercups on a green floor. The mermaid cheered me up. She was in limbo, unaffected by the disappearance of the Oersteds, by the slick packaging of death.

Of course, the funeral parlour was another detour. Going through my aunt's drawers, reading her stories, her notes and lists, finding her caches of food and money, walking through this house, seeing the mermaid, all this has been a deflection, meant to indulge my appetite for prying and speculation. As I expected, it was my sister who got down to business.

When I returned to Margaret's apartment, Ardith was already back from the lawyer's. She was at the kitchen table, sitting on her raincoat, which she had thrown across the chair. She was flushed and animated. Something was making her excited and keyed up.

"You're not going to believe this," she said.

"Believe what?"

"Margaret left a lot of money."

I sat down.

"You and I and Hiep Tieu are each to receive a third of the estate, which I estimate to be about $150,000. I'll have to go to the bank to get the investment certificates out of her safety deposit box before we'll know the exact amount," Ardith said.

"Where on earth would she get so much money?"

"The Irish aunts. That's the only explanation," Ardith said. "Margaret was the one who kept in touch with them, not Mum. I remember, during the war, Margaret used to send them food parcels, tinned meat, fruit cake, cookies."

"She certainly didn't spend the money on herself."

"Maybe she didn't think of the money as hers," Ardith said. "Maybe she was saving it for us. The money would have been our grandmother's if she had lived long enough. I remember

Margaret gave Mum a sum of money once. It must have come from the Irish aunts."

I remembered this. After my father had left Liverpool, he had used this money to help keep his rope-making business going in Cape Breton. Eventually the business failed.

"Dad was right after all," Ardith said. "He always maintained Margaret was loaded."

Ardith and I had been sceptical whenever our father claimed someone was loaded. We dismissed his comments about money, probably because he had so much trouble holding on to it. According to our father, his brothers and his sister, Harriet, were loaded. So were his second wife, Inez, and Harris Erb. Harris had sold the rental properties and the theatre years ago, but he still lived alone in the family mansion in Liverpool.

I told my sister about Margaret's forgiveness list, about Harris and Laddie being on it. "I thought Dad was on it because he had the nerve to marry Mum," I said. "Maybe losing Mum's money had something to do with it too."

"That was part of it," Ardith said. "But there was something else."

"What?"

Ardith turned to the third page of the will without answering.

"There's a section here about the disposition of furniture," she said. "You're to have the maple furniture and I'm to have the oak sideboard and butter churn."

The sideboard and butter churn were early Loyalist pieces from the Burchell side of the family. Ardith had done her doctoral thesis on the United Empire Loyalists. She had a houseful of U.E.L. furniture: blanket chests, washstands, a spinning wheel.

"Everything else is to be given away at our discretion," Ardith said. "I must say Margaret was methodical about her affairs. I suppose it came from all her years in the classroom: keeping school registers, recording marks, filling out report cards, making sure there are no loose ends."

"What was it?" I said.

"You're not going to like it," Ardith told me.

"Tell me."

"Well, after Mum was killed, before Dad and Inez became serious, Dad asked Margaret to marry him."

"Did she tell you that?"

"Dad told me. He was in his cups at the time."

"Maybe he was in his cups when he asked her."

"It's not uncommon for a widower to marry his sister-in-law," Ardith reminded me. "Dad was lonely and needed the money."

Ardith was right about my not liking it. I thought there was something shameful about our father's lack of pride. I thought he should have known Margaret disliked him. I thought he should have been more loyal to our mother.

Margaret's committal service was brief. There was a raw wind, fast-moving clouds, splatters of rain. One of Margaret's Quaker friends brought a bouquet of mayflowers and put them in a jar on top of the grave, beside our mother's. Margaret's urn was placed into a small, square hole, the sod put back and tamped down. The United Church minister, who had not known Margaret, said a few words about Margaret Burchell, about her long teaching career, the help she had given the boat people, her kindness to the sick and the needy. I had wondered about having this minister, but Ardith said we had to remember that our aunt was part of the town. After the service, about thirty townspeople came to Margaret's apartment for sandwiches and tea.

That evening there was a prayer service in one of the Quaker homes, a white farmhouse set in an apple orchard about fifteen minutes' drive from town. I took the books on self-help and the occult with me and set them on the table in the farm kitchen. A bread-maker myself, I recognized the warm, yeasty odour of newly baked bread. Ardith and I followed our host, a brown-haired middle-aged man who intro-

duced himself as Ted Bowering, down the narrow hall into
the front room with its high ceilings and hardwood floor.
There was an ivy in the dormer window, a rocking chair, a
black woodstove set up on bricks. Nine Quakers sat in a semi-
circle around the stove. There were two chairs for Ardith and
me. Except for brief introductions, no one spoke. We sat and
stared out the window at the dark, furrowed field, listening
to the snap and spit of the fire. After a while, Ted Bowering
took a square of paper from his sweater pocket and unfolded
it. The awkward way he kept shifting in his chair and his
broad-knuckled, chapped hands told me he was used to working outside, ploughing fields, mending fences, splitting wood.
Ted cleared his throat and read from the paper. Margaret, he
said, had a musical laugh. That was what he remembered best
about her. Sometimes, if a joke or a situation were particularly
amusing, she would get carried away. Her eyes would stream
and she would laugh louder than anybody. I had forgotten
this, how Margaret snorted and giggled when she thought
something was funny. Ted folded the paper and put it away
and we sat in silence, thinking. Then a Dutch woman with
white hair and a narrow, patrician nose, whose name was
Henny Schmidt, spoke about Margaret, the bird-watcher.
There wasn't a bird she couldn't identify. Before her health
deteriorated, Margaret and she used to go on long walks
through the woods and fields, and Margaret would repeat
different bird calls. She was particularly good at imitating the
black-capped chickadee. This testimony was followed by
another silence. Then someone else spoke, this time about
Margaret's generosity. And so it went round the circle.

   During the silences I thought about my aunt, what she had
kept, what she had given away, what she had hidden, what
she had revealed. I thought about her relentless drive to
improve and instruct, her fierce will to survive. I thought, I
wanted to think, that all the snooping and rooting through
my aunt's life had probably been a haphazard and slapdash
attempt to find a fitting testimony for her. I told myself that

if I hadn't pried, I wouldn't have recognized the testimony when it presented itself.

The day before, when I was burning Margaret's material in the barrel behind the hotel, a scrap of paper had fallen from a sheaf of notes and fluttered to the ground. I picked it up. It was a list intended to help my aunt get herself through the night. My guess was that she had used this list recently, when she couldn't sleep because of breathing difficulties. I put the list in my sweater pocket, the same sweater I was wearing now. Sitting in the warmth of the farmhouse, I decided to share this list with the Quakers. When the last of them had spoken, I took the scrap of paper out of my pocket and read:

To Make Better Use of Conscious and Unconscious
Time

9-12 p.m. – *Sleep*

12-2 a.m. – *Stay Awake, Snack (tea, crackers, yogurt).*
Listen to Mozart tape as reward.

2-5 a.m. – *Sleep.*

5 a.m. – *Get up. Put on clothes, makeup. Drink*
warm water. Sit at desk.
WRITE.

Point No Point

When Madge was a child, she became lost in the woods. She would have been about seven or eight. It was during the war. Earlier that spring a small plane piloted by two young airmen had gone down in a thickly wooded area near Beech Hill Road not far from Liverpool. The airmen had been aiming for a field close by an abandoned farmhouse and had ploughed into the woods instead. The bodies had long since been taken away. A truck had come for the fuselage and wings. There were tire tracks and flattened bushes where the truck had gone in. People went out there on Sundays to see what could be found in the way of souvenirs. Because Madge's father and Buddy Titus worked shiftwork at the paper mill, they were able to go out on a weekday afternoon. Madge would have been taken along to make sure the house was kept quiet while her mother had a nap. In Grade One Madge went to school half days, so maybe she was closer to six, young enough to hold her father's hand as they followed the rough path left by the truck.

The plane crashed near the bottom of a hill. There were trees with their tops snapped off, bits and pieces of wreckage all over, on top of ferns and moss. Laddie and Buddy discussed how they thought the plane had come down, at what angle, what happened when it actually hit. They walked around, drawing pictures in the air with their hands.

Madge had to pee. Laddie told her to go behind a tree. The trees were tall and skinny, Buddy would see her if she went behind a tree. Madge saw some bushes at the top of the hill, beyond a fallen log. She walked up the hill and climbed over the log. Her father was busy talking and didn't see her go. As Madge was squatting behind the bushes, she saw a brown rabbit hop along a path in front of her. This was a deer path, not a rabbit path. Madge pulled up her underpants and followed the path through the bushes. The bushes were far apart, so it was easy to do this. The path ended, spread out, became three paths going off in different directions. There was no sign of the rabbit. Madge went along the path to her left and followed it some distance until she came to some trees. She had never been lost, so it didn't occur to her to be afraid. Behind her were shapeless bushes splashed with sunlight; ahead were dark, narrow trees lined up like soldiers. Madge was about to turn around when she noticed sunlight coming through a slit in the trees. She walked toward it. The slit widened as she squeezed through it, turning sideways so the brittle spokes wouldn't scratch her arms.

She found herself in a small, grassy clearing. It couldn't have been more than twenty feet across. There was a large, flat rock near the centre. Madge sat on the rock and ran her hand across the grey lichen spread over the top like a rough tablecloth. The sun was directly overhead, warming her arms and legs.

After a while she got up and wandered around the clearing. She saw a scattering of yellow toadstools on the grass. She knelt down and pretended to be under them. She heard a voice. She knew it was her father's. She didn't answer but crouched lower beneath the toadstools. Something inside her head had shifted and clicked into place. This wasn't anything defiant or mischievous. She wasn't playing hide-and-seek. It was more like indifference. She had completely shut out her father. She had put herself in a place where he couldn't come, where no one could get through. It was a secluded, peaceful place, suspended in the warm air like a large soap bubble. The bubble floated up and hovered above the circle of trees.

Of course she was spanked for this. Laddie steamed across the grass, sat down on the stone slab, and put her over his knee. When they got home, she was told what a nuisance she'd been, that with the time he'd wasted looking for her, he'd only managed to find a single ball-bearing. Buddy Titus had found the propeller.

One spring, forty years later, Madge is on the other side of the country walking through the woods at Point No Point, on the south side of Vancouver Island. Since moving to the West Coast, Madge has come to think of Point No Point as a place of celebration. She and Stan come here every spring to celebrate the day they met twelve years ago at a farmers' market. By then they were both divorced, their previous partners remarried, though not to the same people involved in their marriage breakdowns. Between them, Madge and Stan have nine children. One of Stan's sons lives in Winnipeg, another in St. John's; his other three children live in the States. Theo, Madge's eldest son, is in Guelph studying agriculture; Alison is in Montreal studying French. Madge's other two children, Shelley and Eric, live nearer, in Vancouver. Recently Shelley has got herself engaged to Travis Stiles, an anthropology student at the University of British Columbia. He and Shelley are coming across on the ferry this afternoon and will be here in time for a supper intended to celebrate their engagement.

Madge is walking along the cliff, high above the water, Stan following not far behind. They have just come from having tea. At Point No Point, an English tea is served in a glassed-in porch. The tea comes in a china pot. There are cups and saucers, date bread, tea biscuits, cake. The woman who showed them to a table was dressed in a tweed suit, a virgin-wool sweater. She wore a pearl necklace and stout Oxfords. After they had finished their tea, she asked them to sign the guest book and showed them the photograph on the wall. It was an aerial photograph of Point No Point. "One of the earliest surveyors named it," the woman explained. "From one direction you can see the point, from another, you can't. It's an optical illusion caused by several points that block each other."

Every year Madge hears this and every year she makes several false starts before finding the point. Not that she and Stan are serious about finding it now; they are more interested in walking off their tea.

They enter a narrow, green tunnel that cuts through the salal bushes growing over the headland. There are miles of these tunnels, forming a network of narrow paths leading down to the beaches and coves. The point is at the end of one of these tunnels, but Madge can't remember which tunnel leads to it. It's as if the path to the point shifts its location each time she comes, switching positions with another path, tacking on new side-trips and detours which distract and confuse. She's decided the point is something she must stumble on, that will elude her if she tries too hard to find it.

She chooses a path that leads upward for several hundred yards before arcing down to a broad stretch of shoreline where there is a beach house containing tables, benches, a firepit. To the left of this house is a huge, moss-covered log. Spruce and ivy have grown around the log, concealing it. Madge sees an opening and comes out on a small beach enclosed by overhanging alders and willows. This is the beach where she once played hopscotch with Nonie. She takes off her shoes and splashes through the water to a rocky promontory that separates this beach from the larger one beyond. The water is cold against her feet, but not as cold as the beach where she spent her childhood summers. Although there are beaches in Nova Scotia where the water is as warm, if not warmer, than the one on which Madge is standing, she thinks of the Atlantic coast as cold and instructive, a place of harsh realities and unequivocal truths. The wind is raw, the coastline spare, the trees stunted; there is the sharp sting of salt in the air.

The West Coast has a soft underbelly. The winds are gentler, less demanding. The air is mild, scented with flowering trees, overgrown with salmonberry, wild broom, holly, rhododendron. Cedar and Douglas fir grow straight and tall, becoming gigantic and mysterious. This is a place where borders dissolve, where there are contradictions, talking trees, enchanted masks, mermaids.

When Stan catches up to her, Madge is sitting on a promontory looking across the water. She sees the top of Mount Olympus, white and spectral, rising beyond the far shore like a backdrop sketched in chalk. Stan has also taken off his shoes. He sits down beside her, sticks his feet into a small tidal pool. He and Madge stare out over the water, watching the swell of waves nudge floating logs toward the shore.

After a while, Stan says, "See that rock out there." He points to a rock that is in a line with the end of the promontory in deep water. Each time a wave rolls over the rock, it disappears, reappearing after the wave has passed. "There was a mermaid sitting on that rock earlier. I saw her when I was down on the beach. She must have slipped into the water as I was climbing up here."

Stan claims to have seen a mermaid in Puget Sound. Another off Pender Island.

"Maybe she's gone to join her sister mermaids," Madge said.

"Never," Stan says. "Mermaids are solitary, romantic creatures. She was probably looking for me." He delivers this straight while looking over the water, arms resting on crooked knees.

Looking sideways, Madge sees a thick mat of kinky grey hair, a chin that is only now beginning to thicken, a nose with a prominent bridge that prevents his glasses from slipping down. He shades his eyes with one hand.

"I don't see her magic cap," he says. "She must have taken it with her. If she had left it behind, I would have gone out there, put it on, and swum away with her. That's all I ever wanted to do, swim away with a mermaid." He sighs, "Missed again."

"What did she look like?"

"Oh, they all have blonde hair," he says. "Didn't you know? Long, blonde hair and green eyes."

Madge has recently dyed her hair black.

"Do you know that one of the first sightings of a mermaid in North America was in St. John's in 1620?" Stan says.

Whenever they travel, this is the sort of information Stan digs out of museums and libraries. Stan's van has taken him across Canada to places like Kaslo, Batoche, Little Heart's Ease. Next year he wants to drive up the Alaska Highway to Anchorage. Madge hasn't decided yet if she'll go with him. When Stan goes off alone on a trip or to visit one of his children, Madge ignores her neighbours and the telephone. She holes up inside the walls of her townhouse, a secluded clearing where the doorbell is as distant as a cowbell in an alpine meadow. This is when she works, eating at irregular hours, wearing the same clothes for days on end, staying up half the night. She can go a long time living like this, missing no one. She thinks there's some danger in this, that she might get to like it too much, that she might turn loneliness into a profession like her Aunt Margaret. Madge is unwilling to go this far, to deny herself indulgences, pleasures like this weekend, most of all to deny herself Stan.

She and Stan put on their shoes, scramble down the promontory, and go through the hole under the log. This time they take a small, winding path that enters the woods behind the beach house. The path follows a small brook that spills over moss-covered rocks and around clumps of fern. They pass dark caves of uprooted trees. High above, giant firs rock and groan. The forest floor is damp, spongy with wet leaves and decaying wood. The air is a dusky green colour; not much sunlight penetrates this far down. When they gain the headland, Stan, who has been walking around, quickens his pace.

"If we're going to catch a salmon for supper, we'd better get a move on," he says.

While Stan is getting out his gear, seeing the proprietor about renting a boat, Madge phones Laddie, who is in Nova Scotia in a nursing home he's trying to get out of. The nursing home is well run, staffed by women who know how to joke with her father, who go along with his stories and complaints. Her father says he would rather die someplace else, he has no particular place in mind. Madge likes to get the phone call over with early, so the weight of his dissatisfaction won't spoil the weekend.

Laddie is seventy-nine. His memory is going. He has delusions. Today when she calls, he has a story about two specialists he met in a hotel lobby who told him they wanted to put a needle up his rectum so they could scrape out something that was growing there. For someone as prudish as Laddie, this story comes as a surprise. Her father asked these doctors for their credentials. He wanted to see their authority written on paper – proof that they were what they said they were, not imposters. When the doctors couldn't produce the evidence, Laddie told them to go away; they weren't to lay a finger on him. Her father had a good laugh over that one. He wasn't about to be pushed around by anybody pretending to be anybody else.

Laddie will get a lot of mileage out of this story, telling and retelling it whenever she phones. He will change the details. Perhaps it won't be his rectum, but his throat. Perhaps the so-called specialists will turn up at the nursing home, not the hotel lobby, and speak to him there. Despite refashioning, the story will have Laddie's stubbornness and recalcitrance at the root of it, his need to have the upper hand. And each time he tells it, the story will have the terrifying urgency of a dream.

Last month, Laddie had another story. When Madge flew to Nova Scotia in May to visit him, he told her his wife, Inez, was having an affair behind his back. According to her father, Inez had put him in the nursing home so she could carry on with a man from Mahone Bay who spent the weekends with her. This man had gotten her pregnant. Inez is seventy-six and has heart trouble. When Madge told her father it would have required divine intervention for Inez to become pregnant, Laddie became angry and told her graphically what had transpired. Madge laughed. That was a mistake. This was a serious story about betrayal and deceit. Gone were the old stories: his sister-in-law stealing a wedding present, his brothers threatening to lock him out of his rope-making plant, the Royal Bank manager telling merchants in town he was a poor risk. Walls have collapsed, openings have been sealed, tunnels blocked off. Madge's father doesn't remember the ugly scenes with her mother, scenes of recrimination and despair. All of this has gone underground, percolated down through cracks and fissures, and is now buried under layers too thick to penetrate. There is a deep pool beneath all this, a residue of bitterness and savagery. Every once in a while, not often, some of this will find its way to the surface, will belch up like a sour smelling gas.

"What's wrong with you that you couldn't hold on to your husband?" he'll ask Madge, referring to her divorce. Madge is the only one on Laddie's side of the family who's divorced. Or he will make a remark about the lines around her neck, the brown spots on the back of her hands. "You're no spring chicken, that's for sure."

During these visits, Madge takes her father for drives in a rented car. These trips are a family ritual, a carry-over from Madge's childhood. When her mother was alive, their family used to go on Sunday drives. After a heavy noon dinner, their mother would make sandwiches from the leftover chicken or roast and a thermos of tea. About four o'clock, Laddie would come from work and take them for a drive over back country roads, most of which were unmarked or had crooked signs with arrows pointing the wrong way. They quickly became lost. Entreaties to stop at a farmhouse and make inquiries were rebuffed. Madge's father continued to drive until they came to some small confectionery store that was open to pick up business from people such as themselves. It was usually part of someone's house and had a large calico mongrel dozing outside the door. Laddie would park the car, go inside the

store to ask for directions, and disappear for up to an hour.
Madge's mother and Ardith would toot the car horn, slam
doors, send Madge inside to tell their father to hurry up. These
tactics seldom worked, because it meant Laddie had to stay
inside longer to save face. He regarded Sunday drives as
opportunities to meet his customers; most of these places
stocked the all-purpose rope Laddie made. When Laddie eventually came out, bathed in surprised innocence, ignoring their
sullen faces and snippy airs, he would explain that he and that
fella inside had merely been chewing the fat. They would
return home more or less the same way they had come, eating
their supper by the side of the road.

These drives stopped abruptly the day Ardith refused to set
foot in the car. Madge thinks she herself might have continued
these drives until she moved away from home. She always
found something to interest her, a meandering stream, bulrushes, a snake warming itself on a rock.

On the last visit to her father Madge had driven him to the
beach. Laddie's balance was poor. He held onto her arm until
he got off the boardwalk and onto the hard, flat sand. He
managed to walk all the way to the end of the beach, where
the river entered the sea, where sandpipers skittered through
flattened waves and gulls splattered their olive-streaked white-
wash on the sand. On the way back to town, they stopped at
a snack bar for lobsterburgers and pie.

When they got back to the nursing home, before they went
inside, they took another walk down the street. It was early
evening. There were lingering patches of light on roofs and
trees. They passed a wooded area of elm and maple whose
branches were leafing out in a burst of new green. There was
a creaking sound coming from the other side of the trees.
Madge's father stopped shuffling.

"Listen," he said. His hearing was acute.

Madge looked through the screen of branches into a narrow
grass clearing. A young girl was using a swing. Whenever the

swing went up, the sun caught her hair in a nimbus of gold. With each movement, there was a slight, almost imperceptible, shift of colour and light. Madge thought of Monet's paintings, the changes in light, the gentle blurring of colour.

"Imagine that!" her father exclaimed. "Isn't that something!" He stood there, shaking his head and staring at the girl, swaying dangerously on his feet.

The creaking stopped. The girl slid off the swing and ran off somewhere.

"That reminds me," Madge's father said. He looked in the direction the girl had gone, as if he expected her to reappear. "That reminds me," he said again.

He didn't look cross or upset that he had forgotten what he wanted to say. He wasn't gesturing impatiently for Madge to prompt him, as he sometimes did. He looked bemused, transported. Madge thought something inside him had flown away with the girl, had flown over the trees and rooftops, back to another place. Or perhaps it wasn't back at all, perhaps place didn't have anything to do with it, or time. Borders had disappeared. Madge felt there was no forward or backward, up, down, or sideways. She thought that inside her father's head, boundaries didn't exist, they didn't exist any more.

Travis has given Shelley a sapphire engagement ring. As soon as his Honda rolls into the parking lot, Madge, who has been watching from the window, hurries outside and heads for the passenger side of the car. Shelley gets out and holds up her left hand, watching her mother's face with the same shy, hopeful expression she used when presenting a floppy valentine made from a paper doily and red cardboard. The sapphire is flat and octagonal. It looks expensive without being ostentatious. One point in Travis's favour is that he has good taste. He knows how to display quality without flamboyance. This conservativeness has been good for Shelley, whose previous boyfriend was a pothead who used to panhandle in the parking lot of the Bayshore Inn.

"What a magnificent colour," Madge says, "a clear, watery blue."

"It's my birthstone," Shelley says.

Madge has forgotten this.

Travis, who has come round the front of the car, gives Madge a peck on the cheek, then puts an arm around Shelley's shoulders, leaning on her. Travis is several inches over six feet and thin. Madge has noticed that he leans on any object that is shoulder height: a mantelpiece, a bookshelf, her daughter.

"I figured I'd kill two birds with one stone," Travis jokes. "I was hoping you'd get her a fur coat for Christmas and we could go halves on her teeth."

Shelley bares her teeth at him and jabs an elbow into his ribs. Shelley's teeth are small and straight. So is her nose. Her hair is natural blonde. Last fall Shelley was approached by a modelling agency which offered to pay for a course if she would sign a contract. She refused. She said she didn't want to get into a rat race, to be flying off to fashion shows in Toronto, Tokyo, and New York. She wanted to stay near Travis, to continue with her job. Shelley works as a desk clerk at the Hotel Sylvia.

Travis gets the luggage out of the car, one small bag because they are only staying the night. Travis is entering a windsurfing race on Sunday.

Stan is waiting at the top of the stairs. He gives Shelley a hug, shakes hands with Travis.

They have the upper half of the cabin, two adjoining rooms and a kitchenette. There's a balcony with a view of the water. This is where Stan has barbecued the salmon he bought in the fish store in Sooke. He didn't get so much as a bite this afternoon. Madge has cooked wild rice, mashed sweet potatoes, made a salad. Stan opens a bottle of wine and they toast Shelley and Travis, clinking glasses round the circle. They do this joyously, rambunctiously, spilling wine onto the carpet.

Stan pours more wine, lifts his glass, and shouts, "May they live well together!"

This is the light-hearted conviviality that Madge was hoping for, a heedless, merry celebration. Madge will celebrate anything, any accomplishment, any piece of good news will do, the new paint job on Stan's van, the arrival of a queen for her beehive, her son Eric's promotion. Eric has managed to work his way up to the position of headwaiter in a Vancouver steak house. Alison, Shelley's older sister, has gained nine pounds, but that isn't the sort of occasion Madge celebrates. Since moving from Toronto to Montreal, Alison's anorexia has improved. She has continued to gain weight. Several times during the past few years, she has gained weight then lost it again. For the last six months she has managed to keep it on.

Stan brings the salmon inside on a cookie sheet, which he lifts high on one hand as if he were balancing a platter. The others are already seated, their plates heaped with vegetables and rice. Stan lowers the cookie sheet and holds it while Madge and Shelley help themselves to the salmon. When it's Travis's turn, Stan says, "I wouldn't eat too much of this if I were you, Travis. This salmon pulled the boat over two miles before I could land him. He was that strong."

"A super salmon," Madge puts in.

"If you were to eat too much of his powerful flesh, you'd be up all night," Stan says slyly.

Shelley blushes.

"I thought fish provided brain-power, not muscle-power," Travis says severely.

Madge wonders if this is why Eric doesn't like Travis. Eric could have driven over on the ferry with Travis and Shelley. He had the weekend off. He told Madge on the phone that he was helping a friend move to a new apartment.

Travis is in his last year of anthropology. Next year, he plans to take law. He still lives with his parents in North Vancouver, in the British Properties. He and Shelley get together in her apartment, seldom in his parents' house, because of his younger brothers and sisters. Travis is a conscientious student. He has told Shelley that, until he finishes law school, he cannot see her more than twice a week.

"Did you know that some of the coastal native tribes used to consider masks, dances, and poems their most valuable commodity?" Madge asks in a gay, party voice. She doesn't expect anyone to ask how she came by this information, which she read in an art magazine. "How's that for an enlightened view?"

"That's not quite accurate, Madge," Travis says kindly. "It's true that masks, dances, and poems were highly valued by the Haida, but their most prized possession was the copper. It was the most sought-after object. Before the potlatch was outlawed, one copper could bring as much as sixteen thousands button blankets. That was the price tag."

"Price tag," Madge says. "I thought potlatches were barter."

"They often gave away cash along with other possessions," Travis explains. "The first day, a man might give away one hundred dollars cash, a few sacks of flour. The second day, he might give away furniture, wooden boxes, and trunks. The third day, it might be two hundred dollars cash, button blankets, canoes, sewing machines, adding more each day until the last day, when he got rid of everything he owned: clothes, washtubs, beds."

"Sounds like something we should all do more often," Madge says, "disassociate ourselves from possessions."

Stan gets up, pours more wine. As he moves behind Madge's chair, he places his thumb against the nape of her neck and presses down gently.

"The Haida didn't disassociate themselves from possessions," Travis says. "They regarded possessions as weapons. Potlatching was a kind of power. It was territorial. You determined your boundaries by the size of your property, property meaning possessions. The more possessions you amassed and gave away, the greater your power. Eventually the price of a copper became so high a man would plunge himself into penury in order to pay. It was runaway inflation. That's why the government stepped in." Travis shakes his head. "When you look at those coppers today, you wonder why they were considered so valuable. Masks, yes, they're works of art, but coppers? I can't get over how ordinary they look, that anyone would . . . "

"Travis," Shelley says, "you're talking too much."

She says this with difficulty, staring down at her plate, but at least she says it, which is a good sign.

"Sorry, Shell," he says. "I guess I got carried away, but it was Madge who got me started."

Later, after they have gone to bed, Madge hears her daughter moan on the other side of the door. The moan continues for what seems to Madge a cruel, almost punishing, length of time, ending with a whimper which Madge associates with a young animal caught in a trap. She doesn't know if she herself makes this sound.

"Must be the salmon," Stan murmurs.

Madge lies beside him in the moonlight, watching the breeze filling the curtains like sails. Now that her daughter is grown, Madge cannot bring herself to make love within her hearing. This is coy, prudish, even miserly, since she nurtures the belief that if she and Stan were also to make love, all four of them would wake up in the morning smiling and cheerful, full of generosity and affection. They would make breakfast together: Stan cooking bacon and eggs, Travis buttering toast, Shelley and Madge getting the coffee ready, setting the table, slipping past each other in the tiny kitchen with a benign and comfortable ease.

Early next morning, Madge and Stan dress quietly in order not to waken Shelley and Travis, and go outside for a walk. The sky is clear, the sun well up, but it's still too early for yellow light to penetrate the woods. The salal tunnels are a dark, forest green, almost black in places where they meet.

"This time," Stan says, in the lead today, "I'm taking us straight to the point, no detours, no mistakes or false starts."

And he does. He chooses the lower tunnel, which plunges downhill toward the water. He ignores the paths going off to the right, the windows of light opening toward the sea. He

continues inside the tunnel until he comes to a small bluff
overgrown with wild roses and holly. Here he follows a path
down a muddy embankment. Madge sees one of the red
benches, set along the cliff edge to make a vantage point. The
path right-angles sharply and crosses a Japanese bridge that
spans a deep cleft in the cliffside. The bridge itself is light
green, the soft, muted colour of weathered copper. The railing
has been painted with so many coats of bright vermilion, it's
taken on the shiny brittleness of lacquer.

They stand on the bridge, looking down at the clear water.
The water gathers and recedes as the tide moves in. On the
other side of the bridge is a flat area, covered by waist-high
salal kept trim by its exposure to the wind. It looks as if a
formal garden of paths and hedges has been built on the headland. The point itself is an enormous slab of smooth, grey
rock jutting into the sea. The rock is low, which explains why
it's hidden by the higher promontories on either side, and bare
except for another red bench set beneath a sitka spruce. Cradled in this slab is a small pool of water with a thick fringe of
yellow scum around its rim. Madge sees tadpoles the size of
carpet tacks darting through the water.

They go to the end of the point and lie down on their backs,
heads pillowed on their arms, listening to the waves wash
against the rocks. Madge sits up, takes off her shoes and socks,
and tests the water with her toes.

Stan lies back, hands behind his head, and watches her.

"How does the engagement strike you the morning after?"
he says.

"Well, I'm glad Shelley's happy," Madge says, "but I think
I should warn her before it's too late."

"Warn her about what?" Stan says irritably. "Just because
you're wary of marriage doesn't mean she should be."

"Warn her about taking better care of herself."

Before her ex-husband left, Madge had never changed a
tire, made a mortgage payment, replaced a tap washer. She
wouldn't drive on the highway unless Doug was with her,
never questioned being put on an allowance, did not protest,

during the births of her two sons, when her legs were held together until the doctor arrived. Now, when Madge thinks about those years, she's amazed how much she put up with, how little she demanded for herself.

"I'd feel better if she were committed to something besides their relationship," Madge says. "Travis certainly is."

"You mean a career."

"Yes," Madge says, though she doesn't think of her own work as a career. She thinks of it being more pervasive than that, like sleeping and breathing, something she can't live without. Madge thinks of a career as something you do as a separate self, something that comes with a blueprint, a list of guidelines. Madge doesn't want to be hemmed in by schedules, consumed with ambition, every ounce of laziness and spontaneity squeezed out of her. She has enough money. She got the house when she and Doug divorced. There was the inheritance from Margaret. Madge is frugal with money. She knows how to spin things out, make them go a long way. She buys clothes from thrift shops, gets her neighbour Em to trim her hair, grows her own vegetables. Now that her children have left home and she can spend more time on her work, she's able to support herself.

"I don't want her living through Travis is all," Madge says. "I want her to make room for herself."

Stan doesn't answer. His eyes are closed. He's drifting someplace else.

Madge has her own places. She closes her eyes and imagines herself slipping into the water, growing a long, seductive tail, swimming out to sea. She swims far out, away from land, entering an endless, watery clearing where there are no boundaries or enclosures, where the horizon is a shimmering filament overhead. She swims through the strange buzzing silence, moving weightlessly, kicking her powerful tail, her body undulating beneath the waves. If she stayed out here long enough, she would never go back. She's enchanted by her own muteness, by the flowing gestures of the mime, the soft, filtered light. She doesn't think about the children who once slid from her womb. She doesn't wonder where they are, whether they have swum away to other oceans, other lands. She doesn't wonder where Stan is, or her father. The point is, when she's swimming like this, none of this matters, none of this matters any more.

When Madge finally swings around, it isn't disenchantment or defeat that reels her in, sleep-drowned and yawning on Point No Point, but something as mundane and familiar as a voice complaining about the weather.

"The wind's up," Stan says. "It's cold. Let's go back."

He shivers, gets to his feet.

Still yawning, still slumberous, Madge sits up and slowly puts on her socks and shoes. She's still on the edge of not caring whether she stays or goes.

When they return to the cabin, they find plates sticky with salmon bones and cold rice stacked higgledy-piggledy beside the sink, the cookie sheet coated with buttery grease, night-clothes thrown across the chair. Nothing in the room has moved, but it's not the same place. While they've been gone, the sun has risen higher in the east. Now a narrow wedge of sunlight enters the room between the curtains, making a path of gold across the floor to the unmade bed.

The Train Family

Years ago, after I moved from the East to the West Coast, I started dreaming about railway tracks. I didn't have this dream while I was on the tracks, travelling, but only after I had been here a while, after I had bought a townhouse and my children and I had settled ourselves in Victoria. In other words, the dream began when I had reached the end of the line and was looking back from where I'd come.

In my dream I'm in the middle of the country, on the prairies, sleeping in the lower berth with my daughters. While I'm asleep, I'm dreaming the tracks are being taken up as soon as we pass over them. There are workmen in heavy jackets and peaked caps outside in the dark. They're picking up the railway ties, carrying them off to build houses, barns, fences. I see iron rails, loose and disjointed as dinosaur bones, sliding into gullies and ditches. The earth closes over, grows miles of rough prairie grass. You understand I was dreaming about dreaming, that the panic came when I wanted to wake up and couldn't, when I wanted to get off the train to stop the workmen but was immobilized in my berth.

Stan and I have talked about this dream. He says it shows my contrariness, that just when I finally get myself going forward, I want to turn around and go back. He says this jokingly, fondly. It's meant to tease me about being a home-

body, of not wanting to spend half my life on the road with
him. I tell him the dream has to do with what I left behind.
Ever since I drifted out of childhood, one way and another
I've been trying to get back. I see childhood as the wellspring
of pure being, a source of unbridled self-centredness and joy.

It's true men have been taking up the tracks in places like
Catalina, Port Mouton, Blissfield, you can pick them off
across the country. I sometimes wonder what the railway has
done with the defunct passenger cars: the dining cars, the club
cars, the cabooses. I like to imagine them as being regrouped
in a place of their own. Caboosetown. No Petro-Canada or
Midas Muffler here. It's strictly residential and pedestrian, the
paths named after places where the train no longer goes. I see
window boxes, picket fences, shutters. Even when they are
on the end of the train, cabooses look as if they were meant
to be cottages. In Caboosetown, wheels are out of sight, hidden behind latticework, hollyhocks, shrubbery. Maybe this is
a retirement colony, one of those busily humming communi-
ties with an active Golden Age club. There are a lot of pastel
colours, hearts and flowers, angels stencilled on the walls.
One of the passenger cars is a movie theatre. The dining car
is, of course, a restaurant. The mayor and the minister use
the club car for ceremonies, weddings, burials. Though no
one is travelling anywhere that you can see, they are unwilling
to give up their rites of passage.

When I was thirteen and living in Sydney Mines, Cape Breton,
I had a train family. This was during the time when my father
was trying to make a go of his rope-making business and there
was a lot of uncertainty about money. There were four children in my imaginary family, a boy and a girl, a boy and a
girl, in that order. There was a mother and a father. They
lived in a caboose. I wasn't in the family. I was their manager.
These people were faceless. They had no personalities. They
were cardboard figures. Age and sex were important only
because of the clothes they wore. I ordered their clothes. I

can't remember ordering food; apparently this family never ate. I ordered clothes for two seasons, spring/summer, winter/fall. Sometimes I gave in and allowed a small indulgence: an Easter hat, a corduroy weskit in forest green, a magenta shorty coat. Mostly I was strict with my purchases and stuck to the basics, underwear and pyjamas for everyone, skirts and blouses for the girls, pants and shirts for the boys. The mother wore a cotton-print housedress, the father a windbreaker and trousers in cotton drill. I didn't have a job picked out for the father. He wasn't a coal miner, I knew that much. I wanted to keep his clothes clean. He wasn't a doctor or a dentist. They made more money than I had to spend. Probably I saw him as a telegraph operator, a ticket agent, some job connected with the railway.

At first I parked the caboose in a vacant lot next to the graveyard, above Greener's Cliff. When winter came, I worried about the wind sweeping off the ice in the Gulf of St. Lawrence. I moved the caboose out of town and into the woods, where the family would have enough fuel for their stove and there was shelter from the weather. I had never been inside a caboose and imagined it larger than it was. I saw space for two bedrooms curtained off, girls on one side, boys on the other. The mother and father slept in the living room on a dropback davenport. Each bedroom had a double bed and a chest of drawers: one drawer each for inner wear; one drawer for outer wear. The clothing and furniture were ordered from Eaton's catalogue. I spent a lot of time making lists. When a new catalogue came out, I abandoned my old lists and made up new ones. I was bewitched by newness, by yards of unsullied paper stamped with patches of gaudy colour. The hypnotic instructions drew me in: *move softly in supple rayons, weather the winter in style, spot a winner.* I mooned over the captions in the girls' wear section: *top honours, lively twosome, chipper checks.* I was wooed by matching outfits: a cherry red tam and red mitts, a velveteen hood and velveteen muff, twin sweater sets.

I wanted a matching living-room set. It wasn't as friendly as odds and ends of furniture, but it was more hopeful. A living-room set invited people to sit down together and have serious conversation. It put order and decorum into their lives. I wanted my family to have a wine velour chesterfield with two matching chairs, a walnut coffee table and walnut end tables, all of which I could buy for $183.55. If I bought this set, I would have to get rid of the davenport to make room for the chesterfield. There was something indecent about expecting parents to share a narrow chesterfield. There was no other place inside the caboose for them to sleep. They would have to go. I orphaned the children and revised the budget. The children didn't miss their parents, but I did. They thrived on adversity, but the responsibility of supporting the family on my own put too big a strain on me. I needed a father to bring home the bacon, to balance the budget. There was no question of the mother going out to work. She had to put the wash through the wringer on Mondays. She had to darn socks and scrub the floor.

I took away the matching set and reinstated the parents' along with the davenport. Now the family had to make do with leatherette hassocks and an unfinished drop-leaf table with the legs sawn off. In struggling with these decisions, it never occurred to me to shop in the town stores. The management of my family had to be carried out in secrecy, in the privacy of my bedroom. Besides, even in a poor town like Sydney Mines, stores provided more choices than I could handle. As my train family became older and the children outgrew their clothes, more money was required to keep them dressed. I had to have more than a cretonne curtain separating the girls from the boys. I worried how I would manage these changes. I picked at my food, bit my fingernails, lost sleep. I thought about moving my family into a house I passed on my way to school, but it didn't suit. The house was too grand, too prosperous-looking. I was afraid that, if I moved my family into so large a house, my budget would get out of hand. I looked around town for something more modest, a bungalow, a four-room cottage. There were plenty of those in town, but I rejected them all. The truth was I couldn't imagine my family living anywhere but inside the caboose.

My father wasn't at all like the father in the train family. My father didn't like working for anyone else. He ran his own show. He started his rope-making business, his spice-bottling plant, got into real estate, kept a second-hand store, whatever he could do to keep himself employed and support a family. I don't think my father was suited to supporting a family. It put too big a strain on him. He wanted too much for us. I don't think he was suited to business. He had been brought up in a business family in Cape Breton, entrepreneurial Scots stock, people who talked about figures in two colours, red and black, who linked pride with being self-employed, being beholden to no one, marching to your own tune.

My father kept a ledger for his accounts. It was a heavy book with a grey cloth cover, steel rivets on the spine. Inside were alphabetized dividers with green leather tabs embossed in gold. My father carried this ledger with him wherever he went. He kept it in a brown, zippered briefcase my mother gave him one Christmas. When business wasn't going well, my father would sit at the dining-room table with the ledger and overhaul his accounting system. He would make new categories, label more pages, move figures from one column to another, so that what had once been a debit would now become a credit. After working for hours at the table, he would stand up and pace the floor, chain-smoking, gesturing with his hands as he explained the new system to my mother, who sat on the chesterfield listening, nodding occasionally. He used words like depreciation, promissory note, accounts receivable. I didn't know what most of these words meant. I wasn't interested in them, but I understood that once again my father had managed to move money from one place to another and, in so doing, had created more than he had before. I knew that he was feeling pleased in the same way my mother did after she rearranged the furniture in the living room. I understood the power of this, that by transforming the room, she had transformed herself. She had made a fresh start, given herself another chance.

Somewhere along the line my mother had chosen to sit on the chesterfield and listen to my father. She could do this because she could see her life stretching ahead of her on the tracks in a way my father couldn't. My mother could have left my father, left all that anxiety and worry about money, gone back to being employed as a nurse, lived on real money. She didn't mind working for someone else. Maybe she was waiting until my sister and I left home. Maybe she left it too long. Maybe she decided leaving would require too much physical and emotional strain, that it would take more energy than she had, that it wasn't worth the effort. My mother wasn't ambitious. She didn't make sweeping gestures. She didn't have a grand design for herself, not like my father, who often spoke of becoming a millionaire. My mother reached a point where she sat back and took my father as he was. This humbled my father, made him grateful. If she thought he was foolhardy or mistaken, she never let on. I think my father had an oversupply of ambition, more than was good for him. His ambition hyped him up, made him uneasy and fretful, difficult to live with.

Stan says he gave up ambition when he resigned from the nine-to-five rat race. Stan lives with me, though it's probably more accurate to say he camps here when he's not somewhere else. Stan is a nomad. A onetime computer man, he speaks of himself as programmed to go forward. He got into computers early, when he owned an advertising agency in the States. Like me, Stan married young. He spent twenty-five years working ten hours a day to support a wife and five kids. He made hundreds of thousands of dollars, which went out faster than they came in. He says that, when he moved to Canada, he cut up his credit cards, cashed in his stocks, and left the money market for good. Now he does carpentry and key-cutting to support himself. Recently Stan remodelled a house in Nanaimo, extending the dining room into the garage to make an atrium. Now that he has enough money to keep him going for three months, he's gone back on the road, this time to Alaska. Stan says he doesn't need a home base. Not me. I need some place to come back to. I've been on two long trips with Stan: one driving to Arkansas and on to Mexico, the other across Canada as far as Newfoundland. Stan is the perfect traveller. He'll eat anything, stop anywhere, go down any road. When we're travelling, I depend on him to make arrangements, solve problems. He knows how to repair tires, make a fire from damp wood, cook bannock over a primus stove. He enjoys luxury, small indulgences. For the Alaskan trip he installed a skylight in the van roof, added a detachable screened porch with a folding table and chairs, built in a compact-disc player. I watched him do all this knowing he was assuming I would come along.

Three weeks ago, I was invited to give a one-woman show in Halifax, in the gallery at The Mount. This is something I've been waiting for. I've been in a dozen group shows, but I've never had a show of my own. The lead time is a scant five months, which means I'm probably a substitute for someone else. I told Stan I wouldn't be going to Alaska, I would be staying home to work. "Bring your buckets of papier mâché and your paints with you," Stan said. "You can work in the porch while I cook supper and poke around." I told him he'd missed the point, that I didn't want to work on the road. I wanted to be left alone. I wanted to give my full attention to my work, not what was left over. Stan offered to cut the trip from three months to two. I refused the offer. Stan told me I'd been unfair, leading him along, saying I might go. He said I should have told him earlier that I wouldn't be coming so he could have made other arrangements. He packed his clothes, both summer and winter, carried his wood-carving tools, and his CDs out to the van. Before he closed the door behind him, he said he might not be back. I didn't watch him go. I didn't wave from the window. I kept my head down, feet rooted to the floor. Stan drove away. I unplugged the phone, went downstairs to the basement, and got to work.

Some critics call me a sculptural primitive, others a primitive sculpturalist. They don't know what to do with my work, where to put me. There has been some argument as to whether I'm an artist at all, whether what I do is closer to being craft than an art form. I think of my work as theatre, entertainment. I compose stage sets, think in scenes. I call these scenes set pieces. Some of my set pieces are open. My park-bench series was like that. Grass trailed off at the edges; there were no walls or fences. In the series I'm making for the Halifax show, the set pieces are closed. The scenes take place inside rooms, boxes, cars. *Cow Pad* is a scatological set, an apartment for cows. Everything in the pad is round and brown: rugs, stools, tables, pictures, plates. The wallpaper design looks like Danish pastry. *Loony Bin* is a large box filled with pairs of loons. Some are singing duets, some are in straitjackets, some are in bizarre sexual positions. There is something less serious about an artist who recycles newspaper, perhaps because the materials are cheap. As an art form, papier-mâché is labour intensive. It doesn't require expensive equipment, doesn't need firing, it simply dries out. It takes paint well, is easily turned to caricature and decoration.

I work on a table made from a discarded door, one window over from the washer and dryer. My tools are often kitchen utensils: paring knife, spoon, fork, skewer, basting brush. Most of these tools are used to make patterns, which I paint over in bold colours so they look like fabric designs. This gives my work the kind of folksiness associated with Grandma Moses, or a sampler stitched with Home Sweet Home.

For the past week I've been working on a set piece entitled *The Train Family*. This is a circus family of animals who live in a caboose, open at the top. I have already made the figures, painted a caboose a fire-engine red, and printed Barnum & Bailey on both sides in canary yellow. There are four children in this family. The eldest boy is a brown monkey with a hula hoop, the eldest girl a seal balancing a ball on the end of her nose. The other boy and girl are a poker-playing rhinoceros and a hippo. It takes most of a day to paint these figures. Each article of clothing has its own design. Afterwards there will be the walls and floor to paint, and a matching set of furniture.

I am contented doing this. It is all I want. It is all I need, for the time being. The days pass, a week, then two. When I'm not working in the basement, I drive out to Kost's orchard to check my beehives or I go for a long walk in Beacon Hill Park. In the evenings I bake bread. I read. I visit Em, talk to my children on the phone.

The father in my train family is an elephant. Like Stan, his torso is heavy and thick, his legs short. I have chosen an elephant because he looks bulky and comfortable, the same as Stan. I paint on blue-striped overalls, a railwayman's cap, put the elephant in the caboose window, reading a map. I try not to think what Stan had in mind when he said he would have made other arrangements for the trip. Did he mean asking one of his children along, another woman?

I'm tall for a woman, taller than Stan. The mother in this family is a giraffe, a somnambulant, slow-moving animal who towers over the others in the caboose as she stands on tripod legs, staring backwards, looking down the tracks. As a final touch, I give her a telescope.

At last *The Train Family* is finished and I give it two coats of varathane. Before I cover it with plastic and store it on a shelf, I spin it around on a lazy Susan, eyeing it critically, checking the view from all directions. I'm pleased and not pleased. It will sell, I know that much, but it's too literal to suit me. There is something conventional and plodding about it. Perhaps there's too much of myself in it. Uneasiness sets in, as it always does after I've finished something and haven't begun another. This has to do with energy draining away, being transferred to an inert lump of paper and paint. It has to do with seeing the result of my efforts in front of me, diminished, circumscribed. I liked *The Train Family* better when it was inside my head.

Stan could be anywhere between here and Fairbanks. He could have decided to go somewhere else, gone in another direction. There have been no postcards or letters. I know he will eventually return, if only to pick up his wine-making equipment, his Elvis records, his carpentry tools. Now, when I go downstairs to work, I plug in the phone, as a concession.

I think about the last time I was in Toronto visiting my sister. I think about a man and a woman I saw come out of a large brick building and walk along Maitland Street. They were wearing plastic raincoats, belts loose at the back. He was on the outside with his arm around her waist. The other hand held an umbrella over their heads. She had her arm crooked on his shoulder which was a natural way to embrace, given the difference in their heights. She was a good six inches taller than he and had her head tilted sideways to accommodate the umbrella. They looked about the same age, in their mid thirties. They may have been no more than good friends, but I saw them as lovers. They had that relaxed companionableness and gratitude of people who have recently made love. I saw an aura around them, a soft, intimate light they carried with them outside. I saw a room in a first-floor apartment, a painted radiator, a hide-a-bed folded out, blankets on the floor. I saw a man and a woman walking around the room naked, in no hurry to put on their clothes, free from vanity and regret. These are the moments I would miss.

In our years together I have pushed Stan and myself into four or five of these separations, not all of them having to do with travel. I can't remember the details of Stan's other departures, but I could probably have made adjustments, been less perverse. This time I could have gone with Stan as far as Fairbanks or Anchorage and flown back, or done it the other way around. Instead I dug in my heels, proclaimed independence, was careless with my lover and friend. After managing a family, I covet aloneness. What som might call loneliness, I call solitude. I think of my ~~~~~~~~ solitude as an air-raid drill, an emergency plan. From time to time I am compelled to go underground and test my survival equipment for what lies ahead. I am always surprised to find it still works. There is something exhilarating about this discovery. I emerge from my bunker rejoicing, grateful for my aliveness, my sense of well-being. Which is why, given the chance, I will probably risk love and do it again.

Swimming Toward the Light

When Laddie Murray went into the Manor, it was being shut away that bothered him, not the place itself. He could see the nursing home was more convenient and up-to-date than what he'd left behind. There was a tap that delivered boiling water into his cup, railings along both sides of the corridors, wall-to-wall carpet underfoot. The Manor occupied three acres in the centre of town. It was surrounded by lawns, trees, gardens. There was a small bridge crossing a stream. From a distance the nursing home looked like an estate. It was a low, ranch-style building with two wings that came together into a lounge. On one side of the lounge were large windows that let in the light. There were hanging plants, budgies, a cat that sunned itself on a rocker by the patio door. The lounge was where church services and bingos took place. Craft classes were held here and rhythm band. Laddie never took part in these activities. He thought they were for people who had led a life of ease, people who had made a lot of money and retired, which he could not afford to do. He regarded the Manor as an inn or hotel, a place where he could continue his work while keeping up his social contacts. Most of his socializing was done after mealtimes. The dining room in the personal-care wing where Laddie spent the first year was called Happy Landing. Laddie ate at a table with Colin

Peterson and Herman Schwindler, two bachelors who looked on eating as a serious task and were offended if it was interrupted by talk.

It was the women at the other tables who talked, making polite inquiries about one another's children and grandchildren, the results of blood tests and X-rays, what various people in town were up to. These exchanges were not altogether courteous and civil. Sometimes a question was met with a sharp retort, especially if it had been asked by an untidy eater or someone who was thought not to be all there. Sometimes one of the women would take it upon herself to bake gingerbread in the kitchenette and pass it around for dessert. On St. Patrick's Day, a deaf woman named Jessie Johnson made shamrock cookies and put them on the tables, at each person's place. It was women like this on whom Laddie relied for conversation and companionship. After the dishes had been cleared away, he would fetch cups of tea and coffee, offer peppermints, cough drops, and cigarettes. Laddie was a yarn-spinner, a story-teller. He was willing to offer gallantries and put up with any number of errands and delays in order to gain an ear. Several of these women would sit for as long as an hour and listen to his stories. At that point in his illness, Laddie could go an afternoon without repeating himself. Usually these women had the sense to restrict their visits to the dining room, so it was possible to slip away when they'd had enough, to go into their bedrooms and close their doors, saying it was time for a nap. These tactful exits gave Laddie the opportunity to nod his head in agreement and say he had to be getting a move on himself, he had work to do in his office.

Early one afternoon, as Laddie was shuffling back to his room after one such visit, he came across a pair of pink slippers that had been left on the floor in the lounge. Recognizing them as belonging to Phoebe Winstanly, Laddie backtracked to Phoebe's room, tapped on the door, and managed to seat himself in her velvet wingback chair, light a cigarette, and launch into one of his war stories without being asked to leave. Phoebe had served in the war as a WREN; she may have told a story or two herself. Perhaps this explained why she did not at first notice the smell of burning cloth coming from the wingback chair, between the cushion and arm, where Laddie had dropped his cigarette. Laddie often forgot he had lit a cigarette. He did not own a pair of trousers without burn holes in the legs. This time his cigarette burnt a hole the size of a bottlecap in Phoebe's chair before she knew she had a fire on her hands. As a result of the chair burning, Laddie had to keep his cigarettes at the nursing station and request permission to smoke. He could no longer smoke in his room.

Laddie's room was his office. In addition to the standard institutional furniture, he had a desk, a chair, and a filing cabinet. Laddie spent hours hunched over his desk, writing figures in his ledger. The figures were part of a bookkeeping system he hoped to sell. He told Madge that he had discovered a new way to set up a balance sheet which was far more efficient than anything an accountant had come up with. He was secretive about this system. Madge had never seen it. Laddie told her that, as soon as he had the wrinkles ironed out, he was going to patent the idea and make a fortune. Except for the seventy-five dollars in comfort money the Manor gave him each month for incidentals, Laddie was penniless. He had eighty-two dollars in bills and change in his strongbox at the back of his closet. Laddie had not opened this strongbox since his first weeks in the Manor. He had lost the key and was unaware that it was inside his night table drawer in a Sucrets tin. One of the housekeepers had found it under the bed when she was mopping and put it into the tin. Laddie couldn't remember how much money was inside the strongbox. He once told Madge he had thousands of dollars stashed away on the premises.

Before his knees gave out, Laddie would walk downtown and wander along Main Street, looking in store windows and talking to anyone who would stop. He might be gone for two or three hours before someone at the Manor noticed he had disappeared and phoned the police to pick him up. Once Laddie went to the town docks and got aboard a rusted trawler that was tied up for repairs. He managed to get below deck, where he found himself a sleeping bunk. The Mounties had spent the night looking for him. When he didn't turn up, they thought he must have jumped off the bridge into the Mersey River.

It was Inez, Laddie's second wife, who blew the whistle on Laddie. Madge and Ardith lived too far away to know how bad Laddie was. They did not know how he disappeared for hours in Inez's car, once for days when he was trying to find his way back to Cape Breton, how he drove the car on the opposite side of the road. They did not know that he messed his pants and would go a week without changing his clothes, that he forgot to take his diabetic pills or took too many. (He would never allow Inez to monitor how many pills he took, in case she was poisoning him.) When he blacked out in the bathroom one night and was taken to the hospital, Inez refused to take him back. She phoned Madge and Ardith instead.

Within a year of being in the Manor, Laddie forgot Inez. He forgot he was still married, that he had ever had a second wife. He forgot Margaret, his first wife's sister. He forgot the names of Ardith's two sons, Madge's four children, but not that he had grandchildren. He remembered the name of his sister, Harriet, though she had died years ago. He knew the names of his brothers, Malcolm and Bruce, in North Sydney. One day he said to Madge, "How did your mother die?"

During his second year in the Manor, Laddie's legs no longer supported him and he went into a wheelchair. He was moved to the nursing wing, what was referred to as the "bad side", and took his meals in Sleepy Hollow with Captain Toby Swain. He also shared a bathroom with Captain Toby. Captain Toby had spent most of his life in the merchant navy. Though he was Laddie's age, he looked much younger. He had smooth, pink skin, a child's small features, and china-blue eyes that had retained their colour though they never

focused. Captain Toby was blind. After meals he would sit
with his chair against the wall, hold his head between his
hands, and say "I love you, I love you" over and over until
wheeled away to bed. There was something docile and bewildered in his voice, as if he were doing penance, making
amends. Madge thought he might have gone through life without saying these words to someone he loved, that he had
discovered their importance too late.

Madge saw Captain Toby for the first time in July when
she came East to visit Laddie soon after he'd been moved to
the nursing wing. She flew to Halifax, rented a car, and drove
to Liverpool with Alison, who had been visiting her father in
Halifax. After Madge and Doug had split up, Doug remarried
and returned to college to study pharmacy. Now he owned a
chain of drugstores and sent his children large cheques. Alison's cheques went to pay for her university expenses. She
was taking a degree in French at Concordia, not to qualify
for a teaching job or to work for the government. She was
studying French mainly because she wanted a second language. Partway down the coast, near Chester, Madge and
Alison stopped for lunch at a roadside restaurant. Madge
watched her daughter lift chunks of potato out of her chowder
and line them up along the rim of her plate. Alison cut up her
roll into six bite-sized pieces, of which she ate two. Alison
was anorexic; she counted her food. She had lost the gaunt
hollow-cheeked look and had begun to menstruate again, but
she still played games with her food, she still phoned Madge
in the middle of the night to accuse and blame, to go over past
wrongs.

Madge's marriage breakup had been messy. There had been
scenes that were impossible to explain, many of which Madge
brought on herself. One Saturday night, she put her four
children into the station wagon while Doug was asleep and
drove around Halifax all night. Alison would have been about
nine years old at the time. She had pleaded with Madge to go
home, but Madge kept driving in circles, parking in school
grounds and shopping centres, turning off the engine so she

wouldn't run out of gas. The police eventually found the five of them asleep in the parking lot of Alison's school. Madge's other children seemed undamaged by this sort of incident, but Alison hadn't yet recovered. Perhaps she never would. That was what Madge thought now, that Alison would never forgive her, that no amount of atonement was enough. They could go days without any of these incidents surfacing. Then some comment or word would trigger an outburst. The most innocuous conversation could take a sudden downturn. Madge had come to think of the words that passed between her daughter and herself as unpredictable and explosive; they couldn't be relied on.

Madge and Alison drove to the cottage Madge had rented at the beach and unloaded their bags to make room in the compact for the wheelchair. Then they drove to the Manor to pick up Laddie. Together they got him out of the wheelchair and into the front seat of the car. They drove back to the beach and parked at the end of the road, near the clam flats. It was a hot, muggy day. As soon as Madge and Alison had Laddie settled in the wheelchair, they put on their bathing suits and went for a swim in the river, which was flooded with seawater. They stayed upstream from the trestle. The train tracks had been taken up years before, but the trestle had been left standing as a bridge. On weekends people stood on this bridge to fish. This was a tidal river that flowed in and out of the sea. Herring and whitefish came up the river. Sometimes a seal followed them in.

The tide was beginning to turn. The water eddied in slow circles as the river started draining back to the sea. Madge and Alison lay on their backs in the amber-coloured water and let the current carry them as far as the trestle. Then they swam ashore and ran upriver, their feet sinking into the soft, wet sand, and floated to the trestle again. This was a safe, easy way to swim. There were no waves, no undertow to pull them out to sea. When they came out of the river and returned to the wheelchair, Laddie squinted at Alison, at her bony hips and ribs, her flat breasts, the rack of vertebrae down her spine.

It was difficult to say if he was displeased by what he saw or trying to figure out who she was.

"You should put on some flesh," he said. "A man likes a woman with some flesh on her bones."

Madge thought her father had got Alison and her mixed up, that he was talking to Madge when she was Alison's age. Both of them were tall and dark-haired. Both of them had grey eyes. Madge was mistaken. Laddie knew who Alison was, all right.

"You don't want to pay attention to what I say," he told her. "Your grandfather talks a lot of foolishness these days." He looked shamefaced, embarrassed. He had taken off the cap Madge had put on his head to prevent sunburn and was fidgeting with it, turning it around and around.

Alison laughed. "It's okay, Grandpa," she said. She was quick to forgive most people.

Later, when they had returned Laddie to the Manor, Madge and Alison went to The Privateer for supper. The restaurant was beside the Mersey River, which flowed through town at a stately, unhurried pace, sweeping beneath the bridge, past the docks and the lighthouse, then on past the paper mill, where it became part of the sea. The restaurant was a few doors up the street from the house where Madge's grandfather, Norman Burchell, once lived with his second family. This house, which had been built by a sea captain in the 1850s, stood on an acre of land backing onto the river. It was large, twelve rooms, three storeys, which was probably why the owners found the house difficult to maintain and had let it go. Despite its shabby, rundown appearance, the house had managed to retain some of its former elegance: elaborate scrolled cornices and shuttered bay windows, a heavy iron lamp above the front door. After supper, Madge and Alison stood on the sidewalk and looked at the hooded upper windows.

"There used to be a secret room on the third floor," Madge said. "I wonder if it's still there. Ardith used to think the sea captain who built the house stored his contraband inside the room. She was convinced he was a pirate." Madge stepped off the sidewalk. "Come on. I'll show you where I learned to swim."

"Didn't you learn at the beach?"

"I learned to swim in the Mersey River. So did Ardith."

The lawn in front of the house had been stripped of grass from the passage of cars. Some gravel had been spread over the mud to make a parking lot. This wasn't the sort of well-kept property that anyone was likely to object to strangers passing through. The garden behind the house, where Madge's grandfather used to raise dahlias and gladioli, was thick with crabgrass, pigweed, and thistles. The tool shed had been torn down, but the arbour where he had grown grapes was still standing, though now it was taken over by some kind of wild vine. Beyond the arbour were the crooked, bent shapes of her grandfather's fruit trees. When she looked at them through the arbour, the trees appeared wobbly and blurred, as if they were bleeding onto wet paper.

Madge led the way through the garden to the river.

"There used to be a boathouse down here where we'd change into our bathing suits," she said. She pointed to the largest rock along the shore. It was partly submerged now that the tide was in.

"That was Canada. That was the rock we started from. The other rocks were countries we used to swim to." She pointed to two rocks further out. "Those were Scotland and Europe."

"Europe's a continent," Alison reminded her.

"We weren't fussy how we named them," Madge said. "The point was that the water around those two rocks was over our heads. We had to swim to get to them." She pointed to a small, stubby rock midway between Canada and Scotland. "That was Ireland. Ireland was in shallow water. You could crawl on the bottom to Ireland."

"Did you ever swim to Scotland and Europe?"

"Not at first. I was afraid of sharks."

Alison laughed. "Sharks? Here?"

"Well, they weren't here, of course, but I used to imagine, as children do, that one would get me if I went over my head. That it would come for me, seek me out."

"But you eventually got there."

"Oh yes. I could swim, all right. The funny thing was I did it at night. It was just getting dark. I remember the water was silky and black. My father had brought Ardith and me over for a swim before bed. My father was a strong swimmer. At the beach he would sometimes swim a mile out to sea and back. Anyway, he and Ardith were sitting on Europe and Scotland. One of my cousins was out there too, Audrey, I think it was. They were calling to me to swim out. It was low tide, so it wasn't all that much over my head. My uncle Dillon was out there in a rowboat. He used to patrol in the boat whenever any of us went swimming. He had a flashlight and was switching it on and off like the Morse code. Who knows, maybe he was pretending to be a lighthouse. My father kept urging me to come out. He told me to swim toward the light. And that's what I did."

"Were you scared?"

"I was terrified. I only did it once. I came back in the boat with Dillon."

"Dillon was retarded, wasn't he?"

"Yes."

After Dillon had been put into an asylum, he stabbed himself in the chest. He didn't die from those wounds, but from pneumonia. Madge couldn't remember if she had ever told Alison this. It happened when Alison was a child. Madge had no intention of telling her now. She didn't intend to give her daughter any more ammunition. Alison already had enough. Twice she had starved herself to the point where she had to be hospitalized and fed intravenously.

"Dillon was musical. He had perfect pitch. He used to whistle along with canaries. 'Singers' he called them. That side of the family was musical. They even had a music room."

As they were walking back to the street, Madge pointed toward the bay window to the left of the front door.

"That was the music room," she said. "It had a Persian rug and blue velvet drapes. There was a grand piano, a violin, a trumpet my cousin used to play. The piano belonged to Cassie, my step-grandmother. She was a music teacher. That was how she met my grandfather. He used to sing in the choir in Welland. She was the organist in the same church."

According to Madge's mother, Norman Burchell had become involved with Cassie Lewis while he was still married to Nelly, Madge's grandmother. Madge's mother seemed convinced of this. She was convinced that her older brother, Dessie, had said something insulting to Cassie and that was why Norman had disowned him, not because he'd gotten into trouble with the law. Madge had grown up believing that this side of the family, what she thought of as the Irish side, was unlucky and unfortunate, that it was doomed to attract trouble, that it had more than its share of misfortune, as if misfortune was something that could be parcelled up and passed around. Early on, Madge and Ardith had lined themselves up on what they saw as opposite sides of the family: Ardith on their father's side, Madge on their mother's. They didn't see this distancing as a survival tactic, as a way of giving each other a wide enough berth. They saw it as something that bore significance, that marked their futures in some inevitable, relentless way. They had often argued about this, about which characteristic ran in whose side of the family. After their children were born, they would go to ridiculous lengths to prove one child or the other favoured a particular relative on one side of the family, this one's curly hair, that one's buck teeth. The sisters continued this practice, even though they knew that their forebears, as Great-Aunt Flora used to call their ancestors, did not fall as much into two parallel lines as they did into an untidy scribble.

When she was researching their family tree, Ardith came up with the information that Norman Burchell had no Irish in him at all. He was a mixture of English and Scots. And Nelly Payne's mother, Madge and Ardith's great-grandmother, was partly French. This knowledge made Madge feel misguided and foolish. It seriously reduced her claim to Ireland, where she had never been. She had exaggerated this claim, had given it more weight than it deserved. She knew she had continued this pretence because it was useful, because it helped justify her mistakes, dressing them up in the guise of bad luck, making her appear helpless against the odds that supposedly dogged the Irish side of the family. The fact was the Murrays' luck was no better than the Burchells'. Later on, when the truth about Agnes Murray's death surfaced, it came out that it wasn't the heavy skirt that dragged her beneath the water. Laddie's mother drowned herself in Sydney harbour when she was forty-four. Agnes had been a strong swimmer and left no note. It was thought she might have had cancer or some kind of dementia. Madge's mother had been told this by Marilyn, Malcolm's wife. Laddie never talked about it, nor did his sister or brothers, though the suicide was common knowledge around Sydney. There was a streak of mental weakness in the Murrays, a rash of depressions and nervous breakdowns. Aunt Grace had been one of these casualties; she suffered three breakdowns before she died. These breakdowns were never discussed, except by the Murray in-laws. The Murrays themselves tended to view weaknesses as mistakes. The family had a pragmatic bent. If they came across something that was of no use, something that couldn't be fixed and made to work, they sidestepped it. They kept questions to themselves and did not invite any from others. Madge thought the Murray behaviour had a lot to do with Presbyterianism. She thought the Murrays had been taught that speculation was a sin, that it was mischievous and irresponsible. There was some truth in this. Madge often speculated on little evidence. She liked to review different possibilities, try various scenarios. Sometimes she was careless with the truth. She wasn't above dragging a red herring across someone's path.

Ardith regarded speculation as part of her job. She was a historian. She looked for chain reactions, switchbacks. Ardith maintained that Laddie's failure in business was explained by the fact that he wasn't really a Murray. The Murrays were businesspeople, opportunistic and calculating. Laddie had been the black sheep in the family because he took after his mother's side, the Fergusons. The Fergusons were investigative and sociable. Laddie would have been better off working as a teacher or a reporter than trying to make it in business. Although Madge had given up looking for family connections, she had to admit Ardith was on to something when she talked about Laddie's natural instincts and inclinations. It was true that he seemed to have spent much of his life working at the wrong things, listening to the wrong advice, some of it from his brothers. Though he took their advice, Laddie never went into business with his younger brothers. Maybe he balked at the idea of taking instructions from them. Maybe he was never asked to become a partner. His brothers may have regarded him as a poor risk. Without him they made a lot of money, mostly in real estate.

Alison stayed another two days. She was missing her new boyfriend, Jean-Luc, and wanted to get back to him. When her anorexia had been at its worst, Alison lost interest in men. Madge thought Jean-Luc could be credited with much of the improvement in Alison's health. Before Alison left, she and Madge brought Laddie to Summerville Beach one last time. They wheeled him along the boardwalk and parked him in front of the dunes so he could watch the waves. Madge wondered what he was thinking, if he was thinking at all. He made no attempt to flag down sunbathers and beachcombers who wandered past. He was no longer capable of sustained conversation. Laddie didn't know he had Alzheimer's. He knew there was something wrong with him, but he was past understanding what the word meant, of having it explained to him in a way he could understand. The disease had also taken away his anger. He no longer bullied people to get his way. He no longer reviewed his disappointments, brooded over injustices and slights. Without anger he had become accommodating, benign.

After they had returned from the beach, Laddie and Madge sat on the patio of the Manor while Alison went inside to make them tea. Madge was pointing out the flowers in the garden, trying to engage Laddie's interest. Laddie closed his eyes. Madge thought he was too tired from the outing to pay attention to what she was saying. She stopped talking. Laddie opened his eyes and looked at her.

"It's no use. I don't know what anything means any more," he said. "I don't know the words. I need another language."

"You know your own name."

"True."

"And mine."

"When I forget that, I'll be in trouble." He laughed. "What was that girl's name?"

"The girl who was just here?"

"Yes."

"Alison."

"My granddaughter."

He smiled, pleased with himself.

Madge imagined the inside of Laddie's head as a switchboard of crossed wires and tangled cords that were plugged in at random. Whenever some bit of information or conscious thought was retrieved, a tiny square on the board lit up with a flash of light.

One afternoon, when Laddie was sleeping, Madge had a close look at the ledger he had left open on his desk. She turned the pages, idly at first, then deliberately looking for the system her father had planned to sell. There was no balance sheet. Most of the pages were blank; there wasn't a mark on them. In the entire ledger there might have been twenty pages with figures written in. Some of these figures were written in red ink; most of them were in pencil. A few pages were dated. One of the pages had *January, 1950* written across the top. That was the year her father narrowly missed bankruptcy by closing down his rope-making business. The system was pretend, something her father played at to keep himself going, to give himself something to do. Madge wasn't surprised by this. It was what she'd expected. Even so, she was alarmed. This was the kind of delusion she was afraid of. It was the kind of thing that could land you in the loony bin if you weren't careful. It wasn't far removed from what she did herself. As an artist she made things up, faked it, created illusions, sculptures made from papier-mâché whose crude lumpiness she camouflaged with brightly coloured paint. Illusions, delusions, what was the difference? Both had to do with deception, fakery. Madge thought that earlier on, before his memory short-circuited, Laddie might have known he was deceiving himself. Madge thought she and her father were compelled to make these transformations because they had looked around at what was there and decided it didn't suit. They had to put an overlay over whatever they came across, to make it palatable. They were too perverse and proud to accept what had been handed to them as it was.

After Laddie had been in the Manor two years, Ardith phoned Madge with the news that he had taken a bad fall. Malcolm and Bruce had come from Cape Breton to visit him, which made him feel well enough to think he could walk, perhaps to follow them. He had been buckled into a lounge chair for the visit and, after his brothers had left, had managed to get the buckle undone. One side of his hip was badly jammed. The injury wasn't something that could be operated on. It wasn't likely to get better. For the next few weeks Laddie would have to lie flat on his back. Ardith went to see him first. Madge made the journey two months later, in October.

This time when she walked into her father's room, Madge no longer recognized the old man asleep on the bed. She thought she had walked into the wrong room. She looked at the dark breathing-hole that had been a mouth and thought *orifice*. She looked at the bony knobs of knees and toes beneath the sheet, the outline of the skull against the pillow, and thought *cadaver*. She got her bearings only after she looked at the wall above the bed and saw the Murray coat of arms, showing a mermaid and a lion, which Ardith had embroidered and framed for Laddie.

Madge spent most of this visit sitting on a chair beside the bed reading, while her father slept. Sometimes he talked in his sleep, ramblings, snatches of conversation he uncovered as he followed roads no longer there. These were dirt roads, country roads that had been paved over years ago. Laddie was like a gypsy, wandering the hemispheres, hawking his wares, picking up something here, something there, buying, selling, turning things over. *My father gave me a pair of pants once. I sold them. . . . Maybe if we had something your uncle wanted, he'd lend us his horse and wagon. . . . I bought a rowboat this morning. The man selling it was easy to beat down.*

Both Laddie's father and grandfather had owned stores. From them Laddie had learned a businessman's view of the world, which was that people were out there ready for you to do business with; they were all fair game; you bought low and you sold high; to stay in business you had to keep turning things over; you had to make a profit. Madge's mother used to say Laddie's problem was that he couldn't make a profit. He wasn't hard-nosed enough to sell high. If someone gave him a hard-luck story, he'd look for a way to lower the price. He regarded this as smart sales psychology, a way of keeping customers happy.

When Madge was nineteen, a few days before she married Douglas Ogilvey, Laddie had taken her into an appliance store in Halifax and told her to pick out a wedding present. He walked around the store, pointing out the latest models of stoves, fridges, washers and dryers, demonstrating their modern features, their gadgetry. "Pick anything you want, anything," he said to Madge. Then he struck up a conversation with the sales manager, leaving her alone to choose. Madge knew her father would have bought her any of these large appliances without batting an eye, that he would never have embarrassed himself in front of the manager by admitting he couldn't afford one. She knew that, beneath the generosity and expansiveness, her father was counting on her to rescue him, that he was trusting her not to be greedy. Madge picked out an electric teakettle.

In January, three days before he died, Laddie was moved out of his bedroom and into the guestroom. This was a room across the hall from the nursing station that was occasionally used as a spare room for overnight visitors. Mostly it was where the dying were kept.

Madge arrived in Liverpool the day her father died. It was cold and blustery, appropriate weather for dying. Madge thought the storm took the sting out of Laddie's failures, acknowledged his ambitions, his striving, gave him more significance than he'd enjoyed in life. By the time Madge reached the nursing home, Laddie was in a coma. His eyelids were shut, his skin mottled and bluish. Madge pictured the organs and muscles inside the body as limp and useless, the arteries drained and slack. But the heart continued to beat, pushing air from the lungs. Madge sat in the chair beside the bed and waited, while rain slammed against the building and wind shook the windows in their frames. She noticed a loosening in the surface of the sheet the nurse had folded across Laddie's chest. With each breath the sheet became lower and flatter, like the end of a wave. By evening this rhythm had changed. There were long moments when Laddie did not breathe, when the sheet lay motionless. At these times, Madge thought her father might be dead. Just when she thought he wouldn't breathe again, he took another breath. These breaths had become light puffs of air, as fragile as the wings of a butterfly or moth, trembling slightly as they came together. Laddie's dying had that languid pace, that lingering slowness. At last, about nine o'clock, Laddie's eyes opened. An eyebrow lifted imperceptibly, his jaw dropped, and an expression crossed his face, fleeting, transient. Madge didn't know if it was reluctance or surprise. She didn't know what her father's capacity for these emotions was, what had been left inside. Whatever it was, he let go. His mouth clamped shut and his eyes locked sideways. They looked as if they had seen something amazing and miraculous, as if they had been shocked open by wonder or light.

Madge left the guestroom and went into the hall just as Evelyn Sarty, the night nurse, was coming out of the nursing station. Evelyn was the mother of married children, a grandmother of six, one of the easy-going, good-natured women who had teased Laddie, listened to his stories, and bent the rules whenever she could. Evelyn crossed the hall and put her arms around Madge.

"He was so proud of you girls," she said. "Before he got so bad, he used to talk about you all the time."

Madge knew this. She and Ardith had both known it from a long way back. Laddie had seldom praised them to their faces; instead, he had done it behind their backs. The sisters had been embarrassed when this sort of bragging came back to them, when they heard the outrageous claims their father had made. Madge felt she hadn't earned her father's praise, that there had been more of it than she'd been able to live up to. Her father's pride in her hadn't been enough to make her want to take him in, to put up with wet sheets and soup-stained bibs, to lift his body in and out of the wheelchair. She didn't think Laddie would have wanted her to do any of this, to see his nakedness and withered organs, to see how useless he had become, but she thought he had wanted the chance to refuse, that there was a point when he had been waiting for her to offer.

Madge went outside into the winter night, which was becalmed now that the storm had blown itself out. The combination of high winds and freezing rain had brought down power lines. The electricity in town had been off for several hours. The nursing home had been operating on emergency generators, so Madge had been unaware of the blackout. She was surprised to find the street outside in almost total darkness. There was barely enough light for her to find her rented car. She groped around for her keys, but they wouldn't go into the lock. It was frozen, the handle iced over. There was a thick coating of ice on the windows. Madge decided to walk back to the motel and return in the morning for her car.

She walked slowly, gingerly. It was well before midnight, between ten and ten-thirty. Here and there inside a house, there was a flicker of light in the darkness where a candle was burning. Madge thought of the blackouts during the war, when streetlights were turned out and blinds were drawn. She had always been in bed during blackouts. She thought this must have been what the streets looked like from outside, rows of dark houses you could barely make out. As her eyes became accustomed to the darkness, Madge began to separate one house from another. She could see which house had a car parked in the driveway, which houses had garages. She passed the rectangular expanse she recognized as the tennis courts, the tall, white courthouse whose columns gleamed faintly in starlight. Madge looked up through the branched intricacies of the elms, toward the stars. The clouds had gone and the sky was clear. The stars shone cold and bright from distant galaxies. Madge thought about the light, the distance it travelled, the years it took to reach Earth. She thought about the names of galaxies, the Andromeda Spiral and the Milky Way. She thought about the names of stars, Altair and Vega. Giving names, putting words to stars, was a kind of taming, an attempt to establish outposts, connections. But the main connection with the stars wasn't words, with their misdirections and limitations, their predilection to confuse and misguide. The language of the universe was light. It was light that people who had died and come back to life claimed to see. In all that darkness, they claimed to see the light.